TOMB OF PENDRAGON

THE ABDUCTION CYCLES

JOHN CRESSMAN

MAVERICK-GAGE PUBLISHING

ISBN: 978-1-954524-07-1 (Paperback)
ISBN: 978-1-954524-00-2 (Hardcover)
ISBN: 978-1-954524-05-7 (Amazon Kindle)
ISBN: 978-1-954524-06-4 (Audiobook)

Any references to historical events, real people, or real places are used fictitiously. Names, characters, and places are products of the author's twisted imagination.

Front cover image by Christina Myrvold

Editing By Celestial Rince.

Printed by Maverick-Gage Publishing in conjunction with IngramSpark, in the United States of America.

First printing edition 2021.

Maverick-Gage Publishing
Allentown, PA
info@maverick-gage.com
www.maverick-gage.com

John Elijah Cressman
www.johnecressman.com

PROLOGUE

E than shot up in bed, awakened by the movement next to him. He turned to look at Nia lying beside him, dagger in her hand. Like him, she was naked, and he briefly wondered where she'd gotten the dagger from. The woman's fox-like ears were back, but they twitched as she sniffed the air.

Nia was a foxling, an alien race of humanoids. Her body was that of an attractive athletic human woman with some notable exceptions. First, she had the coloration of an Earth fox, with short, soft rust-colored hair all over her body. Her face and front torso were cream-colored, as was the tip of her tail. And that was the second thing, she had a large, puffy, fox-like tail, as well as fox-like ears that stuck out of long, rust-colored hair.

Those ears were back at the moment as she glared at the door and continued to sniff the air. Like the canines of Earth, Nia had an exceptional sense of smell. She could identify people and creatures by smell, as well as track them. It was something that had come in useful many times.

"Open up, wizard-boy," came a gruff female voice. "I don't care if you two are up to something, this can't wait!"

Ethan groaned as he recognized the voice as belonging to Ainslee, his female dwarven companion. He growled. What time was it? He felt like he'd just closed his eyes after the rather robust lovemaking he and Nia had engaged in. Or should he say, his wife.

According to the foxgirl, because the two of them had sex, they were married - at least, according to the customs of her world. Ethan wasn't so sure. After all, there had been no ceremony. But he hadn't had the chance to ask anyone how things worked on this world and if they had actual weddings on his world.

Ethan thought back to his own world, Earth. He hadn't been on this new world long. He'd actually lost track of exactly how long it had been since he'd been abducted and dropped on this world, but it couldn't be more than a few months. And it was definitely a very different world.

First, it wasn't even a planet. It was a moon of some enormous ringed gas giant. Second, this solar system had two suns with a black hole between them. It was like something out of a science fiction movie. He was just missing tall, blue-skinned aliens.

The other weird thing was how much this world was like a video game. It had a HUD, heads up display, that showed skills, stats and abilities. There were even classes. In the beginning, not knowing what he was doing, Ethan had chosen wizard. Once he did, he could do magic. Real magic.

It was impossible, he knew, but he could throw fireballs, create portals and even freeze things. It was all very... magical. Part of him thought that he was in some sort of super advanced alien virtual reality game. But if so, it was light-years ahead of anything Earth could develop. The level of detail was staggering, down to bodily functions and body odor - things you never worried about in Earth MMORPGs.

He glanced at the foxgirl next to him as she slipped the dagger under her pillow. Nia's class was acrobat, though the foxgirl was an incredibly skilled warrior. Normally, she carried two scimitars they'd found in the library of Patheos, but at the moment, she appeared to only have the dagger under the pillow.

"I know you're in there!" came Ainslee's voice. "Get some clothes on and get out here. Michalus arrived. And he's hurt."

Ethan and Nia exchanged glances and immediately began scrambling for their clothes. Michalus was a kindly, old elf wizard they'd met a few weeks ago. He was also the only other wizard Ethan had met since arriving. The old elf had offered to pay him a visit after he had escorted some elven children Ethan had saved to a city to the north called Moonpoint. But now Michalus was back and apparently injured.

His group had just arrived back in Hawkshead early that evening. Or was it after midnight already? He wasn't sure. He had been really looking forward to sleeping in a real bed again and, if he were honest, sharing it with Nia. Getting woken in the middle of the night was too much like journeying.

Nia, with her better fox eyes, didn't seem to have an issue with the dark interior. Ethan on the other hand, struggled to find his clothes in the near pitch black. Finally, dressed in the bare minimum clothes to be decent, they hurried to the door, unbolted it and threw it open.

In the doorway stood Ainslee. She was an ebony-skinned

dwarf. Yes, a dwarf, just like in the fantasy books. She stood about 4'8" tall but was broad, with a large chest and ample bosom, thick arms and short, stocky legs. Her white hair was normally up in a topknot but at the moment, lay sprawled across her shoulders and down her back.

Her class was knight and she was the group's tank, as Ethan thought of it in gaming terms. She seemed to be somewhat decent at combat but was able to take a lot of punishment and still stay up.

"I knew you were naked." The dwarf grinned, throwing them a knowing look. Ainslee saw their disheveled appearance and snorted. "Come on! Yuliana is with him now in the inn, trying to heal him."

As they hurried after the dwarf, Ethan thought of Yuliana. She was the last of his original companions. Like Michalus, Yuliana was an elf. But unlike Michalus, who had been born on this planet, Yuliana had been abducted like Ethan, Nia and Ainslee. She was the group's druid, their healer.

Nia and Ethan followed the dwarf up the street to the inn, the Crow and Pick. Pushing open the door, he immediately saw Fearghas, the dwarven innkeeper, Par'karr, his kobold companion, and Yuliana, leaning over one of the inn's tables.

Yuliana was dressed in nothing but a sheet that she held around her runway model-like body. The sheet had slipped down her back, revealing a perfect, tanned back and the hint of round buttocks. Her long, green hair covered most of her back but not her perfect bottom.

Ethan hadn't even realized he was staring until he felt a sharp poke in his side. Flinching, he turned to see Nia glaring at him. He felt his face grow hot from being caught and Nia gave him a disgusted look. "You males are all the same. Always looking for more wives!"

Before he could try to defend himself, Par'karr saw them and turned. The little kobold had joined their group after another tribe of kobolds wiped out his tribe. He was a summoner, a class that could summon creatures from some other world or dimension. In Par'karr's case, he summoned demon rabbits. At least, that's how Ethan thought of them.

"Elf hurt bad," the kobold squeaked.

Ignoring the pain in his side, Ethan rushed over to the table and saw the wizard lying on the table. He had a large gash down the front of his chest and into his upper abdomen. It appeared he had tried to bandage it, but the injury had become infected. The old elf's eyes were closed, and he muttered incoherently as Yuliana's healing magic sealed up the wound.

Fearghas glanced up at him grimly. "We heard him collapse against the front door after knocking. I ran out and found him like this. The women say you know him."

"His name is Michalus and he's a friend." Ethan nodded. He purposefully left out the fact that the old elf was a wizard. That might not be the best thing to mention at the moment.

Since becoming a wizard, he'd learned that something had been systematically hunting down and killing wizards, by sucking their brains out. The people in the town knew he was a wizard and were jumpy about having him around. They were afraid of becoming collateral damage.

Ethan wasn't sure what the people would do if they learned that a second wizard was in the village. That might be too much for them to handle.

"Can you tell how he is?" Ethan asked Yuliana.

"I cannot say," the elf responded. She looked tired and he wondered how much healing she'd already used on Michalus. "His wound was not deep, but it was long."

Noticing how pale Michalus was, Ethan guessed the old wizard had lost a lot of blood. If this were Earth, he would have gotten a transfusion and probably an injection of antibiotics. Unfortunately, in this world, none of that existed.

The group watched in silence as the druid slowly moved her hand over the wound. The magic knitted the skin together and even some of the redness disappeared, leaving a long scar.

Finally, Yuliana was done, and she sagged back. Par'karr grabbed a chair and pushed it over to her. The green-haired elf smiled at him and sat down. "That is all I can do for him. I am out of karma and stamina."

"Me get you water!" Par'karr said and before anyone could object, the little kobold grabbed two pewter mugs and ran out the door to the river.

Ethan remembered how doctors always said to drink lots of fluids. "When he wakes up, make sure Michalus gets lots to drink. More water than anything else. The mead might dehydrate him."

The people in the room gave him blank stares so Ethan just shrugged. "Just make sure he gets lots to drink.

"Do you have an extra bed for him?" Ethan asked the innkeeper.

Fearghas shook his head. "All the rooms are being taken by women and the kobold."

"He can sleep in my room," Yuliana said. "I will stay with him until he awakes."

Ethan shook his head. "You need sleep too so you can

restore your karma and stamina. We can take turns staying with him until he's awake."

Yuliana started to protest but he put a hand on her shoulder. "You get some rest. He might need more healing when he wakes up."

The druid seemed to consider his words. She appeared to be about to voice an objection, but it was cut short by a yawn. Slightly embarrassed, the elf nodded. "Okay, I will sleep..."

"You can sleep in my room." Ainslee grinned. "I've got two beds in mine!"

Yuliana looked like a deer in the headlights and Ethan and Nia suppressed laughs. The reason no one slept in the dwarf's room was because Ainslee snored - loudly. Of course, Ainslee insisted she didn't snore, but the rest of the group knew she did.

Ethan looked down at the scar on the old wizard's chest. It was straight and whatever had made it had been very sharp. A sword? It had to be some sort of weapon. There was only a single, long wound. What type of creature would only have one claw? Nothing he could think of.

Maybe Michalus had run into some of the followers of Hel. Now that slavery of elves, foxlings and other races was legal in Castlehaven, the followers of Hel had been buying and taking slaves to sacrifice to their dark goddess. Ethan and his friends had run into such a group themselves and put a stop to their slaving activities.

Looking at the wizard's pale form, Ethan searched his brain for the complications of losing too much blood. But even if he did know what the complications were for humans, he had no idea if they would apply to elves. He just hoped that Michalus recovered.

Reaching down and taking the old wizard's hand, he squeezed it. He wasn't sure whether or not the elf could hear him, but he tried to make his voice soothing. "Hang in there, Michalus."

1

Michalus hadn't recovered by noon, which was when Ethan had finally gotten up for good. He'd awakened briefly when Nia had slipped out but had immediately fallen back to sleep. After getting dressed, he went to check on Michalus. Nia and Ainslee were waiting for him outside the inn.

"Sorry, wizard-boy," Ainslee growled. She didn't appear to have gotten much sleep either. "He ain't awake."

"Can Yuliana tell if he's any better?" he asked the two women.

Nia and Ainslee looked at each other and shrugged but it was the dwarf who answered. "No idea."

Ethan nodded. Yuliana only had her healing magic. She didn't seem to have any special knowledge of anatomy or physiology. If anything, Ethan's basic anatomy courses in school had taught him more than the elf knew. If he could actually remember most of it.

"But there is another problem," Nia added grimly. "We were waiting until you got up before we told you."

"Well, thank you for that." He flashed them a grin. Neither of them returned it and he sensed this might be serious. He allowed the smile to fade. "What's wrong?"

"We should let Fearghas tell him," Ainslee said. "Get it right from the goat's mouth."

Nia bit her lip but nodded. The dexterous foxgirl spun with a swish of her tail and walked to the door of the inn. Ethan and Ainslee followed her.

As they came through the door of the inn, Fearghas peeked his head into the common room. Seeing it was Ethan, the dwarven innkeeper came around the corner with a stern look on his face.

Ethan sighed inwardly. No doubt this was some issue with the town that he, as mayor, would have to deal with. The last big issue had been a tribe of kobolds that were intent on destroying the village. He wondered what it would be this time.

"Mayor," the innkeeper started, and Ethan knew by the tone of his voice it was serious. Or, at least, the dwarf thought it was serious. "We have trouble."

"Trouble?" Ethan raised an eyebrow. "What sort of trouble?"

"Well," the innkeeper said, looking down and wringing his hands. "We don't rightly know."

Ethan suppressed the urge to roll his eyes at the dwarf. Instead, he took a deep breath, just like he did when he was a computer tech and one of his clients was being particularly obtuse and saying something like "My computer is broken" or "My computer doesn't work". He smiled at the innkeeper, trying to make sure it didn't look too fake. "Well, can you describe the problem?"

"We're starving," the dwarf said, looking him in the eye. "That's the problem."

"Wait," Ethan said, looking around. "What do you mean, you're starving?"

"After the kobolds burned the farms, some of the farmers moved into the homes in town, just like you said," Fearghas replied. Ethan thought there was a hint of accusation in the dwarf's tone, but it wasn't overt. "Anyway, that's all fine and the neighborly thing to do, but there won't be enough food to feed them all. Not with the few chickens and the small garden we have."

"I thought we set up hunting parties?" Ethan asked. He phrased it as a question, but he knew the answer because he had been the one to help organize them after the kobold raid.

"We did." The dwarf bobbed his head. "And they worked for about a week. But we either killed all the game in the area or scared them off, I reckon."

Ethan felt his face scrunching up. That didn't make any sense. This area was teeming with game. He and the others had found no problems finding food. "Maybe it's just the area around the town itself. What about..."

Fearghas shook his head. "It's all around and as far south as the last farm."

Ethan looked at Nia. "That doesn't sound right. I'm sure many of these farmers probably supplemented their food by hunting."

"It does not sound normal to me," Nia agreed. "Prey does not normally leave the territories unless the food runs out. Or possibly, if a new predator enters the area."

The innkeeper bobbed his head in agreement. Ethan

thought back to Earth animals and got an idea. "What season is it?"

"End of summer," the dwarf replied quickly. "Two more weeks and we'll be into fall."

"Do the animals around here migrate?" Ethan asked. He remembered birds migrated, but he was sure other animals did too. But he would have guessed they would have done so closer to winter, maybe at the end of fall.

"Some," Fearghas replied. "But there are always deer and pheasants, not to mention squirrels, groundhogs and rabbits. We ain't got any of that now."

Ethan nodded. He wished he knew more about small animals like that, but he was pretty sure they didn't migrate. If anything, some of them probably hibernated and it was much too early for that if it were still summer.

Was it some sort of predator? Maybe something like an ogre? But that didn't make much sense considering they'd found game even around the ogres they'd encountered on the road of the library in Patheos.

"Has this ever happened before?" Ethan asked. If it had, maybe the dwarf had some idea of what might be causing it.

"Not since I've been here," Fearghas replied, scratching his beard. "And I've been here since the beginning."

"What is it? Dragons?" Ainslee asked and Ethan saw the innkeeper's face go pale.

"Dragons?" Fearghas swallowed, eyes going wide.

Ethan gave Ainslee a sharp look and shook his head. "Have you seen any dragons flying around?"

"No." The innkeeper shook his head violently. "But you think it might be a dragon?"

Ethan sighed. "No. If it were a dragon, it would most likely be flying around. Probably burning things down."

"What do you think it is then?" the innkeeper asked.

"I don't know, but we'll scout around and see if we can find something," he replied.

"The whole village would be much obliged," Fearghas said. "If'n you don't. I ain't sure how much longer we can hold out - especially since winter is coming."

> You have received a new quest "Starving Villagers I"
>
> Your town is running out of food. You have told Fearghas the Innkeeper that you will look into the lack of game in the area surrounding the village.
>
> Discover why there is no game around Hawkshead (0/1).
>
> Reward: 500 experience, +250 reputation with Residents of Hawkshead, +250 reputation with Farmers of Arrowpoint Valley
>
> Failure: -150 reputation with Residents of Hawkshead, -150 reputation with Farmers of Arrowpoint Valley, Loss of population
>
> Accept quest (yes or no)?

"Winter is coming," Ethan echoed. The little gardens the villagers had and the crops from the surviving farms wouldn't be enough to get them through the winter. If he didn't find some solution, he doubted any of them would survive. No pressure.

"Wait," Ethan said, thinking of the nearby river. "What about fish?"

The dwarf smirked. "That's all we been living on lately. Now, the river up and down for a day's walk has been fished almost clean. At least, the fish ain't bitten much if there are any left. Personally, I'm kind of tired of fish but if that's all we got, then that's all we got."

Ethan frowned. It sounded like this couldn't wait. They needed to figure out what was causing the issues with the nearby game.

"Nia, Ainslee." He turned to the women. "Get your gear and let's scout out the area. Ainslee, can you ask Par'karr and Yuliana to get their stuff and come too."

"Yah, yah," the dwarf said. "You think we could get some lunch first?"

Fearghas looked embarrassed and Ethan wondered if the man even had enough food for his family. He gave the dwarf a meaningful look. "We still have some jerky left over. We can eat that on our way out to scout the area."

Ainslee started to open her mouth but at that moment, Sawney poked his head around the corner. Sawney was Fearghas' son and was only about as tall as Par'karr. "Da, I'm hungry. Do we have any food?"

Fearghas' face flushed an even darker scarlet and he turned and hurried over to his son, whispering something to him and shooing him off.

Ainslee closed her mouth, brows furrowing. She looked from the innkeeper to Ethan. When she spoke, it was in a tone that was clearly meant to be overheard. "Yah, we should eat on the road to save time. I'll go get the others."

Ethan flashed her a smile and a nod but Ainslee just bit her lip, spun and hurried up the stairs.

Fearghas walked back over to them. "I'm truly sorry, but I only have enough right now for my family - a bit maybe for the elf upstairs. If I had more..."

Holding his hand up to stop the dwarf, Ethan gave him a genuine smile. "I know you would, Fearghas. We still remember the porridge you set outside for us, back when you didn't even know us."

The innkeeper didn't smile but nodded gratefully. Then, his face grew grim. "We're not the only ones. With most of the crops burned by those kobold devils, and now the game gone, we're barely scraping together enough food to survive."

The dwarf looked troubled but resigned. "I'm afraid, for the time being, you and the women will need to fend for yourselves."

Nia nodded curtly. "We will take care of our own needs. You must take care of your pack... your family. This is the way."

Ethan saw the innkeeper's eyes grow moist and the dwarf nodded.

There was a clamor on the steps and Ethan turned to see Ainslee and Par'karr coming down with their gear.

"Yuliana is going to stay here," Ainslee said as she followed Par'karr down the steps. "She said that her head is aching, and she would like to be here if Michalus wakes up. She said she'd look after the horses."

He hadn't known the elf to ever complain of a headache before but considering how much magic she used on the old wizard and the fact that she probably hadn't gotten much sleep with the dwarf snoring, he couldn't blame her.

Ethan didn't like going out without their healer, but he did understand the elf's desire to stay and keep an eye on the old wizard. If he had his way, he'd stay too. It was also good she'd be keeping an eye on the horses, considering the food shortage.

"We go on adventure?" the kobold asked cheerfully as he reached the bottom of the steps.

Ethan couldn't help but grin at the enthusiastic kobold. "Yes, Par'karr. It looks like we are going on an adventure."

2

The group swung by Ethan's place so he and Nia could grab their gear. As they did, Ethan noticed the horses were skittish, neighing and running around the makeshift corral they'd made.

"Do they smell a predator?" Ethan wondered aloud.

"There are no strange scents in the air." Nia sniffed and shook her head. The foxgirl looked Ethan up and down. "Though you could use a bath."

Rolling his eyes, he opened the door and led the foxgirl back to their bedroom so they could get the rest of their gear. When the two of them returned everyone looked at him for the next steps. But he was used to being the leader at this point - for better or worse.

"So where do we go? How do we find the missing animals?" Ainslee asked. Then her mouth became a frown. "And whatever beastie is scaring them off?"

Ethan turned to Nia. Of all his companions, she had the most experience hunting and tracking game. "What do you think?"

Nia rubbed her temples and shrugged. "We should scout the area and look for any tracks, spoor or other signs of a new predator."

He nodded. That had been his plan too, mostly because that seemed like the common sense thing to do. If something new had moved into the area, then there should be signs of it. If they could find traces of it and track it back to its lair, hopefully they could kill it. Unless it was a dragon. He prayed it wasn't.

"So, we just walk around until we find something?" Ainslee grumbled.

"Unless you have a better idea," Ethan retorted with a raised eyebrow.

The dwarf rolled her eyes. "Let's just try to make it back before dinner. Fearghas says his new batch of mead is ready!"

"If we wish to make it back before nightfall," Nia said, looking between them, "we must leave now."

"Fine! Then let's leave!" the dwarf huffed.

Nia said nothing else. The foxgirl spun with a swish of her tail and began marching south out of the town. Ethan thought she seemed irritated, but he knew sometimes the dwarf did that to all of them. The rest of them filed after her.

As they walked, Ethan looked back over his shoulder. For some reason, his first thought had been to go north. He couldn't say exactly why. It was like a hunch or feeling he had. But he wasn't a tracker, or a hunter and he deferred to Nia's experience.

Once out of the town, Nia cut west into the forest. She was only a few hundred yards into trees when she stopped. The foxgirl rubbed her temples while her ears twitched. "Do you hear that?"

"I don't hear nothing," Ainslee grumbled. "Except birds."

"Precisely," Nia retorted. "There are birds around. But I have yet to see a single prey animal that is not a bird. I do not even hear the scampering of prey."

"No rabbits." Par'karr nodded. "Par'karr always look for rabbits. There none."

"So, what does that mean?" Ainslee demanded. "Something ate them all?"

The foxgirl took nearly a minute sniffing the air. As she did, Ethan saw her massaging the sides of her temples. He frowned. He'd been around Nia for well over a month and he'd never seen her do that before. Did she have a headache?

"Are you okay, Nia?" he asked.

"I am fine." Nia dropped her hands to her sides immediately. Ethan thought she was lying but before he could say anything, the foxgirl continued. "I smell no predators and no prey in the area. Not for days."

"Let us go back to the river," she said and, without another word and without giving Ethan a chance to say anything else, Nia spun and went back east towards the road and the river.

When they reached the river, Nia began following it south. The foxgirl occasionally made small noises and stooped down to look at muddy patches of the riverbank. After a half hour of that, she finally stopped and faced the rest of the group.

"The creatures are fleeing the area," she said. "And all of the tracks are heading south."

"South?" Ethan echoed. "Why south?"

The foxgirl began to rub her temples but immediately brought her hands down, glancing around as she did. "They may merely be following the only source of water. But I see only the tracks of prey that I have seen before or predators that are too small to have caused all of the animals to flee."

"Unless it flies," Ainslee blurted out. "You know, like a dragon!"

Nia shook her head and gave the dwarf an annoyed look. "If it flies and is a predator to birds, why have they not fled?"

Ainslee screwed up her face. "I don't know. Maybe dragons don't eat birds."

"Dragon eat lizard bird!" Par'karr offered helpfully. "At beach."

They all seemed to remember back when they'd hit the coastal road on their way to Castlehaven. They'd found that the ocean was a tumultuous collection of random waterspouts that were hundreds of feet high. Feeding on the fish that the spouts carried were some sort of prehistoric looking pteranodon creatures.

As if those creatures weren't strange enough, they later encountered a dragon - "hidden from a dragon" was probably a better description. The dragon had gone after the pteranodons and ate several of them before flying back to wherever it had come from.

He smiled at the small kobold. "Good point. Although, maybe these birds are too small for a dragon? IF it is a dragon."

Ethan rubbed his chin. He had been shaving with a knife since he arrived, but today he hadn't had time and his stubble was rough against his fingers. Could it be a dragon? He knew nothing about real dragons. For all he knew, it could be the same dragon they saw previously, and it was tired of pteranodons.

The real question was: why would the creatures be fleeing south? The obvious answer was that they were fleeing something from the north. But what? A dragon, like Ainslee thought?

In the disaster movies, there were always birds flying away from a natural disaster like a volcano eruption or a tidal wave. And yet, the birds were still around. Was that just Hollywood taking creative license? Maybe only the mammals fled in real life? Or at least, maybe on this world only mammals fled.

But what kind of natural disaster would they be fleeing? A volcano? That was a possibility. An earthquake? Also, a possibility, if that were common on this planet. Not a planet, he corrected himself, this was a moon. A moon with two suns and a black hole that revolved around a ringed gas giant like Saturn. He couldn't begin to comprehend what sort of gravitational influences those might have on this world.

"I'm not sure it is a dragon," Ethan said, realizing everyone was looking at him. Part of him felt good that they all seemed to think he was smart and deferred to him. It made him feel smart. Another part didn't like the pressure.

Sure, he had the knowledge of a high school and college education in a technological society. The jury was still out on how much that knowledge translated into being able to figure out things in an effectively medieval society where dragons and magic were a thing.

"Why has no one seen it flying around?" Ethan said as Ainslee opened her mouth.

The dwarf closed her mouth, looked thoughtful and then looked smug. "Maybe it's only flying at night."

"That's a fair point," he conceded. "We saw it during the day, but that could have been a fluke."

Ainslee looked around the group with a smug smile.

"However," Ethan continued. "Why no attacks on the village. It would seem that the village would be like a buffet for it."

Ainslee frowned and deflated. She opened her mouth as if to speak but then closed it, brows furrowed.

"Perhaps it does not like human or dwarfkind," Nia said.

"That's a fair point too," he said. "But we need proof before we tell the villagers they have a dragon on the loose."

"Like what?" Ainslee demanded.

"Like us seeing it or a footprint or something," he replied.

"And how are we going to find that in all these woods?" the dwarf asked with her hands on her hips. "Run around the entire forest?"

Ethan shook his head. "The animals were headed south, not north. It makes sense that whatever is causing this is in the north. We should check there first."

The dwarf let out an exasperated breath and threw her hands up in the air. "Great! Let's just go walk right into the dragon's lair! What are we? Daft?"

"We will not walk into the lair of a dragon," Nia said between clenched teeth. Once again Ethan saw her fingers massaging her temple.

"And..." the dwarf started but Ethan held up a hand to stop whatever she was about to say. He was looking at the foxgirl, who had dropped her fingers from her temple.

"What's wrong?" Ethan asked her. He gave her the sternest look he could muster. "And don't tell me nothing."

The foxgirl gave him a momentary look of defiance but then she sagged. "It is a... pain in my head. It does not go away."

"A pain in your head?" he repeated. "When did it start?"

"I first noticed it yesterday, when we arrived in the

village," she replied. "But it got worse. It is a little better right now, but it is always there."

Ethan remembered something the dwarf had said earlier. He turned to Ainslee. "Didn't you say Yuliana complained about the same thing? A headache?"

Ainslee looked thoughtful for a moment before nodding. "Yah. She had an ache in the head."

"Do you get headaches often?" he asked Nia.

The foxgirl shook her head. "I have never before had an ache of the head."

Ethan cocked his head. Must be nice to have never gotten a headache. He got them all the time. He stopped. Actually, he used to get them all the time. He couldn't remember having a headache since he was here that wasn't related to his first arrival or using too much magic.

And now, out of the blue, two of the women - different species really - had gotten headaches at the same time. To Ethan, that seemed too coincidental. What were the chances of two people in his party having the same affliction at the same time? He needed to find out when Yuliana's headache started. Maybe there was something else going on. But what?

"Let's go back to town," he told the others. "I want to find out when Yuliana's headache started."

"What does that have to do with anything?" Ainslee asked.

"I don't know," Ethan said. And he didn't. There was something in the back of his head. Something he couldn't quite put his finger on. Hopefully, talking with Yuliana would help him to figure it out. "Besides, there's mead back in town."

Ainslee grinned and clapped him hard on the back. "Now, you're making sense! Let's go!"

3

———

On the way back to Hawkshead, they had stumbled upon a group of ducks in a wider section of the river. Nia was bringing out her bow, but Ethan stopped her. Instead, he reached out with tendrils of <u>Air</u> and captured four of the ducks. Unfortunately, focusing his attention across four different creatures seemed to be his limit.

Ethan and his companions carried the quacking, flapping animals into the villages and gave them to Fearghas. He'd thought about killing them where they were, but this way, they'd be fresher.

"You found some ducks!" the innkeeper exclaimed. "I bake these up for you. You want them for lunch or dinner?"

"Lunch!" Ainslee said, licking her lips.

Ethan gave her a hard look, but she shrugged. "What?! I'm hungry!"

Rolling his eyes, he turned back to Fearghas. "If you can do anything to maximize how far they go, that would be appreciated. And keep one for yourself..."

Ainslee's eyes went large and she opened her mouth to object, but Ethan cut her off with a glare as he continued to talk. "Since you are taking care of Michalus."

"Maybe a duck soup or a stew." The innkeeper nodded and looked thoughtful. He called his son and the young dwarf came racing into the room.

"Yes, Da?" Sawney asked and waved at the group.

"Take these ducks and put them in the pens," the older dwarf told his son. "Be careful with them. I don't want to be chasing a duck around the inn!"

"Yes, Da!" The boy bobbed his head and hurried over to Par'karr. He and the kobold extracted the duck from Par'karr's pack, and the boy carried it in the kitchen.

Fearghas' expression grew more serious once his son had left the common room. "Did you find out anything about the game?"

"Only that anything land-based seems to have headed south," Ethan replied.

"Yah," the innkeeper snorted. "Cause there's nowhere else to go. The mountains become impassable to the north, east and west. South's the only way they could go."

Ethan considered the innkeeper's words. He hadn't realized the mountains were impassable in the other directions. The mountains near the mines certainly were impassable, that much he remembered from their brief excursion to find the former mayor. At least, they were impassable unless you were a mountain goat or bitten by a radio-active spider.

Knowing that the mountains east and west were also impassable seem to lend more credence to his theory that the cause was to the north. Could it be a dragon? Or some other monster they hadn't seen? Or was it some pending natural disaster that the creatures somehow sensed and were fleeing?

"Has there ever been any volcanic activity in this area or earthquakes?" Ethan asked the innkeeper.

Fearghas looked surprised at the question but then scratched his head. "These aren't volcanic mountains, lad. As for quakes, I can't say that we have had any in this area. Never even heard of them this far north."

The innkeeper nodded. "Along the equator. That's a hotspot for quakes and tremors."

The equator on Earth was the warmest because there was more direct sunlight. Could there be more quakes at the equator of this world because there was more gravitational pull there? He had no idea. It wasn't exactly the type of thing that showed up on a college or high school exam.

"You okay, lass?" the innkeeper asked, glancing at Nia.

Ethan looked over at her to see her brow wrinkled and her fingers once again massaging her temples. Her face looked pained, more so than before.

The foxgirl looked at Ethan. "The ache of the head is more noticeable now. And... uh, nevermind."

"And what?" he insisted. He stepped closer and put a hand on his shoulder. "Any detail could help us figure this out."

"There is a ringing in my ears." She winced. "It is like when a thunderclap strikes too near to you, but it is constant. I noticed it before, but it had almost disappeared outside the village. Now it is back."

Noise on the steps caught Ethan's attention and he turned to see Yuliana coming down. She had one hand to the side of her head and stopped halfway down the stairs. "I heard you talking. I too have an ache in the head. Not only that, but this morning, Luna was missing. She was whining most of last night and I let her out. She has not returned."

That something which had been nudging at the back of his mind suddenly jumped into his consciousness. High-frequency audio waves! Only last year, he had bought one of those ultrasonic pest control devices that were supposed to repel mice. It had worked pretty well but whenever the neighbor walked his dog past his house, the dog began to howl.

It made sense. Most animals heard frequencies which were too high for humans to perceive. Ethan was human and wouldn't detect them. Dwarves may be in the same boat, especially since Ainslee had never demonstrated any extraordinary level of hearing.

Par'karr hadn't shown any exceptional hearing. But he was a reptile, or at least reptilian, and Ethan had no idea how a reptilian's sense of hearing even worked. It wasn't like the kobold had ears.

But then there were Nia and Yuliana. The elf had already demonstrated hearing that was far superior to humans, even better than Nia. It was entirely possible that elves could hear ultrasonic frequencies.

The foxgirl obviously had some animal characteristics. Her sense of smell was on par with a bloodhound, so it was possible her other senses were enhanced as well. Foxes were canines. Perhaps Nia's hearing wasn't as good as the elf's, but she was probably able to pick up ultrasonic frequencies in the same way a dog could hear a dog whistle.

"You know something," Nia said, her eyes searching his face. The corner of her mouth turned up. "You are smiling."

Ethan realized he was smiling and nodded. "I think I know what's going on."

He immediately had everyone's attention. Ainslee gestured impatiently. "Don't keep it to yourself, wizard-boy. Tell us. Is it a dragon?"

"Dragon?!" the innkeeper gasped, eyes going wide.

Ethan turned a glare on Ainslee, but the dwarf just stood there with her hands on her hips, waiting. He let out a sigh and turned back to the innkeeper. "There is no proof it's a dragon...."

"There's no proof it isn't," Ainslee cut in. When he glared at her again, she shrugged. "There's not. Just sayin'."

Letting out an exasperated breath, Ethan continued. "I don't think it is a dragon..." He saw Ainslee's mouth beginning to open and turned to glare at her again. "... BECAUSE... of the headaches."

"The headaches?" the group repeated at nearly the same time. As they did, the innkeeper's son reappeared and walked over to the dwarf.

"What does an aching skull have to do with it?" Ainslee asked with a scrunched-up face. She handed her duck to Sawney and the boy disappeared into the back room again. "That doesn't make any sense."

"If you'll let me explain," Ethan continued. "I believe the headaches are being caused by sounds that humans and dwarves can't hear. Elves and foxlings have more acute senses of hearing and can pick them up even though we can't hear them."

Both Ainslee and the innkeeper looked skeptical, while he caught Yuliana and Nia nodding. Par'karr, always his advocate, seemed to accept what he said at face value. He bobbed his head up and down.

"Ethan right," the kobold exclaimed. "Par'karr rabbits not

like to be here. Par'karr not summon them since get in village."

"Wait," Ethan turned on the kobold. "Your rabbits have the same problem?"

Par'karr nodded. "Par'karr see they not happy. Par'karr send them home."

"And Luna," Ethan added, casting a glance to the steps where Yuliana was sitting. The elf was rubbing her temples, just like Nia. "The mountain lion left as well. If I'm right, she went south to get away from the sound."

"She was going south before I lost all sense of her," Yuliana confirmed. Her voice was haggard, as if she had been up all night. For all he knew, she had been.

"So," the innkeeper squinted at him with one eye, "you think a sound is causing all this? A sound we can't hear?"

"Yes," Ethan replied. He looked at Nia, remembering her superior sense of smell. "Think of it like a scent that we can't smell, but which certain animals can not only smell it, but actually track using scent."

"And you think this sound is coming from the north?" Fearghas asked.

"That seems the logical choice," Ethan replied, "since all of the animals are running south."

"What do you think is causing the sound?" the innkeeper asked.

"I don't know," he replied. "Have you ever heard of anything like this happening anywhere else?"

"Can't say that I have," the dwarf said, scratching his beard. "I think I'd recall hearing of a sound no one can hear scaring away all the animals."

"So then maybe it's something unique to this area," Ethan replied.

"Like what?" Fearghas asked.

"Is there anything unusual about the area up north?" Ethan asked. "Any sort of technology? Ruins? Anything at all?"

"Ain't nothing up there," the dwarf responded. "Except for the mine. And that's been up there for years and we never had no problems - not even when it was active."

"And nothing's changed? No landslides? Earthquakes? That sort of thing?" Ethan pressed.

"Nothing," the innkeeper insisted. "Mine's been abandoned for years."

"Except for those bandit fellows," Ainslee chimed in. "Digging around and opening up passages."

Ethan turned to look at Ainslee. "You're right!"

"Of course, I'm right," she said smugly. "But just digging around ain't going to cause some sound no one can hear."

His mind was going into full MMORPG and roleplaying game mode as he thought about the possibilities. The bandits had been hired by the former mayor to terrorize the town while they dug out and looted a tomb that had been discovered inside the old mine. They'd found the tomb but before they'd had the chance to explore it, Ethan and his group had put an end to their reign of terror.

In fact, Cuthbert, the previous mayor, had actually tried to go into the tomb himself but had been found dead in the entrance - the victim of some sort of spike trap. They'd brought back his body to the village and that had been the end of it.

Right after that, they'd had to deal with the kobolds and then he and his group had left for Castlehaven. They'd never gone back to the tomb or sealed it back up. Was it possible the bandits or Cuthbert had awoken something in the tomb?

Were undead a thing on this world? It was a disturbing thought, if true.

He glanced around the people in the inn. "I think we need to go have another look at the tomb Cuthbert and his goons opened."

4

____

Knowing they could make it to the tomb and then back to town before sunset, Ethan had urged the others to leave immediately. They hadn't been happy, especially Ainslee who wanted some lunch. Once the innkeeper explained that it would take several hours to make the duck stew, and gave her two mugs of mead, the dwarven knight finally relented.

"Mead makes everything better," Ainslee said, as she finished the second mug. "Fine. Let's go up there, fix this sound and be back in time for dinner!"

Ethan doubted it would be that easy, but he could hope. Once again, Yuliana opted to stay at the inn, so it was just Ethan, Nia, Par'karr and Ainslee. The four of them piled out of the inn and set off to the north.

They'd walked about a mile before he saw Nia stagger to the side, holding her head. She immediately recovered, but he could see the foxgirl was in pain. He guessed that the closer they were to the source of the sound, the worse it would be for her.

"Nia," he told her. "You don't have to come. We can scout it out and then come back. Why don't you head back to the inn."

"I... am... fine," she said through gritted teeth in a tone that said she was anything but fine. Her breath was coming quick and he knew she wasn't out of breath from the walk.

"You're not fine," he said, walking over to her. As he got closer, he could see perspiration beading on her forehead. "The sound is worse, the closer you get, isn't it?"

"I... am... fine," she repeated.

"No, you're not," he repeated. "We're turning around."

"No," Nia protested.

"That's fine with me." Ainslee shrugged, already turning around. "Dinner won't be ready, but the mead will be."

"We go back?" Par'karr asked, looking between Ainslee, Ethan and Nia.

"No," Nia said weakly. Her eyes were slits, but he could tell it was from pain and not menace.

"We will return," he told the foxgirl. He needed to put it in terms the woman would understand. "Think of this sound as a foe. Right now, it has us outnumbered, so we will retreat and come up with a winning strategy. We cannot take on this foe head on."

It wasn't his best analogy, but the foxgirl was a warrior. She understood battle tactics. Hopefully, he hadn't gone completely off the mark. After all, until recently, his idea of a battle was an online game.

"You think you may know a better strategy," she asked.

"I have a few ideas," he told her, and it was true. He had an immediate idea of how to give her a short reprieve from the headache and he also had an idea of a longer-term solution. Maybe.

"Then let us return and formulate a better plan," she nodded. When she did, he saw her face tightened in pain. Ethan guessed she must be experiencing something like a migraine.

He'd never had one himself, but he had experienced some nasty hangover headaches where it felt like any light that entered your eyes was boring a hole through your brain and into the back of your head. If it was anything like Nia and Yuliana were experiencing, he hoped his idea would work.

THE FOUR OF them returned to Hawkshead. On the way, Ethan managed to use his magic to snag a few quail from a nearby tree. The birds were small and quick, and he only managed to grab three before the others flew off out of his range.

When they reached the town, Ethan handed out the small birds to several of the farmers who had moved into houses in town. They were grateful for the small gesture, but he wished he could do more. Hopefully, they could figure out what was causing the sound and turn it off or destroy it.

When they reached his house, he told Nia to go inside and wrap a blanket around her head while he worked. Once she went inside, he went to the back of the house and used Earth magic to create a hole about six feet long by four feet wide by three feet deep.

He grinned as he remembered making a similar hole to test whether the balweers, long snakelike creatures with many legs, could see well in the dark. Nia and he had hidden in the hole and luckily, the balweers hadn't seen them. That was the first time they'd had sex.

Hesitantly, he pushed those thoughts aside and concentrated on his next task. He had a hole, but he needed to line it with something waterproof. The only thing he could manipulate that would be waterproof was <u>Earth</u>. In this case, stone.

Going down to the river, he used *Air* to pick up multiple stones and bring them back with him. Par'karr was following him, fascinated at what he was doing. "Can you do me a favor?"

"Yes!" the kobold responded immediately. "Par'karr help!"

"Can you go down by the river and see if you can find any reeds. I need a hollow reed, as thick as you can find it," he told Par'karr. When the little kobold looked at him in confusion, Ethan clarified. "A reed is a hollow stick. About this big around."

"Hollow stick. Yes! Par'karr find!" The kobold nodded and then raced away back towards the river.

Ethan carried the stones to the hole and dropped them inside. Then he repeated the process several more times until he had a dozen decent-sized rocks at the bottom of his small pit.

Checking his *Mana* level, he used *Earth* magic to first merge the stones together and then shape the new stony mass into a box shape, open at the top. It looked like an open stone sarcophagus, but it would serve his purposes.

He moved dirt into the stone box, to line the sides and bottom. Then, he gathered some additional stones and formed an inner layer, effectively making an insulated water tank. With the tank done, he created a lid for the tank the same way. Create a thin stone base, fill it with dirt, then enclose it with stone. All except for one small hole, large enough for a reed.

With the tank and lid created, he walked halfway between the river and the stone box and used *Water* magic to bring water from the river and fill up the box. It didn't take long at all and soon he had what looked like a long, stone bathtub. But in actuality, he'd just created this world's first sensory deprivation tank. At least, that was his intention.

As if on cue, Par'karr came up from the river. His head was hung low and his hands were empty. He stopped in front of Ethan. "Par'karr not find hollow stick."

"It's okay," he told the kobold. He held his hands a foot apart. "They may not even have them in this world. Can you go grab me a stone about this big, instead?"

The kobold nodded, ran down to the river at top speed and came running back a few seconds later with a stone. "Me have stone!"

"Thanks, Par'karr," he told the kobold as he took the stone. He once again used <u>Earth</u> magic to shape the stone, but this time he formed into a three-foot-long, hollow stone tube. It was a bit heavy, but it would do.

"What that?" Par'karr asked, cocking his head.

"A tube," he told the kobold. "For breathing through when you're underwater."

He demonstrated by putting the tube to his mouth and wrapping his lips around it. He took several breaths in and out. Just like a snorkel, only heavier.

"Now to test it out," Ethan said and stripped off his clothes. He started to get into the water but quickly withdrew his foot. It was freezing. Using his <u>Fire</u> magic, like he had to heat up the water in the bathtub at the inn, he warmed the water to a comfortable temperature.

Slipping back into his large tub of water, he once again put the tube in his mouth and then submerged himself in the water. Using *Air*, he levitated the lid over top, sealing the chamber and then stuck the tube through the hole.

After a moment of getting used to breathing through the tube, he was able to relax. Then he listened. There was nothing. No sounds of the river. No sounds of the village. As he had hoped, the chamber drowned out all sounds of the outside. Now, for the real test.

Levitating the top off the chamber, he went inside and found Nia. The foxgirl was lying on their bed, blanket around her head and hands pressed against her ears. He tapped on her and she groaned and turned to face him.

"Do you want to not hear the noise?" he asked.

"Yes," she said hopefully.

"I have something you can try," he said and reached out for her hand. "Come with me."

Ethan led her to the chamber at the back of his house and explained how it worked. She listened, a pained expression on her face the entire time.

"I breathe through the tube?" she asked, looking through the opening in the tube.

"Yes," he told her. "Try it out without the top on."

Shrugging, the foxgirl started to undress when she noticed Par'karr nearby. She glared at the little kobold, who immediately cowed under her gaze.

"Par'karr go... uh... check on elf," he stuttered and then hurried off.

Ethan warmed up the water again while Nia finished stripping her clothes off. Not bothering to tease him with her naked body, the foxgirl slipped into the water with the tube.

It only took her a few minutes to get used to breathing through the tube and then she sat up.

"This is very interesting," she said. "I can still hear the noise, but it is not as loud."

"For the full effect," he told her, "we have to put the top on. That should block out nearly all of the sound. Just raise and lower the tube three times and I'll move the top. I'll move the lid in five minutes if you don't signal me sooner."

"Okay," she said and sank back down into the water.

Moving the lid onto the chamber, he sealed her in. Then he began counting. When he reached 300 Mississippi, he tapped on the tube and then moved the lid.

Nia emerged from the water smiling. He saw her cringe a few seconds later but she still grinned at him. "It worked! I could not hear the sound. It was so nice for that short time."

"Good," he said. "It should give you and Yuliana some short relief while I work on a better solution."

"A better solution?" She furrowed her brow.

He grinned. "Ever heard of noise-cancelling headphones?"

5

———

The next day, Yuliana and Nia took turns using the sensory tank. The short bursts of relief seemed to help both of them immensely and improved their mood. While the two of them took turns in the tank, Ethan worked on creating magical items.

From the talks he had with Michalus previously, Ethan knew the basics of creating a magic item. To his mind, it worked much like an electronic circuit in many aspects. Instead of electricity and microchips, it used magic and Chymera crystals.

Casting spells and enchanting, or "programming", the Chymera crystals worked on the same principle: the will and intent of the wizard. And while spells were generally quick and he didn't need to hold his focus long, enchanting was a slow, meticulous process that required long periods of focus. Something that apparently Ethan wasn't great at.

Ethan knew what he wanted. He needed to create a neck-lace that acted as noise-canceling headphones. He knew the basic concepts. Read in sound waves and send out the inverse wave, effectively canceling out the sound. Technology did it on Earth but the same should be possible with magic. He hoped.

The problem was focusing on what he wanted. While solidifying air into a shield or creating a ball of fire were both straightforward, it turned out that creating noise-canceling technology with magic wasn't.

His first attempt was an abysmal failure and nearly deafened him when he put it on. Even an hour later, his ears were still ringing. But he had created a magic item. A real magic item. He dubbed it the Necklace of Deafening Sounds +10!

Since he could find no practical use for the necklace, other than torturing someone, he decided to dismantle it so he could reuse the crystals. Unfortunately, he knew this to be more difficult than it seemed. Once the crystals were set up in a "circuit" they didn't want to be pulled apart. The only way to break the circuit was to smash one of the crystals. And not just any crystal.

There were two types of crystals that went into making a magic item: battery crystals and spell crystals. They were both Chymera crystals and identical in every way. The difference was how they were used.

The battery crystal was just like its Earthly namesake, a battery. There had to be enough *Mana* in the total battery crystals to create the spell effect. If not, nothing happened, and the item would be useless.

In contrast, the spell crystals contained the actual spell, program or wizard's will which would create the effect. When the two types of crystals were joined together with *Mana*, they formed what Ethan came to think of as a magical circuit.

The only way to break the magical circuit, once created, was to smash one of the spell crystals. Michalus had been very clear on that. Destroying a battery crystal could be bad, potentially very bad depending on the amount of *Mana* in the crystal.

Once in a circuit, the circuit somehow recharged the battery crystals. If a fully charged battery crystal was shattered: boom! There could be an explosion relative to the amount of *Mana*. Apparently, people had lost limbs doing that. Some had lost entire city blocks.

Smashing a spell crystal, like he had done with the library gateway in Patheos, not only broke the crystal, it also broke the enchantment completely. That meant there was no way to salvage any work he had done or repair a broken magic item.

Instead, he had to gather the intact crystals and start from scratch. That included charging the crystals. While charging the crystals wasn't difficult, it required dumping nearly all of his *Mana* into the crystal. That was the easy part.

The time-consuming part was waiting for it to recharge. He had actually toyed with the idea of trying to convince Nia to have sex to recharge his *Mana*, but considering that she, quite literally, had a headache, he didn't even try.

Instead, he waited and helped around the village while his *Mana* recharged. He helped rip boards from some of the old houses, helped other villagers fix their roof and other menial tasks that didn't involve magic.

Part of him was helping out of a sense of altruism. He genuinely enjoyed helping people. But another part was to show that, even though he was a wizard, he was just a normal guy. Considering how people shied away from him, he could use a little goodwill.

After lunch, he finished recharging the battery crystals and tried again. He channeled the spell, program, magic or whatever you wanted to call it, into the spell crystals. Once all three spell crystals were created, he had to quickly form the circuit with the battery crystals.

He used the same 5 crystals in the same necklace as before, just adding a new spell crystal. The necklace was just a simple piece of silver jewelry they had taken from one of the bodies. Using the blade of his knife, he'd pried the existing stones out of it and managed to replace them with the Chymera crystals.

All the crystals were charged with *Mana* or loaded with the spell. Now it was time to test his invention. Ethan willed *Mana* into the necklace and he sensed the circuit take hold. And just like that... he'd created a new magic item. But would it do what he wanted it to?

Learning from his previous failure, the Necklace of Deafening Sounds, he took some frayed pieces of cloth and stuffed them into his ears. Hopefully that would protect him if he had created a second deafening necklace.

Taking a deep breath, he tensed up as he held the necklace over his head. He was ready to pull it off instantly if things turned out like last time. Taking a deep breath and wishing for the best, Ethan lowered the necklace around his neck.

Nothing happened. At least, there was no loud, deafening noise. He rotated his head around. Not only was there no deafening noise, there was no noise at all. Ethan frowned. He yelled but heard nothing. He pounded on the table he'd been working on. Nothing.

It was deathly quiet, like there was no sound at all in the world. Ethan sighed. He had created a noise-canceling necklace. Unfortunately, it seemed to cancel out all sound, not just the high frequency sounds he needed to cancel.

He took the necklace off and was immediately greeted by the sounds of the river, the sounds of the townsfolk and a plethora of other sounds. Ethan looked down at the necklace and shook his head. Another failure.

Putting the necklace down on the table, he prepared to smash one of the spell crystals. He hesitated. Unlike the Necklace of Deafening Sounds +10, this one didn't cause pain. Given what it did, one of the women might actually like it while they slept or while they weren't in the sensory tank.

Ethan set aside the Necklace of Silence, as he had just dubbed it, and brought out another necklace. He groaned. He'd have to go through the entire process again. Shaking his head and sitting down at the table, he began making another magical necklace.

JUST AFTER DINNER, Ethan took the fourth attempt off his neck. It had done nothing for him. It hadn't caused ear-bursting sound, nor had it dampened all sound. Was it possible it was dampening the high-frequency sounds? Had he actually done it? Sadly, he had no way of knowing.

Stretching, Ethan took the necklace and walked outside. Nia had gone hunting to the south a few hours ago. She was a better marksman than the villagers and had managed to bring down several birds early. Shortly after lunch, she'd done a session in the tank and then went south again for more hunting. She was still out, which meant he'd have to test it on Yuliana.

Ethan walked over to the inn and, going inside, went up the stairs to the guest rooms. The second room was Michalus's room and he knew he'd find her there. He knew Yuliana was wearing the Necklace of Silence so he didn't bother to knock. Cracking the door open, he looked inside.

Michalus was still in the bed, eyes closed, breathing shallow but steady. In a chair next to the bed was Yuliana - and she was sleeping. Around her neck was the Necklace of Silence. He smiled. At least some good had come of the thing.

He walked over to her and tapped her on the shoulder. Despite being gentle, the tapping caused her to start and nearly jump out of her chair.

"It's just me!" he said, forgetting she couldn't hear.

Eyes wide, she recognized him and then looked down at her chest. She pulled off the necklace, blushing slightly. "I am sorry. You startled me."

Ethan grinned. "I guess you're used to relying on sense of hearing."

"More so than I realized," she nodded and already Ethan saw the pain lines creasing her forehead.

Remembering why he had come, he held out the new necklace. "Try this one. I can't tell if it works or not, but I can hear fine with it on."

She handed him the Necklace of Silence and took the new necklace. Slipping it around her neck she froze. The elf cocked her head one way and then the other. As she did so, Ethan saw the tips of her ears twitching slightly.

A huge grin spread over her face and she flung herself at

Ethan, wrapping him in a huge hug and planting a wet kiss on his lips. Surprised, he froze and didn't react immediately. By the time he did, she was stepping back and blushing furiously.

"I'm sorry," she said. "I was just so happy. The sound, the ringing, it's gone! And I can hear everything else! It's so wonderful!"

Ethan forced himself to smile back but his brain and his other parts were both confused and excited by the elf's kiss. He silently chided himself for enjoying it.

After all, he was a married man. Sort of. He still needed to find out from someone whether that was a legal marriage. Not that it mattered. Nia thought they were married and he wasn't about to win an argument with her.

"I'm glad it works," he said finally.

The elf's embarrassment was gone, replaced with a sense of profound relief. She collapsed into her chair. "Perhaps tonight I can actually get some sleep."

"You still bunking with Ainslee?" he asked.

"Yes," she replied.

Ethan grinned and held up the Necklace of Silence, making a snoring sound as he did. "Sure you don't want this one?"

They both shared a laugh and then Ethan returned to his home. He hadn't eaten but he wanted to have one of the necklaces ready for Nia when she returned. The foxgirl had been out hunting for most of the day, catching ducks, quail and other birds for the village. He wanted her to be able to get a good night's sleep.

He went to work immediately and had just finished up when Nia finally returned. The foxgirl carried a half dozen bird carcasses and gave them to Fearghas to hand out to the villagers. Afterwards, she joined Ethan inside and he presented her with a new necklace.

When she figured out what it did, she had the same reaction as Yuliana, but it didn't just stop at a kiss. Her headache gone, they quickly found their way to the bed and she helped him restore his *Mana*. Many times.

6

The next morning, they ate leftover duck stew. He picked the meat out of his and gave it to Nia, while she gave him all of her vegetables, or "prey" food as she called it. None of them were satisfied after the meal but no one in the village was well fed at the moment.

After breakfast, the group gathered again outside Ethan's home. Nia and Yuliana both looked rested for the first time since they returned from their adventure in Patheos. Nia was even smiling, though he knew the grin was from their early morning "mana restoration" activities.

"Alright," the dwarf huffed. "We're all here. We headin' north now?"

"No," he replied, to everyone's surprise. He reached into his pocket and pulled out the leather slave collar he'd taken from Par'karr. The little kobold had given it to him after he explained what he intended, though he knew the summoner was glad to be rid of it.

The slave collars had been Ethan's idea. After he'd learned that Castlehaven's ruler had passed an edict allowing the enslavements of anyone who wasn't a human, dwarf or halfling, he bought some collars for the others to wear to prevent them from being taken as slaves.

While they had resisted the idea at first, he'd finally persuaded them with reason. They'd worn them around Castlehaven and to the library of Patheos and back. But now that they were back in Hawkshead, there was no need for them.

Except Ethan had found a need. He handed the collar to Yuliana, who eyed it for a moment before taking it. Her left hand went up to her own collar. She looked confused until she saw the crystals embedded in the collar. She raised an eyebrow.

"For Luna." He smiled. "If you can find her."

The elf's face split into a huge grin and she threw her arms around Ethan in a big hug. Thankfully, she hadn't kissed him in front of Nia. He wasn't sure, but the foxgirl seemed the jealous type. "Thank you! I must go find her!"

"Good idea. Hopefully, it will work on her, just like it works for you and Nia," he agreed and then turned to Par'karr. "Sorry, I didn't have anything small enough to fit around a rabbit's neck."

Par'karr looked disappointed and nodded but then looked up brightly. "Maybe Par'karr make collars."

"If you can make something that will fit your rabbits," he said. "I'll turn them into noise-cancelation collars. I'm just not sure what will happen when they disappear."

"Stuff fall off them when they go home," Par'karr told him.

"Good," he said. "But that means you'll need to keep track of them. If they disappear during combat, you won't be able to resummon them until you retrieve the collars."

The little kobold bobbed his head in understanding.

"Now," Ethan said, looking around the group. "Yuliana is going to go give the collar to Luna. The rest of us need to help the villagers."

"Hunting?" Ainslee groaned.

"No," he said. "I think that will take too long and we can't hunt and investigate the source of this noise at the same time."

"Then what do we do?" Nia asked.

"The villagers don't have my magic and they don't have Nia's skill with a bow," he said. "So we use traps."

"Traps?" Nia asked.

"Yes," he nodded, looking at the foxgirl. Of all of them, she seemed to be the best outdoorsman. Outdoorswoman? Outdoorsfox? He smiled. "Do you know how to trap birds with cages?"

She screwed up her face. "Capture birds? With cages?"

"Like rabbit?" Par'karr asked with a cocked head. "Me capture rabbits with traps."

"Maybe. Would your traps work with birds?" he asked.

The little kobold shrugged. "Me never use them for birds. Only rabbits."

Ethan had Par'karr describe his traps and how they worked. When he'd finished, Ethan was smiling. It sounded exactly like what he'd had in mind. A cage made of branches, propped up on one side by a stick. A piece of rope or twine was connected to the stick and once the rabbit - or bird in their case - went inside, the person pulled the rope and the cage fell atop of the bird, sealing them inside.

"We just need some breadcrumbs or whatever will attract the birds," Ethan told them. "Once we build the cages and show the villagers how to build more, they can do most of the trapping while we go investigate the noise."

"Why don't we just go break whatever is creating the noise and then come back and do it?" Ainslee asked.

Ethan sighed. That had been his original thought as well until he remembered the deadly trap that had killed the former mayor. He had a bad feeling that wasn't the only trap, and probably not even the deadliest.

If they didn't return right away, or at all, Ethan wanted to make sure the villagers had some way of getting food. Hopefully, the cages would be enough to supplement the few vegetables they still had.

"Fine," the dwarf said, her eyes darting back to the inn. She smiled. "Fearghas still has some mead left, so another day won't hurt."

With all of them in agreement, Yuliana left to find Luna while Nia and Ainslee followed Par'karr into the woods to find the right sticks to make the cages. Ethan stayed behind to work on his own project.

It was actually two projects, but he needed to create a proof of concept first. Luckily, their lovemaking the night before and then again this morning had allowed him to charge enough crystals for his experiments - provided they worked.

He smiled involuntarily as he remembered their "mana recharging" sessions. Ethan still had no idea exactly how or why it worked, but it did and he enjoyed every minute of it.

Another thing he didn't quite understand was HOW he was able to keep up with the foxgirl, and he meant that in every sense of the word.

Not that he had a ton of experience, but he always seemed to "rise" to the occasion. Was it magic? Part of this strange Stamina/Health system or was it something else entirely? He wasn't sure, but he wasn't complaining. Sometimes it was best not to look gift horses in the mouth.

Ethan spent the first hour gathering rocks near the river. Once he had enough, he shaped them into a stone chest and a lid made from stone too. It was similar to his larger sensory deprivation chamber, but nearly airtight. The water, which was fed down from the mountains, was cold. Very cold. With the stone chest in the river, any food put into it should keep like it was in a refrigerator. At least, that was his working theory.

And that was just the first part. He used *Earth* magic to manipulate the inside of the stone lid and create three unique symbols. These he modeled after baseball team logos. Once that was complete, he went back to his house to work on the rest of his proof of concept.

Using the chest he'd taken from the Graycloaks, he used *Fire* to burn three different unique symbols into the bottom left of the chest, just like Michalus had done. Next, he took his largest leather pouch and embedded crystals into it. It wasn't easy and proved beyond his meager skills.

In the end, he'd had to ask Fearghas' wife, Elspeth, to sew them into the leather. She'd looked at him curiously but after mumbling something about "wizard's business," she'd done the job in record time.

When she was done, he'd given her his leather backpack and asked her to do the same thing while he went back to his house. It was time to put his theory to the test.

Like he had done with the necklaces, he "programmed" the spell crystals. Having learned his lesson with the noise-cancellation necklaces, he took his time and kept his will focused on exactly the result he wanted.

Once all three of the spell crystals were programmed, he took a deep breath, said a little prayer and then sent the magic into the crystals to complete the circuit. The crystals flared to life but nothing else happened.

Had it worked? Had he just created his first portal pouch? Unfortunately, there was only one way to know for sure whether or not it had worked. Ethan had to test it.

Wiping sweaty palms on his breeches, he thought about sticking his hand into the pouch but quickly dismissed the idea. What if the spell didn't work properly and his hand ended up in lava, in the vacuum of space or some equally deadly or painful place. No. Best to try it with something inanimate.

He grabbed a nearby candle and took a deep breath. This was the moment of truth. He dropped the candle into his pouch and... it disappeared. Instantaneously, it tumbled into the bottom of the chest. It had worked! He'd just created a portal pouch!

After doing a little victory dance, he tried sticking the edge of his staff into the pouch. Like the candle, it passed through. He pushed it further in, until the staff hit the far side of the chest and then he pulled the staff back out.

Examining and feeling the part of the staff that had gone through the portal, he made sure it looked and felt the same. He tried the staff a few more times before he was confident enough to stick his hand in the pouch.

When he finally did, he found it bizarre to see part of his arm going into the pouch and then appearing in a chest several feet away. He watched with a morbid fascination as he wiggled his fingers and the fingers of his hand in the chest wiggled.

Suppressing a shudder, he withdrew his hand and made

sure everything still worked. When it did, he let out a shout of joy and did another dance. That was when Elspeth walked in with the backpack.

She took one look at him doing his dance and shook her head. "I have your backpack all done, just like you asked."

"Excellent!" he replied, ignoring the heat in his face. "I really appreciate it. If I'm right, this will help the village."

She screwed up her face in confusion. "How is a back-pack supposed to help the village?"

"Two ways," he said. "First, I've created a stone chest in the river. The river is so cold that any food you put in the chest should last for days."

She nodded. "We've done similar things before, but the animals usually find it. No one ever thought of making a stone chest."

"That's only part of it." He grinned, barely containing his enthusiasm. "When I enchant the backpack, anything you put into the backpack will appear in the stone chest."

"You're going to magic the backpack? What good will that do?" She frowned.

Ethan was proud of this part of his plan. He'd gotten it after overhearing Odelina saying how it was no good hunting so far south because it would take too long to get the meat back to town. With the backpack, hunters could go south where the animals were, kill them, dress them and put the meat into the backpack and it would appear in the chest. Problem solved.

He quickly related his idea to the dwarf, who listened with a sour face. When he was done, she shrugged. "It's wizard magic though. People ain't gonna want to mess with it."

"Maybe," Ethan said. "But if it's a choice of starving or

using an enchanted backpack, I'm hoping they'll use the backpack."

Elspeth shrugged again and set the backpack on one of the shelves before turning and stepping through the door. She paused and looked back. "Even if they don't use it, me and my husband appreciate you and your women friends helping the village." She glanced at the backpack again. "I pray it will be enough to keep us going."

"We'll figure out what's keeping the animals away," he told her.

The dwarf nodded unconvincingly. Then she turned, walked out and shut the door behind her.

Ethan went over to the backpack and brought it over to his work table. All of the crystals were sewn in. He'd used almost twice as many crystals on the backpack as he had on the pouch. He wasn't sure why he'd felt compelled to do it that way; considering how many crystals the library portal had contained, he thought he was right.

The backpack was ready. The crystals were ready. Now, he just needed to do his part. Ethan smiled. It was time to make some magic.

7

———

Ethan had just finished enchanting the backpack when he heard a pounding on the door. It persisted, so he stood from his table and walked through the shop area to the door. Throwing it open he saw a young boy who couldn't be older than seven, with a pock-marked face, dirty flax-colored hair, tattered clothes and no shoes.

The boy looked familiar and Ethan thought he'd seen the kid playing with some other children around town since he'd returned.

Looking up at Ethan with wild eyes, the boy stuttered. "Pa says... mm.... monsters ... comin' to town!"

He started to run away, but Ethan caught the kid by the arm. "Where?"

The boy looked terrified but Ethan wasn't sure if it were the monsters the kid was scared of... or him. He pointed north. "North... they're...coming from the... north. My mum was out looking for berries and saw it!"

Ethan released the boy and the child fled south. Looking

north, Ethan saw several townspeople gathering at the bridge. One of them carried an axe, another carried a pitchfork but the other two carried the long-spears they'd used to defend the town from the kobold attack. He smiled. At least some of them had kept the weapons.

Ducking back into his shop, Ethan grabbed his long knife and his staff and rushed back out. Running over to the villagers, he called out, "What's going on? I heard there are monsters?"

"Aye, mayor," said the nearest man. He was a tall man with long dark hair and a full beard. Ethan remembered he was one of the farmers who was staying in town while they rebuilt his farm. "A cyclops from the mountains."

By habit, Ethan scanned the man.

```
Zachary
    Human
    Farmer
    Level 4
```

"Cyclops?" Ethan groaned. "Those are a thing here?"

"Aye," Zachary said. "Don't usually come near humans. I reckon it's cause the game went south."

"You're probably right." Ethan nodded. He brought up his HUD and checked his scores.

```
Health: 30
    Stamina: 38
    Mana: 57
```

His *Health* was maxed out, but from all his work today,

his *Stamina* was low and his *Mana* hadn't quite fully recharged from creating the magic backpack.

"What is happening?" Nia asked as she, Par'karr and Ainslee came running over.

"Some sort of cyclops is coming towards the town," he replied, glancing back at them.

"Cyclops?" Nia asked, furrowing her brow.

Ethan shrugged. He knew what a cyclops was supposed to be from ancient Greek stories. According to Greek myths, cyclops were one-eyed giants. Were they the same on this world? Or something completely different? "In the stories of my world, they're one-eyed giants."

"Aye." The farmer nodded. "One big, ugly eye right in the middle of their foreheads."

"One eye, huh? You gonna magic his cyclops thingy, wizard-boy?" Ainslee asked. "Or should I go get me stuff?"

Ethan had handled ogres before, could cyclops be any worse? Still, it was best to be prepared. "Go grab your stuff. Best to be ready for anything."

"Fine," huffed the dwarf and she ran back towards the inn.

Nia moved up beside him. He glanced over at her and smiled. The foxgirl always had her weapons with her, even in town.

Par'karr had no weapons either, but normally the kobold's summoned rabbits were his weapons. But would the rabbits be any good in combat with the high-pitched sound? Ethan was looking over at the kobold when Nia gasped beside him.

Turning to face north, he saw the reason. Around the bend, lumbered the cyclops. The creature was large, though not quite as tall as the ogres. Ethan guessed it to be about nine or nine and a half feet.

Like the Greek stories, this cyclops had only a single, large eye in the middle of its forehead. Beneath its large eye was an equally large, flat broad nose. Then came an over-sized mouth filled with jagged teeth.

The creature had leathery skin and virtually no hair on its head. It seemed to make up for its bald head with an overly hairy chest, legs and arms. The hair wasn't thick enough to be fur and seemed to grow in uneven patches that gave the cyclops a disheveled look.

It was garbed in what Ethan thought were large bear hides that were tied or slung over its body haphazardly. In its left hand it held what looked like a piece of a tree trunk, which it was obviously using as a club.

The creature stopped as it spotted the town and then its mouth formed into a broken smile as it spotted the horses near Ethan's house. A deep, gravelly voice spoke a single word. "Meat!"

The farmers shifted uncomfortably and although his nose was nowhere as good as Nia's, he could smell the fear on the men. These farmers had fought a horde of kobolds, but a nine-foot, one-eyed giant was something different.

"Steady, men," Ethan said, trying to encourage them. If it worked, the men gave no indication.

Resuming its lumbering walk, the cyclops began coming straight for the horses. Ethan had no intention to let it have their mounts but he didn't want to kill this poor hungry crea-ture if he didn't have to. Maybe he could scare it away with some magic.

Summoning a fireball, he sent it hurling at the one-eyed giant. Ethan intended to have the fireball explode just in front of the cyclops and hopefully scare it away. At least, that was what he intended.

What actually happened was the ball of fire flew towards the creature and its large eye turned towards the ball of fire. The cyclops's one large eye grew wide as it saw the fireball and then the ball of fire just... dissolved. One second it was there and the next it sparked out of existence with a pop.

"You changed your mind?" Nia asked, giving him a confused look.

Blinking in confusion, he stared at the place where the fireball had been. Ethan hadn't changed his mind or willed the fireball to vanish. So what had happened? He quickly checked his *Mana*.

Mana: 53

His *Mana* was fine. He'd only intended to scare the cyclops away so he hadn't used much but the *Mana* was gone and no fireball. Ethan quickly tried grabbing at the one-eyed giant with *Air*, but nothing at all happened.

He began to get a sinking feeling as he watched the cyclops advance towards the bridge. Testing out his theory, Ethan sent a small fireball at the creature. This time, the creature was already looking his way and the fireball dissolved before it even finished forming.

Ethan swore loudly, causing everyone to look at him. Zachary and the other farmers, who had already been terrified, turned white.

"I think the creature dispels magic with its eye," he told Nia and Par'karr, making sure to lower his voice.

"Uh-oh." Par'karr swallowed.

Nia opened her mouth to say something but an out of

breath Ainslee chose that minute to run up to them. She had her armor on, though he noticed not all the buckles were fastened. She also had the shield and hammer they'd retrieved from the library in Patheos. Ethan had to admit, the dwarf was looking more and more like a knight.

"That's... a big one," the dwarf huffed. She looked at Ethan. "You... gonna... magick it... or what?"

"My magic doesn't seem to work against it," he replied in a hushed tone.

"YOUR MAGIC... DOESN'T WORK... AGAINST IT?!" the dwarf bellowed, still trying to catch her breath. "Thor's hammer!"

If the farmers were terrified before, the dwarf's shouting had them wide-eyed and ready to run. Despite the villagers being wary, and sometimes even frightened, of his magic, it appeared they had been counting on him to stop the creature using it.

"I think its eye is what cancels out the magic," he explained. "I just need you and Nia to get its attention and turn it away from me."

"You think?" the dwarf growled. "So you don't know?"

"How would I?" Ethan retorted. "I've never met one of these things."

The dwarf snorted and then stepped out. "Come on, foxy, let's go pull wizard-boy's fat out of the fire."

Nia glanced from Ethan to Ainslee and then back at Ethan. She nodded grimly and drew her scimitars. "We will turn this creature away from you."

"Par'karr help!" said the kobold.

Ethan smiled but shook his head. "I think your rabbits will be dispelled and you don't have your spear."

Par'karr sagged and looked hurt for a moment before he perked up, eyes bright. "Par'karr go get spear!"

Before Ethan could say anything, the little kobold spun and darted off to the inn. Nearby, he heard one of the farmers mumble, "I would have given him mine."

The cyclops reached the far end of the bridge just as Nia and Ainslee reached the near end of the bridge. The one-eyed giant looked at the dwarf and the foxgirl and tilted its head. "Meat?"

"I'll show you meat!" Ainslee yelled and barreled straight at the cyclops shield first. Ethan guessed she'd activated the *Charge* ability.

The dwarf closed the distance in amazing time and slammed into the creature's thick leg. There was a meaty thud and Ethan expected to see the cyclops stumble backwards. Instead, Ainslee staggered back a step and then collapsed onto the stone bridge. The cyclops looked down at the unmoving dwarf and reached out its right hand to pick her up.

Nia reached it and sliced both scimitars across the creature's meaty hand. The one-eyed giant snatched back its hand with a howl. As it did, the foxgirl danced around the creature, trying to get it to turn. Unfortunately, the cyclops' attention only strayed momentarily before turning back to the dwarf.

Once again, with single-minded determination, the cyclops reached down to pick up the dwarf. And once again, Nia sliced the creature's hand, causing it to withdraw. It glanced from its hand to Nia and back, then looked at the dwarf.

Ethan groaned. The cyclops was either too hungry or too stupid to go after Nia. Or was it smart enough to know not to turn its back to him? The one-eyed giant didn't seem partic-ularly smart, but maybe some instinct was at work.

The farmers hadn't made a move. They were literally shaking in their boots, having seen what happened to Ainslee and how ineffectual the foxgirl's attacks seemed.

"Par'karr help!" cried the kobold as he came running back at full speed, spear in hand. Before he could run by, Ethan held out a hand for him to stop.

"Par'karr not help?" the kobold asked with tearful eyes.

"Actually." He grinned at the kobold. "I have a special mission for you!"

The kobold perked up and leaned in while Ethan relayed his plan. When he was done, Par'karr nodded and ran off towards the one-eyed giant.

Ethan watched him go and prepared his spell. He had remembered how the Greek hero, Jason or Odysseus, had defeated the cyclops. They'd put out its eye so it was blind. He wasn't sure if using tactics from Greek mythology was wise or not, but he had asked Par'karr to do the same thing. Blind the cyclops.

If Ethan was right and it was the creature's eye that was dispelling his magic, then he should be able to kill it quickly. If not, he would need to think of a different plan and hope that Ainslee was still alive.

The kobold ran full speed across the bridge and when he was within ten feet of the cyclops, he hurled his spear with all of his momentum behind it. The one-eyed giant saw the weapon coming but its reactions were too slow. Its meaty hand rose to block it but Par'karr's aim was true and the spear embedded itself in the thing's eye.

The cyclops howled in pain and dropped the club in his

left hand. It started to bring both hands to its injured eye but Ethan reached out with *Air*.

This time, he was able to grab the spear with tendrils of *Air* and with as much will as he could muster, he jammed the spear all the way through its eye and into its brain.

```
You critically pierce Mountain Cyclops
for 75 damage.
   Mountain Cyclops dies.
   You gain 45 experience. Experience
to next level 2525.
```

The cyclops stiffened, then staggered and started to fall forward. Had it done so, it would have crushed the unconscious dwarf under its massive weight.

Luckily, Nia bounded forward, somersaulted into the air and did some sort of double leg kick to its head which knocked it backwards. The cyclops tumbled backwards and slammed into the ground with a thud.

The farmers nearby were gasping and muttering.

"You see that? The kobold killed it with one hit!"

"The kobold killed it!"

"How'd he do that?"

Ethan smiled and said nothing. He didn't care about who got the credit. Let them believe that Par'karr was the hero. It was about time the little kobold got some recognition.

Grinning, Ethan got up and jogged over to check on Ainslee.

8

———

A cheer had gone up from the farmers when the cyclops had collapsed. Once Nia had signaled it was dead, the group of farmers rushed forward to congratulate Par'karr.

For his part, the little kobold seemed to believe that he had killed the thing. He accepted the praise with a big grin, happy for all of the attention. He had gone from mistrusted or tolerated, to the town hero in one stroke. Ethan wasn't about to ruin it for him.

Ethan checked the dwarf's pulse. It was steady but that's all Ethan knew. His very basic understanding of first aid was limited to the simplest of conditions. But, it was enough to earn him a skill up.

Skill increase: First Aid +1%.

He knew that in the TV shows and in the movies, they always checked the pupils with a flashlight to see for responsiveness. But even if he did that, he had no idea what it would mean or if it would mean the same with a dwarf.

Nia crouched down beside him. "She is still unconscious?"

Ethan pointed to a lump on her head. "From what I can tell, when she collided with the cyclops, the shield must have rebounded and hit her in the head, just under her helmet."

"Will she be okay?" the foxgirl asked.

"I don't know," he replied honestly. He wasn't a medical professional. He didn't really know the outward symptoms of a concussion. Or if those symptoms applied to dwarves. "Yuliana is still gone?"

Nia nodded. "I have not seen her since she went to look for Luna."

"When she gets back, she can heal her and hopefully she'll wake up," Ethan said. "If she doesn't wake up before. In the meantime, let's get her to the inn."

As he thought of the inn, Ethan looked around for Fearghas. He would have expected the innkeeper and some of the other villagers to have joined them. "Speaking of the inn, where is Fearghas?"

"He and some of the others went south to hunt for food," she said solemnly. "It is getting scarce again with all the mouths to feed."

Ethan sighed.

Nia moved close to his ear. "The kobold's spear did not have enough force to pierce the creature so deeply. And yet, you let the kobold take the credit."

The foxgirl's warm breath on his ear made him think that maybe he needed some of his *Mana* restored but he knew there were too many things that needed to be done right now. It would have to wait.

Ethan moved his mouth to her ear. "Let's keep that between us. Let him take the credit. If nothing else, the villagers won't be quite as mistrustful of him from now on."

"But it is your kill," she whispered back. "You are the Alpha. You are Packleader. You deserve the glory."

Smiling, despite himself, he whispered back. She really was taking this packleader/husband seriously. "It was a team effort. You distracted it, he hit in the eye, and I just finished it off."

"But the villagers believe that Par'karr killed it," she replied. "You should get the praise."

"Par'karr is getting the praise," he told her. "And he follows me. So in essence, I am getting the praise... by proxy."

"That makes no sense," she whispered back. She cocked her head and looked him up and down. "But you are not like other packleaders, so maybe this is good."

She stood up then and looked at the cyclops corpse. "I will go scout north and see if there are any others. I have its scent now."

Ethan started to object but nodded. She was right. If there were more of them, they needed to know. It had been blind luck they'd spotted this one. One of the farmer's wives had gone north to look for berries. If she hadn't, it would have been in town before they noticed it. "Be careful."

Nia nodded, stood and then ran off to the north without a word. Ethan watched her go, admiring the woman's nubile body as she ran. As if she had eyes in the back of her head, she turned, rolled her eyes at him and then continued her jog north.

He grinned at being caught. He didn't feel embarrassed

any more. She was his wife. Why shouldn't he check her out. Besides, he'd seen the corners of her mouth turned up when she'd caught him staring at her.

"Par'karr!" he called to the kobold, who was still surrounded by farmers.

The little kobold perked up and pushed through the farmers to come stand by him. The kobold looked down at the dwarf. "Ainslee be okay?"

"I'm not sure," he said. "But I need you to do something for me."

Par'karr straightened up and puffed out his chest. "Par'karr help!"

"Nia went north to see if there were more cyclops..." he started.

The kobold put on a fierce face and dropped into a crouch. "You want Par'karr go with fox girl?"

"No." He grinned. "Nia said Fearghas and some others went south to hunt. I need you to go south and take something to them."

"Something?" Par'karr asked, his face puzzled.

"An enchanted backpack," Ethan replied.

"Enchanted?" the kobold asked, eyes wide. "How enchanted?"

"It's like Michalus' portal pouch," he explained, motioning from the pouch to the stone chest in the river nearby. "But bigger and anything put in it will come to that chest over there in the water. Because it's cold, the food will keep longer."

Par'karr followed Ethan's pointing finger to where the stone chest lay in the riverbank on the far side of the river, near the village. The kobold looked back to Ethan, still puzzled. "They put things in backpack, they appear in chest?"

"Exactly," he said. "If they catch something and cut it up, they can put the meat in the backpack and it will appear in the chest. I'll tell Fearghas' wife to check it regularly."

The kobold nodded. "Par'karr go south. Give backpack to Fearghas. Tell him put meat in backpack, it appear in village?"

"Right!" He smiled. "The backpack is on the worktable in the back room of my shop. Also, if you see Yuliana, tell her what happened to Ainslee and tell her to come back right away."

"Okay, Par'karr go now!" he said and then turned and raced off, leaving the farmers befuddled.

"Can some of you give me a hand with the dwarf," he asked the nearby men. "We need to get her to her room. The rest of you, see if you can find some rope and drag the cyclops further away from the village. The last thing we need is for any more predators to show up."

Fifteen minutes later, Ethan was back at his workshop. Ainslee was in her bed back at the inn and Elspeth had promised to apply cool compresses to her head until she woke up or until Yuliana arrived.

Ethan had also told her about the chest and sending Par'karr south with the backpack. Once he explained how it worked and how it would instantly transport any meat they caught, she was thankful and promised to have Sawney check it every hour.

Now, Ethan was sitting at his work table. He wanted to try and figure out what his next enchanting project should be. He knew he had time to make one more thing before they left but he wasn't sure what that should be. Unfortunately, he couldn't focus his mind on a new project.

Instead, he was thinking of the cyclops and its magic dispelling power. When he'd found that he couldn't use his magic, he felt helpless. More helpless than he'd felt in a long time. It had been too much like his old self.

On Earth, he'd been a nobody computer technician. A geek with a dead-end job that few girls wanted to date. Now, he was a fairly powerful wizard, if he did say so himself, and he had a really hot wife who was, literally, a fox.

But he'd felt that all stripped away when his magic had proved impotent against the cyclops. He wanted to know how the cyclops could disrupt magic. And more importantly, he wanted to know how he could make sure it never happened again.

He hadn't realized until then how much he'd been taking his magic for granted. At first it had been a shock to be able to do magic. Now, it seemed to almost come second nature to him. Like he was born to do magic.

Having that power suddenly unavailable to him, especially when his companions' lives depended on him, had sobered him. He needed to find a way to avoid that happening again. If he couldn't find a way, then he needed to be able to compensate for it. Somehow.

But he wasn't a warrior like Nia and it would probably take years to become half as good as the fox girl. His asset was his mind. He needed to think of something he could use, even if his magic was neutralized. But what?

Thinking back to the combat with the cyclops, he remembered Nia attacking the thing. She'd been wearing the noise-cancelling necklace he'd given her. Had it been affected by the cyclops?

If not, maybe that was the key. He would need to ask her when she returned. If it still worked, maybe only active magic from a wizard was cancelled. Perhaps magic powered by the enchantment "circuits" wasn't affected.

Suddenly, he began to get an idea. Perhaps he could combine Earth technology with magic. If that were the case, then he could make himself some magic-tech to help him if he were ever in a situation where he was out of *Mana* or unable to use magic.

He was still formulating his ideas when Nia returned. After reporting that she had found no signs of any other cyclops, he convinced her to help him charge a few more crystals by restoring his *Mana* after each one. She eagerly obliged him.

9

───────

The next morning, Ethan and Nia went to check on Ainslee. They found her in the common room of the inn, eating some porridge along with a tankard of mead. Even as they closed the door behind them, he saw the dwarf pour some of her mead into the porridge.

The dwarf looked up at them and grinned, teeth full of porridge granules. "Not bad if you put enough mead in it."

Ethan shook his head. "You feeling okay?"

Ainslee took a long draw from her tankard and shrugged. "I reckon. Me noggin still hurts and I don't remember anything after hittin' the one-eyed guy. I take it we won?"

"We did," Nia replied, she glanced at Ethan and rolled her eyes. "Par'karr killed the cyclops."

Ainslee stopped moving with the tankard halfway to her mouth. She looked from Nia to Ethan. "Par'karr... the kobold... killed that one-eyed giant? Loki's balls! You're joking?!"

"He stabbed it right in the eye." Ethan nodded with a grin. "The spear punctured the thing's brain."

"Par'karr did that?" the dwarf asked again and then brought the tankard up to her mouth and downed the rest of the contents in a single swig. She slammed it down and snorted. "Who knew that little runt had it in him."

A number of emotions played over the dwarf's face, too quick for Ethan to follow. She leaned back in her seat and sighed. "That cyclops was a lot more solid than it looked. I hit and me shield bounced up and hit me in the head. That's the last thing I remember. I guess it knocked me cold?"

"You were unconscious," Nia agreed. "We carried you to your bed and had Elspeth checking on you."

Ainslee narrowed her eyes and glanced between them. "Which one of you undressed me?"

Ethan and Nia exchanged looks. Other than taking off some of her armor, they'd left her as she was. He was about to tell her as much when Nia spoke up.

"We had many of the farmers help carry you in," she said. "When we left, a few of them were working on getting your clothes off."

Ethan suppressed a laugh, as well as a look of surprise. Had Nia just made a joke? He couldn't remember her making a joke before? Except maybe about the dwarf's snoring. This was something new.

The dwarf's eyes bugged out and she went white and then red. "Farmers?! Farmers undressed me?! How many? Which ones? Were they cute?"

Ethan had to bite his lip to stop himself from laughing but Nia maintained a straight face and even made herself look thoughtful. "There couldn't have been more than a dozen."

"Dozen?!" the dwarf gasped. "You mean a dozen farmers saw me naked?"

Clearing his throat, Ethan tried to play along. "I lost count. Your room was pretty packed with them."

"And you let them undress me?!" Ainslee demanded. "And see me naked?!"

"They insisted," Nia responded.

"And honestly," Ethan said, now fully committed. "There were so many farmers in your room, we couldn't really see what they were doing anyway. So we left."

The dwarf's face had gradually gone from white, to red and was now approaching purple. She opened and closed her mouth, unable to speak.

"Don't you listen to them," Elspeth said, entering the common room with a new tankard of mead. "Farmers didn't undress you. I did."

Ainslee sighed in relief and glared at Ethan and Nia.

"The farmers just watched," Elspeth added with a wink to Ethan. Head snapping back to Elspeth, Ainslee stared open mouthed at the innkeeper's wife. Elspeth made a dismissive motion with her hand. "It's okay, honey. I charged them a silver piece each to watch and I figure we can split the money fifty-fifty."

Ethan hadn't thought it was possible for the dwarf's eyes to bug out any more than they already were but he was wrong. Ainslee's mouth continued to work but only unintelligible sounds came out.

Unable to hold it any longer, Ethan staggered back against the door as he burst into laughter. Nia broke next, bending over and holding her stomach as she laughed and finally Elspeth joined in too.

"Oh, I see. Very funny," growled the dwarf, crossing her hands over her chest. "Very funny. Have a laugh at the injured dwarf's expense!"

Ethan, Nia and Elspeth continued laughing while Ainslee alternated her glare between them. Her face had resumed its normal color and Ethan even thought he saw a hint of a smile on her lips but she kept up the glare.

"We're just playing with you, dearie," Elspeth told her as the innkeeper's wife got her laughter under control. She handed Ainslee the full mug of mead. "I undressed you. No one else was in the room."

The dwarf snorted and muttered some things under her breath but took the offered tankard. Glaring at Ethan and Nia, she brought the tankard to her lips and drank down the entire thing in one long swig. She slammed the tankard down on the table and let out a long belch.

"I knew you were kidding," the dwarf said.

"Oh?" Ethan asked with a grin.

"Oh yeah," Ainslee nodded with a grin. She pushed her breasts together with her hands and looked around the room. "Any farmer who got a look at this body would still have been in me room when I woke up!"

Elspeth chuckled but Nia and Ethan rolled their eyes.

"We're glad to see you're back up on your feet," Ethan said. "Is Yuliana back?"

"The elf's up in her room," the innkeeper's wife replied. "Her and that cat of hers. I heard them come in last night."

"Michalus?" Nia asked.

"Wasn't awake as of a few minutes ago when I took her some of the porridge," Elspeth replied. "But that's all I got. I ain't got nothing for that cat."

"Are Fearghas and the others back?" Ethan asked her.

Elspeth shook her head. "Not yet. And I just sent Sawney to check that stone chest."

As if on cue, Sawney burst through the door. "Ma! Ma! There's meat in the chest!"

"Is there now?" his mother asked with a relieved smile. "How much?"

"It's full!" The little dwarf grinned. "All the way to the top!"

"Bless them!" Elspeth said and Ethan saw her eyes grow moist. "You go get Froba over at the mill and tell her to come and help me with it. We'll see how much we have and divide it up."

"Okay, Ma!" the boy retorted excitedly and then raced out the door.

"That's a blessing," the innkeeper's wife said. "I wasn't really sure what we were going to make for lunch, let alone dinner."

"I guess this means Par'karr found them," Ethan stated. He hadn't been sure the kobold would be able to and had almost asked Nia, but she'd been scouting for more cyclops. It was good to know the little kobold had delivered it and that they'd actually used it.

"He's quite the little hero," Elspeth agreed.

Ethan smiled. "Yes, he is."

"Once he's back, we need to go check out the mine and find out if the sound is coming from the tomb," he told them. He turned his attention back to Ainslee. "Are you feeling good enough to come with us?"

"If the farmers haven't stolen all my clothes," the dwarf snickered.

Ethan gave her a smile. "Great! Let's try to head out before lunch."

"Nia." He turned to the foxgirl. "Can you talk to Yuliana and tell her we need her to come. Elspeth will watch over

Michalus until we return." He looked over at the innkeeper's wife. "Is that okay, Elspeth?"

"That's fine," the dwarf said. "If what you're doing helps bring back the game, then I'll make the time to check in on the elf."

"Thank you," he told her and then gave her a sheepish look. "I have one more favor to ask."

"Oh?" Elspeth raised an eyebrow.

Ethan explained what he needed to the innkeeper's wife. He would leave the chest with her that his portal pouch was linked to. In it, he would put five stone bottles. All he asked is that they refill the bottles with water from the river a few times a day.

"Fill mine with mead!" Ainslee insisted when she overheard. "Or dwarven spirits!"

Upon receiving a disapproving look from the innkeeper's wife, Ainslee sighed. "Just once a day?"

"The water should be no problem." Elspeth nodded. She turned to Ainslee. "I'll see what I can do about a little mead every now and then."

Ainslee licked her lips and gave Elspeth a toothy grin.

"And," Ethan added. "Any food you can put in there would be appreciated. Hopefully, now that the others have a way to get food to the village more quickly, you may have enough to spare for us."

Elspeth let out a heavy sigh. "I'll do what I can for the food. I can't guarantee nothing."

"I know," he said. "You have to take care of your own first."

"True enough," the woman said. "But you've done a lot for the village, and if you can stop whatever is scaring away the game, that will be even more we'll owe you. I will do my best to make sure there's food in there for all of you."

"Thank you," Ethan replied and then turned to the door. "I need to go make the stone bottles and finish my project."

Leaving the others, Ethan went to gather some rocks to shape into water bottles. He had some corks he'd found in among Cuthbert's things - probably from long-gone bottles of wine. If he shaped stone bottles to have necks the same size, he'd have a way to cork bottles, which would be much better than the tied water jugs they had now.

After that, he had to finish up his personal project and they'd be ready to go.

10

———————

Par'karr returned just after noon and reported that he had found Fearghas and the other hunters and had given them the enchanted backpack. After he related his story, the little kobold grabbed some lunch from Elspeth and they were ready to go.

Ethan, Nia, Ainslee, Yuliana and Par'karr assembled in front of Ethan's house. Luna was there, apparently unfazed by the sound now that the mountain lion wore one of his collars.

"You sure we need to bring all this stuff?" Ainslee complained, gesturing to her backpack. "The mine's not that far."

Ethan sighed. It was the third time the dwarf had brought it up since that morning. "Let's take it to be on the safe side."

"It's just a lot of stuff to carry for a few hours of walking," Ainslee pointed out. "We can be there and back before supper."

"We can be at the tomb entrance, yes," Ethan replied. He

had to consciously keep his voice neutral even though he wanted to scream at the dwarf and throttle her for making him repeat the same arguments.

Part of him understood. They'd never played role-playing games, seen movies or read books where inevitably people got trapped in a cave, buried in some ancient pyramid and in some way cut off from the way they entered.

That was basically the theme of tons of horror movies - most of which involved nearly everyone dying. There was no way he was going into some strange, booby-trapped tomb that was emitting a high-pitched sound that was scaring off all the animals, not without being as ready as possible. That's what the idiots in movies and books did.

"Let's just be prepared as possible, okay?" he told Ainslee.

"Fine." The dwarf rolled her eyes. "You're the wizard. Let's just go already, then. If we're quick, we'll be back in time for supper."

"Sure," Ethan replied, though he didn't think that's the way it was going to work.

They started off then, with Nia in the lead. They didn't expect any trouble, but if there were any more cyclops or other surprises, the foxgirl would hopefully smell them and give the group some warning.

His group traveled north, down the same road that they'd first taken when going after the brigands that had plagued the village when they first arrived. Ethan kept his ears open while they walked, noticing how quiet the forest around them was.

There were still bird songs. Birds seemed unaffected by the high-pitched sound for some reason. Maybe they couldn't hear high frequencies. If he had a cellphone, he'd look it up on Google. As it was, he had to guess.

Even with the birds, the other sounds that he hadn't even noticed previously, were missing. Not only that, but even just the little movements that he'd been used to when walking in the forest were missing. The lack of life in the forest was eerie and surreal. It was almost like being in a video game, where little details were always missing so players got better frame rates.

The lack of all the other sounds and movements was palpable. And he wasn't the only one who noticed. He caught the others, even Ainslee, glancing from side to side, as if looking for any signs of life on the floor of the forest.

Eventually, they passed the old mining headquarters, where they'd fought and vanquished the gang of brigands. The two-story building was now all but unrecognizable.

"They sure did a number on that place," Ainslee said, stopping to survey the damage.

Ethan could only nod. When the kobolds had burned the farms on their way to destroy the village, he'd suggested the farmers cannibalize the unused buildings in the village, as well as the old mining headquarters to help them rebuild.

The farmers had obviously taken his suggestion to heart. They had scavenged the building for lumber and raw materials to help rebuild their own farms. Now, there was barely any building left. Even the thatch from the roof had been taken.

"The farmers needed it," Yuliana said. "It was put to good use."

After a few more moments of staring at the remnants of the building, they continued their march northward. The group began the climb up the side of the mountain and to the main entrance to the mine.

They passed a rough-looking trail that he hadn't noticed

the first time they had come to the mine. Cuthbert, the old mayor, had gone to loot the tomb of any riches and the town had asked them to stop him. They'd been in a hurry, so the side trails hadn't really been of any importance at the time. Now it was.

Nia stopped and bent down, looking at the ground. When Ainslee started to speak, the foxgirl motioned for silence. Surprisingly, the dwarf complied. After several minutes, Nia stood and motioned them all near.

"The cyclops came from there," the foxgirl said quietly, pointing up the side trail. "Its scent is weak, but there is some other scent too, mixed with the cyclops."

"Another one?" Yuliana said in alarm.

The foxgirl bit her lip and looked from the footsteps to the trail. "I cannot say."

Ethan took a deep breath and let it out. So much for a quick trip. "We need to investigate it."

"Loki's balls we do!" Ainslee objected loudly and everyone else immediately shushed her. The dwarf rolled her eyes. "Give me one good reason why we should go looking for another one of those things."

"Because we don't want it sneaking up on us from the rear," Ethan answered and Nia nodded approvingly.

Ainslee opened her mouth and then closed and screwed up her face. She looked begrudgingly at the trail. "Fine, I guess that's a good enough reason. But those one-eyed giants give me the willies."

"Par'karr protect you," the kobold said, holding up his spear.

The dwarf rolled her eyes and looked at the group. "Well, then. Let's get moving. We might still make it back in time for dinner."

Nia nodded and turned off onto the trail. The others followed her but unlike the road they had been following, which had been worn smooth by countless wagons and men, the trail they followed was little more than a game trail. It was rough and uneven, making their progress slow and somewhat treacherous.

"You sure it ain't a mountain goat you smelled," Ainslee complained.

The trail was erratic and Ethan had to admit that it seemed less like something the cyclops could easily navigate. Though, with its larger stride, perhaps some of the rougher areas had been easier for it.

"This is the way," the foxgirl hissed. "The scent is stronger. It is near now."

"Fine. Fine," the dwarf snorted.

Nia didn't say another word, but turned and scrambled up a steeper part of the trail with the dexterity he'd come to expect from the foxgirl. When Ethan attempted to mimic her actions, he found he was neither as strong nor as nimble as his wife.

Nia saw him struggling and gave him a disappointed look. "You are the alpha. You should not be struggling. We must work on your skills when we get back to the village."

Ethan groaned but knew she was right. He'd come a long way since he'd arrived on this world. He was no longer flabby and out of shape. Days of walking and eating a high-protein diet had burned away the softness from stomach, arms and legs. He could actually see muscles now, though he was still far from a six pack.

Considering how much physical strength, endurance and coordination played a role in surviving on this world, he'd come to the same conclusion several times. He needed to get into better shape and he needed to start training in using weapons.

Still, having your wife point it out in front of everyone else wasn't exactly the best way to be reminded. He smirked. "Yes, dear."

Nia nodded, oblivious to the sarcasm and reached a hand down to help him up. He accepted gratefully and once up top with her, he helped the others up. When it came to Ainslee, both he and the foxgirl had to help pull the heavy dwarf up.

When they were all up, Ethan looked over the west edge. The trail had taken them at least three hundred feet above the entrance to the mine. Looking down at it, he felt his stomach lurch. He didn't usually have a problem with heights but considering how treacherous the trail had been, he realized that a bad slip and they would plummet to their deaths.

"How much... longer?" the dwarf asked. She was still puffing from struggling up the incline and her forehead was beaded with sweat.

"I am not sure," Nia told them. "The scent is stronger and the cyclops used this part of the trail frequently."

"Let's... hurry... up then," the dwarf puffed, gesturing at the suns. "I don't... want to... come down this trail... at night."

Ethan looked at the dual suns and nodded. They probably had three hours of light left. They needed to make it back down to the main road before then or they'd need to camp somewhere on the trail for the night. That would be dangerous. Very dangerous.

"She's right," Ethan agreed. "I don't think we want to camp anywhere near the cyclops' den, especially if you think there could be a second one."

Nia nodded, turned and started back up the trail. Ethan turned but noticed Par'karr. The kobold was as far from the ledge as possible and he realized it wasn't the first time he'd noticed it. Not only that, but the little kobold looked scared, if not downright terrified.

Ethan cursed himself for not recognizing it before. "Par'karr, do you not like heights?"

"Par'karr not like high places," Par'karr shook his head violently. "This higher than Par'karr ever be."

"Are you going to be okay?" he asked. "Do you need to go back down?"

Par'karr looked down the trail longingly and then looked back up to Ethan. The kobold put on a brave face that nearly hid the little kobold's terror. "Par'karr go with Ethan. Ethan Par'karr's friend."

"You're a brave kobold," Ethan told Par'karr, earning a smile from his friend. Turning, Ethan followed after Nia with the others coming up behind him.

They followed the trail by the ledge for another thirty minutes before the group reached a flatter area of the mountain. The trail turned away from the ledge and towards the center of the mountain.

Another half an hour and Nia called them to halt, sniffing the air and glancing over the ground in front of her. She motioned them down. Turning, she looked at Ethan and whispered, "The cyclops lair is just up ahead."

11

Nia pointed to a large cave a hundred yards in front of them. Outside the cave were the skeletons of various creatures scattered around the cave entrance. There were piles of bones on either side of the cave, some of which might have been human.

The group quietly readied their weapons. Nia slid her scimitars from their scabbards, while Ainslee pulled out her hammer and strapped on her shield. Yuliana had her club and Par'karr still gripped his spear.

Ethan grinned like a child who was about to unwrap his Christmas present. Reaching over his shoulder and into his backpack, he pulled out his special project. He'd thought of several items he could have created to help him in cases where he couldn't use magic.

He had thought of making a stone hilt that would generate a laser sword or energy sword. The device, similar to the devices used by the space sorcerers in those star battles movies, would be powered by crystals instead of his own *Mana*. It had seemed like a great idea and the concepts were simple enough. But the sheer amount of *Mana* the thing consumed made it impossible to power without using more crystals than he wanted.

Instead, Ethan had gone with something a bit more mundane. At least, it was mundane on Earth. In his hand, he held this world's equivalent of a sawed-off, double-barrel shotgun. Or at least, it was the best replica he could make out of shaping stone.

The barrels were smooth gray stone that he had painstakingly shaped into two-feet-long cylinders. They were mounted in a brown stock he shaped out of a reddish-brown stone he'd found near the bank of the river.

He'd actually shaped a trigger guard and double triggers, though he had no idea how to craft a trigger mechanism. Even if he did, it wouldn't matter. The "shotgun" didn't work on gunpowder. It worked on magic.

Rows of crystals had been carefully shaped into the barrel with an additional crystal on each trigger. Just the slightest touch of his finger on the appropriate trigger and it would activate the spell effect. And the effect was impressive. At least, Ethan thought so.

He'd take the idea from the spikes he'd used to impale several of his enemies in previous fights. Ethan had used *Air* to pick up the spikes and hurl them into the foes to great effect. He'd taken that idea and distilled it into an enchanted stone gun that would propel stone balls with tremendous bursts of *Air*.

In his tests, it had performed well. Ethan had hit a tree so hard with one of the stone balls that the ball had shattered. He had no way of knowing exactly how fast the ball traveled, but if it hit a person, or monster, it was going to hurt. A lot.

Ethan was actually very pleased with his home-made, enchanted shotgun. In fact, there were only two issues.

First, the stone shotgun could only fire what were effectively slugs. He tried loading a handful of small stones but the magic only seemed to affect one stone at a time, no matter what he did. So he'd shaped perfectly round balls, like the old muzzle-loader rifles only much bigger.

Second, the amount of *Mana* required to fire off both barrels was more than the battery crystals could quickly regenerate. Ethan still wasn't sure exactly how the magic circuit regenerated *Mana*, but the regeneration rate seemed directly proportionate to the number of crystals in the circuit.

Because of this, it took a full minute for it to regenerate enough for a second volley of stones. It wasn't ideal, but if he were out of *Mana*, it was still much better than him having to defend himself with a knife or staff.

Everyone in the group turned to stare at Ethan's new toy as he pulled two round stones from a pouch on his belt and slipped them into the barrels.

"What is it?" Par'karr asked, wide-eyed.

Ainslee was literally stopped in her footsteps when she saw it. Her eyes grew wide and then narrowed as she looked from the shotgun to Ethan. "Is that a... blunderbuss?"

"Blunder-what?" Yuliana asked, head tilted.

Nia didn't say anything, she only gave him a curious, yet approving look.

Ethan held it up and grinned ear to ear. "This is my... boom stick!"

No one laughed and they all just looked at him, as if expecting him to explain. Ethan sighed. It was a line from one of his favorite movies, with one of his favorite actors. His friends back on Earth would have gotten the reference.

He quickly explained what it did and how it worked. When he was done, everyone had blank stares except for Ainslee. She nodded at him. "Like a blunderbuss, but you've replaced the black powder with magic."

"If a blunderbuss is a firearm that shoots a projectile by igniting black powder," Ethan replied, "then yes, it's like a magical blunderbuss."

"And it ain't iron," the dwarf observed. "It's all stone. Not sure how that will hold up."

Ethan was about to agree with her when Nia hissed and held up the hand signal for silence and then motioned them to go low.

Instantly, their conversation ended and the group ducked down.

"The wind has shifted," she whispered, "and we are now upwind."

At the same time the foxgirl spoke, a deep growl came from inside the cave. A few seconds later, a large figure emerged. Ethan was expecting to see another cyclops but the creature that stalked out of the cave opening was nothing at all like the one-eyed giant.

Sliding from the darkness of the cave was a huge iguana-like creature. The lizard-like monster looked like some sort of bizarre cross between an Earth iguana and an octopus or squid. While it had four legs and a long, serpentine tail, the thing also had four large tentacles that sprouted from the lizard's back, two just behind each shoulder. The tentacles writhed to either side, showing off wicked-looking barbs at their tips.

"What in Thor's hammer is that?" Ainslee gasped.

"I have never seen anything like this creature," Nia confessed. "It is... wrong."

Ethan couldn't help but agree. There was something about the creature that just didn't feel right, like it was even more alien than most of the other monsters he had encountered. He just couldn't put his finger on it.

"It not from this world," Par'karr squeaked, his hands on his spear clenching. "It from the other world. Like Par'karr's rabbits."

Looking from Par'karr to the lizard beast and back, Ethan remembered what the channeler, Mertin Graystaff, had explained. That sometimes, if a summoner was strong enough, he could pull a creature from the other world - the demon world - over to this world. Was that what this thing was? A creature from the other dimension? From the demon realm?

The lizard roared, a terrible sound like something from one of those jurassic dinosaur movies. Then it charged them. The lizard thing moved remarkably fast for its size and Ethan barely managed to scan it before it reached them.

```
Tatzelwurm
   Level 10
```

Nia rolled nimbly to the right side as it charged them. The foxgirl was quick but she hadn't fully anticipated the reach of the tentacles or their reaction speed. One of them lashed out and nearly caught her leg but Ethan slapped the tentacle away with *Air*.

The creature's head snapped forward and its eyes focused on Ethan. Had it somehow sensed his magic? That was both disconcerting and terrifying and he felt himself break into a cold sweat.

With a bellow, Ainslee rushed past him but judging by her speed, she hadn't used her *Charge* ability. Apparently, the dwarf had learned her lesson about charging into much larger creatures. The dwarf skidded to a halt as the Tatzelwurm reached her and swung her hammer directly at its head.

The blow caught the creature in the side of the lizard's snout, snapping its large head to the side. The creature seemed stunned for a moment, its tentacles slowing for a few seconds.

Those few seconds were all Nia needed. She sprung forward and sliced through one of the tentacles, severing it in half. She almost got the second tentacle but the beast recovered enough to pull it back and lash out, catching the foxgirl with a back-handed blow that sent her tumbling away.

The two tentacles on their left lashed out at Ainslee, trying to latch onto the shield and pull it out of her hand. At the same time, the creature opened its mouth and made a gagging sound.

Ethan thought the thing might breathe fire or have some other sort of attack, and he tried to put a wall of Air in front of its mouth but he wasn't fast enough. Some sort of thick, green-brown mucus-like fluid sprayed out of the creature's mouth, drenching the half of Ainslee's body and face that wasn't behind the shield.

Ainslee screamed and fell back, her hands coming up to her eyes. "It's burning my eye!"

The Tatzelwurm snapped its open maw at the dwarf but Ethan's wall of *Air* had materialized, and it rebounded from the invisible barrier. The tentacles on the left oozed around the barrier and scraped across the dwarf's arm, just behind the shield.

Nia was up and tried to use the distraction to slice the other tentacle but the creature side stepped and brought its tail around, slamming it into the foxgirl's legs and sending her sprawling, then it brought down its remaining tentacle, wrapping it around Nia's legs.

Pulling the struggling Nia closer with its tentacle, the Tatzelwurm turned its head and opened its mouth. Ethan didn't know if it planned to bite her or spit that mucus stuff at her but he wasn't about to let it do either. Extending his shotgun towards the creature's head, he tapped both triggers.

Unlike the intimidating boom of a real shotgun, his enchanted stone weapon made practically no noise, other than a hollow whooshing sound as the two stone balls were expelled from the barrels. He was only a few feet away, so both of the balls hit the creature within inches of each other.

The first hit the lizard in the neck, while the other hit it just to the right, in its jaw. Red blood exploded from its neck and part of its jaw seemed to dislocate where the stone ball had hit.

You crush Tatzelwurm for 27 damage.
You crush Tatzelwurm for 29 damage.

At the same time he fired, Yuliana had moved up and was using healing magic on the dwarf, who was still screaming. Par'karr moved to the left, jabbing at the tentacles with his spear.

Snapping its head back toward Ethan, the creature stared

at him with undisguised hate. Its jaw hung at an odd angle, either broken or dislocated but it reached for him with all three of its remaining tentacles.

That left a newly freed Nia to somersault to her feet and slice the other right tentacle off at the shoulder.

Snarling in pain, the Tatzelwurm tried to slam its tail at her again, but the foxgirl was ready for it. In an acrobatic move, she rolled over top of the lizard monster's back and came up on the opposite side.

Par'karr took a long gash across his abdomen as he didn't quite dodge one of the tentacles and Ethan barely blocked a tentacle to his own face with a shield of *Air*.

Nia sliced at its front leg, while also slicing at the tentacles, forcing the creature to side-step to avoid the blows. This allowed Ethan to retrieve two more balls from his pouch and drop them into the shotgun.

The Tatzelwurm seemed to sense what Ethan was about to do and it narrowed its eyes and rushed towards him, possibly intending to trample him. As it approached, a blur charged past him with a battle cry.

Ainslee, apparently recovered, used her *Charge* ability to slam herself into the other side of the lizard monster's jaw, breaking it with an audible crack. The Tatzelwurm's tentacles went slack for a few seconds, and Nia sliced the remaining two off nearly at the shoulders.

Ainslee continued her battle cry as she brought the hammer down on the creature's head over and over until it slumped to the ground.

Tatzelwurm dies.

You gain 50 experience. Experience to next level 2475.

By the time Ethan had counted to sixty and was ready to fire his shotgun again, the Tatzelwurm had collapsed to the ground. Its head was a bloody mess but Ainslee continued to scream at it and pound its head over and over.

When the dwarf finally stopped, she was covered in blood and gore and there was no longer anything that could be recognized as a head. When she turned around, Ethan saw that the right side of the dwarf's face was horribly scarred and her eye was milky white. Even on her blood-streaked face, he could see the tear streaks from her good eye.

12

"Ainslee!" Ethan gasped as he saw the dwarf's ruined face. As he looked closer, he saw that a portion of her armor and clothes were missing. Dissolved away. By acid. The mucus that it had shot from its mouth had been some sort of acid and had eaten away part of her face, clothes and armor on her right side. It had dissolved anything organic but hadn't touched the chain shirt she wore, her hammer or shield.

Yuliana's magic had healed the skin, but like so many of his own wounds, had left scars. In Ainslee's case, the entire right side of her face, all the way back to her ear was scarred with a bumpy spider web series of ugly scars.

The dwarf let the hammer fall to the ground as she fell to her knees. She brought her hands to her face and began weeping. In between her sobs, he thought he could make out the words "I'm hideous" repeated softly, over and over.

Ethan stood rooted to the ground, feeling awkward and unsure what to do. He wasn't really a touchy-feely guy but he understood that the dwarf was hurting. He couldn't imagine how he'd feel if that happened to him. He wasn't the most attractive guy in the world, but the disfigurement she'd suffered was next level.

Yuliana moved over to Ainslee, dropped to her knees and threw her arms around the dwarf. Par'karr dropped his spear and did the same. Feeling it was the right thing to do, Ethan did the same.

Nia looked around, sniffing the air before pushing her scimitars into the ground and coming over to join them. Even Luna came over and rubbed up against them. The big cat seemed to know something was wrong, even if it didn't understand what.

They all held on to the dwarf as she cried for what seemed like ten or fifteen minutes. No one said anything during that time, letting the dwarf have her moment. Finally, the crying gradually changed to sniffling and it appeared Ainslee had experienced as much group hugging as she could take.

"All right, you people," Ainslee said, her voice hoarse. "Get off me already."

The group slowly untangled themselves from her, and each other. One by one they stepped back from the dwarf, who stood up and wiped her eyes. Her face and clothes were still bloody, though her left cheek had been mostly washed clean but Ethan could see that no tears had flowed down the right side of her face. The acid had destroyed her tear ducts on that side.

"Are you..." Ethan started but realized asking if she were alright would be stupid. Instead, he asked, "Are you in any pain?"

The dwarf brought her scarred hand up to the wreckage of her face. She touched it gingerly, then pushed a little harder on the spider-webbed skin. She sniffed and then shrugged. "I can't really feel much of that side anymore." She turned and spit on the dead lizard creature. "Gods cursed monster."

The dwarf turned her shield around to see herself in the reflection. She cringed and quickly withdrew the shield, uttering curses that Ethan had never heard and he was pretty sure she took every god and goddess' name she knew in vain.

"Do you want anything?" Yuliana asked, a look of genuine concern on her face.

"Yah," the dwarf snorted. "About a wagonful of mead. Maybe even some spirits."

Nia was looking around, sniffing the air. Ethan raised an eyebrow. "You smell something else?"

Everyone tensed and looked at the foxgirl. Nia continued to sniff the air for several seconds before shrugging. "No, but this place reeks of the cyclops and the beast. They lived together here."

"This was the cyclops' pet?" Ainslee frowned. The ruined right side of her face didn't seem to be able to move very well, so only the left side actually frowned.

Nia nodded. "I think that's exactly what it was."

Ethan groaned. "You mean it left its 'dog' here while it came down to town, looking for meat?"

"Maybe cyclops a summoner," Par'karr offered. "Like Par'karr."

"That's right," Ethan said, looking back at the dead Tatzelwurm and remembering the kobold's comment about it not being from this world. "You said it wasn't from this world. It was a summoned creature?"

Par'karr shrugged. "It feel like summoned creature, but summoner dead."

Ethan thought back to the fight with the cyclops. He frowned. "The cyclops didn't summon anything when we fought it in the village. But, the channeler we met in Castlehaven said creatures sometimes cross over into this world. Maybe that's what happened."

Par'karr looked at the dead Tatzelwurm. "Cyclops very powerful. Lizard very big."

Nodding, Ethan turned Ainslee. "We can take you back to the village. You can rest and recuperate there."

The good half of the dwarf's face screwed up in disgust. "What?! And sit around like an eyesore for everyone to stare at? No, thank you. We can stick to the original plan. Let's figure out what's causing the game to leave the area and be done with it."

"Are you sure?" Ethan asked.

"That's what I just said," the dwarf snapped. "I'm going to start down now. The rest of you can follow me when you're ready."

With that, Ainslee spun and stomped away towards the ledge. Yuliana watched her go and then looked at Ethan.

"You and Par'karr go after her," he told them. "We'll catch up in a second."

The elf and kobold hurried after the dwarf and Ethan turned to Nia. "Let's search the cave and then catch up with them."

They moved into the cave and Ethan summoned two floating balls of light to illuminate the large cave. The cave was a stinking mess of rotting furs and piles of bones. Stopping to examine and push aside the bones, he saw more than one set of human-looking bones.

"It looks like some of these bones are human," Ethan commented.

"If so," Nia replied, "they are old. There is no scent of humans or dwarves in this cave any longer."

Ethan scratched his head. "Maybe from the miners? But if that was the case, then why didn't the mining company hire some mercenaries to kill it?"

"Perhaps the humans were killed after the mine closed," Nia suggested. The foxgirl was kicking at some piles of bones with her boot and Ethan heard the sound of coins hitting stone.

Turning, Ethan went over to see that Nia had kicked a rotten pouch, spilling silver coins and nuggets on the stone floor. Bending down, he picked up one of the nuggets. "Fearghas said this was a silver mine. Looks like maybe this came from a miner."

"Then why did they not kill the beast?" Nia furrowed her brow.

Scratching his head, he considered her question. It didn't make sense until he remembered Timberwell. There were scores of lumberjacks and woodsmen in the town, usually drunk at night. Would anyone really miss a single miner? Considering the treacherous terrain around the mine, would they assume he'd fallen to his death?

"Maybe no one even noticed him missing," Ethan offered. "Remember Timberwell?"

The foxgirl scowled. "You mean the sorry excuses for males?"

Ethan nodded. A few men had thought Nia and Yuliana were slaves and had wanted to use them for their amuse- ment. Ethan had taught them the error of their ways by pretending to be an insane warlock and threatening to burn them and the inn to ash. He smiled. Good times.

"Those men and what they intended to do amuse you?" Nia spat.

"No." He gave her a big grin. "But what I did to them was amusing. As I recall, one of them lost control of his bodily functions."

The foxgirl's face lightened and then she chuckled. "You were very frightening. They believed you really would have burned them."

Ethan gave her a pointed look. "If they had tried anything, I would have and wouldn't have felt the least bit guilty."

Nia stared at him for a moment, her eyes searching his face. Then she nodded with a small smile. "As it should be. You are a good alpha."

Ethan rolled his eyes at being called alpha, but inwardly he enjoyed the praise. No one had ever called him "manly" or whatever the human equivalent of "good alpha" was. Then again, he couldn't burn down buildings or pick up items with a thought back on Earth either. Regardless, it felt good.

He walked over to her and kissed her. Nia pushed into him and he felt himself growing excited. Apparently she noticed too. When they broke away, she stepped back and looked him up and down. A sly grin played across her lips. "Do you need your mana recharged?"

Taking a deep breath, Ethan had to shake his head. As tempted as he was, this wasn't the time or place. They needed to finish and then catch up with the dwarf. "Let me take a raincheck on that."

"Raincheck?" the foxgirl asked in confusion. She glanced outside the cave. "It is not raining."

Ethan sighed. "It's an Earth saying. It means, let me take you up on that offer another time."

Nia pouted for a second but then nodded. "You are right. We must get back to Ainslee."

"That's what I was thinking," he said. "I can't imagine how I'd feel if I'd been scarred like that."

"You would still be a good alpha," she said with a shrug.

"You can't tell me that you'd still be attracted to me if I was scarred like that," he snorted.

Nia tilted her head and chuckled quietly. "You are not attractive to me."

Ethan opened his mouth to protest but she kept going.

"You have a pleasant scent and you are a strong alpha," she continued. "This is what I find... attractive."

"But..." he started but she waved off his words.

"You are nothing like what my species finds attractive. You are scrawny and hairless and have no tail," she said, making a face. "You would not be found attractive to my people. Though, as I said earlier, you have a pleasant scent."

"At least you didn't say I was scruffy-looking," he muttered.

Seeing his reaction she moved close to him and reached up to kiss him again. "Do not be troubled. On my world, a pleasant scent and a strong alpha is preferable to attractiveness. Alphas are rarely attractive."

"Well." He smirked. "Then I'm in good company."

Retrieving the coins and nuggets they searched the rest of the piles and found a few more bags of nuggets and some rusted pick heads. When they had completed their search of the cave, the two of them quickly headed down the mountain to rejoin the rest of the group.

13

The group walked back down the trail in silence. Ethan spent the time trying to think of some comforting words for the dwarf but he couldn't think of anything fitting. Despite being the person his friends dumped on when they had issues, he had no experience comforting women. Especially women with the type of disfiguring injury Ainslee had suffered. To him, all of his ideas of what to say rang hollow.

Finally, they reached the bottom just as the suns were dipping below the horizon. By the time they reached the mine entrance, Ethan was lighting the way with balls of light. It had gotten dark quickly but now they'd be leaving behind even the starlight and the moons as they entered the darkness of the mine.

"Let's stop here for now," Ethan told them as they gathered around the mine's large entrance. They'd been in a hurry the last time they'd been here. Now, Ethan thought the entrance reminded him of one of those mines you saw in the westerns with the thick timbers bracing the entrance.

Sitting down with his back to one of the large timbers, Ethan reached into his pouch slowly and felt around. His hands closed on one of the water bottles and he pulled it out. "Water?"

Like Ethan, they were all thirsty from the long climb and subsequent descent. He pulled out all of the bottles and handed them around, finding that one of them had been filled with mead.

"It looks like Elspeth listened to you." Ethan smiled and handed it to Ainslee. "It's mead."

The dwarf didn't look up from the ground as she took the bottle from his hand. She lifted her eyes briefly to him and smiled weakly, then opened the bottle and took a small sip. Then she corked the bottle and let the hand holding it drop into her lap. She didn't say a thing about the mead nor did she swallow most of it down in one gulp.

When he'd been getting the bottles, he'd felt a cloth bundle as well and he withdrew it from the pouch next. Unwrapping it were several smaller cloth-wrapped bundles. As he unwrapped the first, the smell of meat greeted him.

He smiled, trying not to drool over the savory bundle. Instead, he handed it Ainslee. The dwarf looked up, took the bundle and set it in her lap. Then, she immediately resumed staring at the ground.

Ethan tried to prod her. "It smells good!"

The dwarf didn't look up but mumbled something incomprehensible. Ethan sighed and opened up the next bundle. It was meat as well and he handed it to Nia. The foxgirl smiled and took it, scooting closer to Ethan so their knees touched.

The next bundle was some herbs, carrots and some dark leafy plant that he thought might be spinach. He handed that to the elf, who accepted it eagerly. The final three bundles were also meat. One went to Par'karr, another to Luna and Ethan kept the final bundle.

Wasting no more time, Ethan dug into his own meat. It was cold, but he didn't care. The meat had been roasted with some spices and tasted amazing after hours of hiking. Ethan used a bit of *Water* magic to chill the water in his bottle and offered to do the same to the others. To Ethan, the cool water really refreshed him and he instantly felt better.

Then he saw Ainslee. The dwarf hadn't touched her meat, nor had she touched her mead since taking the first swig. He forced a smile. "You should eat and drink to keep up your strength."

Ainslee looked up at him with her one good eye, then looked down at her food and drink. She began to mechanically eat the food and occasionally washed it down with some of the mead.

Everyone watched the dwarf as she ate, noting the stark difference between this Ainslee and the normally lusty dwarf who attacked her food and her mead with gusto. The dwarf didn't seem to notice them and ate robotically until she was done. Then she let the cloth and her water bottle fall into her lap.

"Ainslee want the rest of Par'karr's meat?" the little kobold asked, offering up half of his meat to the dwarf.

At first, Ainslee didn't react. Then she looked up slowly, seeming to stare right through the kobold before dropping her head again.

Par'karr's face fell but he pulled the meat back and began to munch on it.

The group finished up their food and drink and Ethan replaced the empty cloths and bottles back into his pouch, knowing they were appearing in his chest back in town. Hopefully, tomorrow morning there would be more food and drink.

The water he wasn't worried about. He knew Elspeth and Sawney would at least fill up their water bottles. Water was still plentiful. But he had no idea how much food the village had, so food might be sparse.

"We want to go in or camp out here?" Ethan asked the group when they'd finished.

A thought occurred to Ethan and his head shot up. "Can someone test to see if the sound is still here? Maybe the Tatzelwurm was causing the sound."

Ethan scratched his chin. It had been a very strange creature. Perhaps it had been generating the sound and they were done with the quest and could go back to town.

Nia began to slip off her necklace and barely got it over her head before wincing and her ears flattened against her head. She quickly slid it back around her neck and frowned. "It is still there and is much more intense here."

Disappointed, Ethan groaned. He'd been hoping they might have already solved the quest, despite not actually receiving a quest update. Now it looked like they would be exploring the tomb.

Ethan thought back to the tomb where they'd found the former mayor. The thing had been bobby-trapped with pressure plates that shot out five-foot metal spikes from holes in the floor. And that had just been the entrance chamber. What other traps awaited them inside the tomb?

He looked at the dwarf, who still stared numbly at the ground. They'd already paid a high price for this quest. Would any of his other companions pay a price? Considering what had happened to the previous mayor - impaled on metal stakes - Ethan didn't want to think about what that price might be.

These people were his friends. They weren't like his old friends back on Earth. There wasn't that same jovial camaraderie he shared with his buddies. And yet, Nia, Ainslee, Yuliana and Par'karr were his friends. They'd fought and bled together.

Looking around at his companions, his gaze settled on the dwarf's ruined face. He vowed that he would do whatever it took to prevent any of his other friends from suffering the type of harm, or worse, that had befallen the dwarf.

Having made his silent commitment to his friends, Ethan looked around again. "So, are we camping here or going inside?"

"I would prefer sleeping outdoors," the elf said, scratching Luna between her ears. The mountain lion was curled up next to Yuliana and was now purring loudly.

Considering the elf always wanted to be outdoors, Ethan was not surprised. He looked from Nia to Par'karr. "Any preference?"

"Outdoors fine." Par'karr shrugged. The kobold looked into the cave and then back to Ethan. "Par'karr not really like caves."

Ethan nodded, remembering that it had been another kobold tribe called the Cave Clan that had butchered his village. The little kobold had a better reason than most to hate caves - even if this was actually a mine, not a cave. Since he didn't expect an answer from Ainslee, he looked to Nia.

The foxgirl looked around and then into the mine. Her fox-like eyes saw much better in the dark than any of the others but they still needed light to see. And in the mines, there would be no light except what they brought.

"We should camp here," Nia said, gesturing around. "There are multiple avenues to watch, but they are all isolated. An enemy cannot surround us unless they are already in place. The mine may be more defensible, but also more confining and less avenues of retreat since we are not familiar with the passages."

Ethan grinned at the foxgirl's assessment. She seemed to always be thinking of the tactical advantage, which was a good thing. Ethan had some small amount of tactical knowledge, but it was all from video games. Nia had actually lived in a society that was always warring with itself.

Looking around, he realized there were no trees nearby to use as firewood. Considering most of them couldn't see in the dark, that presented a problem. They'd need to get wood and set a fire before turning in for the night.

"That sounds good to me," Ethan said. "Out here it is. Nia, you and I can go get firewood and the rest..."

"I will go back to get wood," Nia interrupted. "You are the only one who can create light. You must stay here so the others can see. I can see in the dark, so I will go get the wood."

"Fine. But shout if you run into trouble." Ethan knew better than to argue with the foxgirl. Plus, she was right. If he left, the others had no way to make or build a fire to see by. They'd be at a severe disadvantage if there were anything else out there that hadn't fled. Nia smirked and then turned and jogged into the darkness.

The foxgirl returned thirty minutes later carrying an armful of wood. She dropped it off and then turned and disappeared back into the darkness. Ethan and Par'karr had collected rocks and made a ring of stones for the fire. They stacked the wood in the circle and then Ethan set it alight with his *Fire* magic.

By the time Nia returned with a second load of wood, their campfire was blazing and everyone's bedroll was laid out. Ethan had even laid out Nia's for her.

"I'll take first watch again," he told them. "You all get some sleep."

"I'll take first watch," Ainslee murmured.

Everyone turned to the dwarf, who hadn't said a word in hours. "What?"

"I'll take first watch," the dwarf repeated.

"Ainslee," Ethan retorted. "You don't even need to take watch if you don't want to. You can just rest."

The dwarf looked up. Her face was expressionless but her good eye was pleading. "I'll take first watch."

Ethan hesitated for a moment but then nodded. "Fine. I'll take second watch."

The dwarf nodded, a nearly imperceptible motion and then dropped her eyes to stare into the flames.

Ethan looked at the others, who shared his concern for the dwarf but they simply shrugged. None of them knew what to do to help her.

Lying down on his bedroll, he prepared to close his eyes when Nia pulled her bedroll next to him, plopped down and snuggled up next to him. She smiled at him and then closed her eyes. Ethan smiled back, laid his head down and closed his eyes as well.

Tomorrow they'd have to explore the tomb and brave whatever dangers and traps might lay waiting for them. For now though, Ethan just enjoyed the feel of his wife's warm body against his as he drifted off to sleep.

14

The next morning, Ethan found some fried meat wrapped in cloth in the portal pouch. Elspeth had come through for them again. Along with the meat were some carrots for Yuliana, and the innkeeper's wife had refilled their water bottles too.

The group ate the meat quickly. It had been seasoned with lots of salt and reminded him of uncured bacon. But compared to Earth bacon, Ethan found it was bland. But it was better than nothing.

Ainslee was quiet and listless through the meal. She ate robotically, shrugging or grunting at any questions directed her way. Eventually, the rest of the group got the hint and stopped asking her questions.

After breakfast, the group packed up their gear and gathered outside the mine entrance.

"Are we sure we wish to go in there?" Yuliana asked.

Ethan caught Ainslee's good eye shooting over to the elf and then to Ethan. The dwarf's expression was unreadable, especially now with half of her face disfigured. Was she hoping he'd say "No"? Or would she think that she had been scarred for nothing if they turned back now?

If they didn't figure out what was going on, the village would fall apart. That meant they'd need to seek a new base camp. A new home. It wouldn't be easy and they'd probably have to travel all the way to Moonpoint - if that was even a safe haven.

He looked at the faces of his companions. "We have to at least check it out. If there's something we can do to stop it, we have to try. If we don't, the villagers will either starve or move out. Even with the portal backpack, and even if I can create more of them, it won't help the farmers who depend on their flocks and herds. They'll have to move on."

"I have to go," Ethan told them, looking into the darkness of the mine. He hadn't been completely sure until that moment but saying it aloud, he knew it was true. Not only was he the mayor, but he wasn't the kind of person who could just let people suffer if there was something he could do about it.

Now, he had magic. Real magic. Real power. And like that line from the superhero movie said, with great power, came great responsibility. Yes, he had to go. He had to at least try to figure out what was happening. But the others didn't.

"If any of you don't want to go, I understand," he said, looking from face to face. He lingered on Ainslee for a moment. "Some of you have already given a lot."

"I go with you," Nia said, stepping forward to stand next to him. He had never doubted the fierce foxgirl would come with him.

"Par'karr go with Ethan," the little kobold squeaked, stepping to his other side.

"I ain't turnin' back," whispered Ainslee, not making eye contact with any of them.

They all looked at Yuliana, who was idly stroking Luna's head. She bit her lip and looked at each of them before finally letting out a sigh. The elf shook her head. "Things were so much simpler in the grove."

Ethan nodded. "I think most of our lives were simpler back on our own worlds."

"Simpler maybe," Nia snorted. She looked at Ethan. "But not necessarily better."

"Par'karr miss rabbit farm." The kobold looked down sadly, kicking a stone with his clawed foot. "But me have lots of fun with Ethan."

"Maybe," Ethan offered, "when we get to the bottom of this mystery, maybe we can claim some of the unused plots of land and plant a garden for Yuliana and set up a rabbit farm for Par'karr. And we can set up the old forge for Ainslee."

The elf raised an eyebrow, considering his idea. Par'karr looked genuinely excited at the prospect of having another rabbit farm. Ainslee's expression didn't change. She just looked into the darkness of the mine and ran her hand along the ruined side of her face.

"It sounds like we're agreed," he said and gestured to the mine, "so let's get going."

Ethan created balls of light to light their way and Nia led the way into the mine. She had only gone about a dozen paces before she stopped and sniffed around. She continued sniffing, moving her head right and then left, for a full minute. Finally she stopped and turned. "Our scent is too weak to follow and I... do not remember the way."

"I wasn't really paying attention either," Ethan admitted

sheepishly. The fact was, he hadn't been paying attention at all when they'd raced to find the previous mayor. The foxgirl had been able to follow his scent and they'd all followed her.

"I know the way," Ainslee said quietly. They all turned to the dwarf, who looked straight ahead. Without another word, she moved to the front of the group. She paused. "More light."

Ethan moved his balls of light to hover just above Ainslee's head. The dwarf grunted and began to lead them through the maze of tunnels.

Trusting that Ainslee knew her way, the group followed her. Realizing none of them would be able to find their way back without the dwarf's help, Ethan came up with an idea. In movies and books, people always marked their way with chalk or some scratching marks into the stone to mark their trail. Ethan had no chalk, but he did have magic.

At each intersection, Ethan used a little *Earth* magic to form an arrow on the floor that pointed back to the entrance. If any of them got separated, or if anything happened to Ainslee, they'd be able to find their way back.

Being a Jules Verne fan, he included his initials just like Arne Saknussemm had in Journey to the Center of the Earth, only not in runes. He carved ECG, Ethan Carl Gower, next to the arrow.

"ECG?" Nia asked when she saw the mark.

"My initials." He shrugged, feeling his face flush. He was embarrassed for being caught in his geeky behavior but then he realized his companions had no idea it was geeky behavior. Maybe to them, it was wizard behavior. "Ethan Carl Gower. So we know I made the mark."

In front, he heard the dwarf snort. "Who else would have

done it. You expect many other wizards to be coming through here putting marks on the floor?"

The dwarf immediately turned back around but Ethan smiled. It was the closest she'd been to sounding like her old self since being burned with the acid. Grunting, the dwarf continued on, forcing them to hurry to catch up with her.

Several minutes and several intersections later, they arrived at a familiar sight. It was the four-way intersection they'd come to the first time they were in the mine. Ainslee looked at the center passage.

Ethan remembered that last time, Yuliana had heard some insect-like noise behind it. There had been some talk of a nest of spiders or something and the dwarf had admitted she hated spiders.

Staring at the boarded-up passage, Ainslee frowned. Ethan guessed she remembered too. Then she turned right and led them at least two hundred feet. At that point, the passage opened into the huge natural cavern they'd been in before.

The space was at least fifty feet wide to his left and right. He could barely make out the edges of the cavern in the light. It stretched out in front of him only twenty feet, ending in a smooth, worked stone wall. It was a wall he recognized.

The wall of stone was smooth except for an archway that was carved out of the same stone. Thick and covered in some sort of writing or symbols, the archway framed two stone doors that were seven feet tall and four feet wide each. The right door had been pried open just barely enough to allow a human to squeeze through.

He knew what was inside. It was the booby-trapped entrance chamber to the tomb. It was where they'd found Cuthbert's body the first time.

"Let's pry the doors open," he said. "And let's block them with something so they can't close behind us."

"Close behind us?" Nia looked at him, head cocked.

"Ancient tombs have a way of... uh... trapping people," he said. "Sometimes, it's not just the traps that kill you instantly, there are other things that trap you inside."

At least, that's what happened in the horror movies and movies where people explored pyramids or ruins or pretty much any other scary place. Someone stepped on a plate or pushed a button or rested on a lever and suddenly doors were sealed or some giant piece of rock fell and sealed them in.

In the movies, there was usually a monster in the place with them and most of them ended up being killed before the star of the movie, and possibly their boyfriend or girlfriend, found a way out and/or killed the monster. But this was reality - or perhaps virtual reality. Getting trapped would mean dying slowly of thirst or starvation.

Of course, he had portal magic and should be able to get them out, plus they had the portal pouch where they could get water and food from Elspeth. And yet, he felt like they should still take precautions. When people ignored those precautions in the movies, things always went wrong.

"We should open the doors all the way and then block them," he told them. "Just to be on the safe side."

"Can't you just do that with your magic?" Yuliana asked. "Like you move things through the air?"

"Uh... yeah. Good point." Ethan looked sheepish and suppressed the urge to face palm himself. Of course she was right. He could just use *Air* to open the doors and then use *Earth* on the hinges. Reaching out with *Air*, he pulled the doors completely open. At least, that's what he meant to do.

Instead he experienced something he'd never felt before. The *Air* magic seemed to just "slide" off the doors.

"What the - ?" he muttered as he blinked in surprise. Reaching out again with *Air*, he tried to pull the doors open. And once again, the *Air* just slid right off the doors like he was trying to grab onto a greased pole. It wasn't like the doors were too heavy. Instead, the magic just "slid" or "rolled" off.

"What is it?" Nia demanded as she heard the alarm in his voice. The foxgirl dropped into a crouch, hands moving to the hilts of her scimitars.

"My magic," he muttered. "It's not working on the doors."

The foxgirl relaxed a bit and looked at the doors and then back to Ethan. "Why not?"

Ethan shrugged. "I have no idea."

Walking to the doors, Ethan examined them closely. He expected to find Chymera crystals with some sort of spell that deflected his *Air* magic. There were none. He looked all over the surface of the door but found no trace of crystals. Yet, there was something. Something he could feel INSIDE the stone.

Reaching into the stone with his magical awareness, like he did with Chymera crystals, Ethan found them. Lots of crystals inside the stone and they were definitely generating some sort of, for lack of a better word, static. It was just some sort of magical interference field to prevent the doors from being acted on by magic.

Stepping back, he tried to shape the stone of the doors with *Earth* magic. As he expected, his magic couldn't get a purchase on the doors. It just slid off. Ethan whistled. Whatever spell they'd put on the doors was ingenious, but putting them inside the stone was even more so.

Ethan could break a magical enchantment by breaking one of the spell crystals. It would cause the entire magical circuit to fail. But with the crystals buried inside the stone, there would be no way to get to them without mundane tools. One thing was clear though.

"A wizard made this tomb," Ethan told his companions, "or at least, a wizard enchanted these doors and probably more stuff inside. Magic doesn't work on the doors at all and may not work on other things in the tomb."

Everyone was quiet as they absorbed what he told them.

"What are you saying?" Yuliana asked.

"I'm saying," Ethan said, looking at the tomb with newfound concern, "things just got a lot more complicated."

15

____

The group took the time to manually pull open the doors. The task took a while, as the doors were heavy and whatever mechanism allowed them to swing open had deteriorated with the passage of time.

Once the doors were pried open, Ethan was able to use his *Earth* magic on the floor of the cavern to form a square of stone. Using *Air*, he managed to drag the heavy rock square between the doors and place it where it would block any attempt they might make to close. He hoped.

"Ainslee," he addressed the dwarf, who hadn't said a word during the entire process, "will that stone block hold back the doors?"

The dwarf looked at him with a sullen expression and then looked at the stone block. He saw her good eye roving over the doors before she nodded. Ethan waited to see if she would add anything - or speak at all - before realizing the dwarf's nod was the only answer he was going to get.

"Now the fun part," he said. Ethan walked over to where

they had found Cuthbert, careful not to step on any of the tiles.

Moving his light to either side of him, he surveyed the entrance chamber. As before, it appeared to be a ten-by-ten chamber. The chamber's walls, ceilings and floors were tiled. The tiles had intricate patterns on them but each of the tiles had a circle in the center. A trail of dried blood led from the center of the chamber, where they'd found the former mayor's body, to the edge of the doorway.

On the far end of the room was a doorway, blocked by a stone door. Experimentally, Ethan pushed at the door with *Air*. Unsurprisingly, his magic just dissolved as it reached that door too. He cursed. "The door on the far side can't be manipulated with magic either."

Looking more closely at the door, Ethan wondered how the door would even swing open. Something about it didn't look right. There was no handle on the door and there were no hinges anywhere.

"I actually have no idea how that door on the other side can be opened," he told the group. He looked back at his companions' faces crowded in behind him. "Any ideas?"

No one spoke. Yuliana just looked confused. Par'karr looked intently but scratched his head. Nia looked up and down the ten-by-ten room but then gave him an apologetic look. "I do not know. This is unlike our structures. We do not build houses or tombs of stone."

Ethan nodded reassuringly and turned to look down at the dwarf. Ainslee's eyes were on the floor and he thought she was lost in thought until she said something quietly.

"What was that?" he asked. It had been too quiet for him to make out.

"I said," the dwarf repeated louder. "The door slides down."

Ethan looked back at the door across the room. He frowned as his brow furrowed. He saw nothing at all that indicated how it would move. Turning back to the dwarf, he asked, "How can you tell?"

Ainslee sighed and pointed to the bottom of the door. When she spoke, Ethan heard a bit of the old dwarf in her tone. "There's a lip there on the bottom of the floor. There's no lip on the top. The top of the door is resting directly against the stone of the doorway. It can't go up, it's got to go down."

Ethan strained his eyes and managed to see what the dwarf meant. He'd missed it the first time but now that she said it, the top of the door and the bottom of the door didn't look the same. He scratched his head. "How do you know it wouldn't slide to the right or left?"

The dwarf sighed. "Unless they got some better technology or magic, you ain't going to slide a two-ton door left or right. They'd make a circular door for that and roll it."

It was more words than Ainslee had spoken since she'd been scarred. Ethan was glad she was talking but there was no real life to her voice. She might have been annoying at times, but he missed the rambunctiousness that the dwarf had brought to the group.

"That makes sense." Ethan nodded. "But we can't rule out magic either. I'm just not sure how that would work, especially since it has the same sort of anti-magic enchantment. So I assume something is holding it up, right?"

Sighing again, the dwarf shrugged. "Probably some sort of gears roll it up and down. Just got to find the trigger switch."

"Trigger switch?" Ethan asked, searching the chamber with his eyes. "What would it look like?"

"Could look like anything," Ainslee muttered. "Probably one of the tiles."

Ethan swallowed. He gawked at the sheer number of tiles in the room. The tiles were a foot wide by a foot long and covered the floor, walls and ceilings. Since it was a ten-by-ten room, that meant 100 tiles on the floor and side walls. Accounting for the space for the doors, it was nearly 500 tiles!

"Might even be a combination of them, in the specific order," Ainslee added.

He let out a frustrated breath. It could be like a combination lock or MMORPG puzzle. He hated those puzzles. He and his friends just wanted to kill things or do quests. They didn't have time to solve puzzles. That's what wikis were for. Only there was no wiki for this.

"Do you already know a way past the spikes?" Nia asked from behind him.

"I do," he replied with a grin. He'd actually figured out several methods last time. One of the methods might not work now, since he was sure the floor tiles couldn't be manipulated by magic. But the other two still held promise, provided they could get the door open.

Seeing that everyone was staring at him expectantly, he smiled at them. "One way is to levitate everyone over there. Of course, to do that, I need the door open so no one ends up on the tiles."

The group looked at the blood-stained floor and nodded. They all knew the consequence of stepping on one of the tiles. Instant shish kabob.

"Ethan know another way?" Par'karr asked.

"Yeah," he replied, gesturing around the cavern. "I can make a ten-feet-long stone plank and two stone risers. I set one riser here, on this side, then levitate one of the risers to the other side. Then I just levitate the plank to rest on the two risers and we can walk across on the plank instead of the floor."

"Like a tree trunk over a river." Nia nodded.

"Exactly," Ethan replied with a smile at the foxgirl. "We'd be stepping on the plank without disturbing the tiles below. But that doesn't help us if we can't figure out how to get the door open."

Ethan knew a bit about encryption and passwords. The longer a password was, the harder it was to break. If you used special characters, that made it even more complicated and difficult to break. This room had almost 500 tiles and any combination could be the key. It could be a single tile or a combination of three, six or even ten tiles. In other words, it was impossible.

"Any clues as to how to figure out which tile or tiles would cause it to open?" Ethan asked. The question was mainly directly at Ainslee, but he was open to any suggestions from anyone.

No one offered any ideas for several minutes. Finally, it was Ainslee who spoke up. "Only way really is to test the tiles. The floor tiles do the spikey thing, but the side tiles... maybe not?"

"Do you think they intended anyone to ever open this up? Or once it was sealed, do you think it was intended to stay sealed?" Ethan asked, an idea starting to form in his head.

"Given the doors were sealed with an actual locking mechanism," the dwarf said thoughtfully. "I'd think they at least planned for the possibility that someone would come back in here."

"What do you mean?" Ethan looked down at the dwarf.

"I mean," she said, a bit of her old self evident now as she talked about something she was familiar with and obviously more knowledgeable than anyone else. "If they didn't mean to have it opened, they would have made a lock on the side that was tripped when the doors were closed. Even something as simple as a bar that slid between the doors would be enough to keep all but the most persistent out."

"That's what I was thinking too," Ethan said. "And if that's the case, they left a way for someone to get back in. They even went out of their way to make the doors anti-magic."

Ethan reached out with *Air* and tested the floor panels. As expected, the magic dissolved as soon as he touched it. He did the same with each wall and the ceiling, and had the same result. He looked down at Ainslee. "The ceiling, floors and walls are all anti-magic. That means there must be a mundane way to open this. If that's the case, then we have to assume there is some safe path across and that whatever combination of tiles opens that door can be reached without magic from the safe path. Right?"

Ethan saw a spark of excitement in the dwarf's good eye as she nodded. "You might be onto something there, wizard-boy. We just have to find the safe path first."

Everyone looked at the deadly room in front of them. From his left side, he heard the kobold mutter, "Par'karr not volunteer to find safe path."

16

"No one is volunteering to find the safe path, and I certainly don't blame anyone," Ethan told them. "So it looks like it's up to me to find it."

"How?" demanded Nia, her voice full of concern. "Did you not just say that your magic does not work?"

"True." Ethan nodded. "I did say that. My magic won't work directly against the floor, ceiling or walls. But I can still use my magic on other objects."

The group looked at him with puzzled faces so he walked a few steps back and reached out with *Air*. He grabbed several rocks in range and floated them to him. "I can use rocks to trigger the panel."

The others nodded and Par'karr gave him a toothy grin. "Ethan smart!"

Ethan chuckled and hoped the kobold was right. It should work, but he didn't know the extent of the anti-magic enchantment. Would it affect just the panels or anything touching the panels? He was about to find out.

Before he started, Yuliana put a hand on his shoulder,

tilting her head towards the door. "The insect sound I heard last time is coming from behind the door."

"Behind the door?" Ethan asked, tilting his own head to listen. He heard nothing.

"Insect sound?" The dwarf perked up unexpectedly, good eye wide. "The spiders?"

Ethan screwed up his face in thought. He looked at Ainslee. "Could it be machinery? Some sort of gear mechanism - maybe something that moves the spikes?"

The dwarf visibly relaxed. "Aye. And that might sound like insects to someone who wasn't aware of it."

"So it is not insects?" the elf asked. "It is... machines?"

"Metal gears and machinery." Ethan nodded. From the little she'd spoken of it, he didn't think the elf's world had metal machinery. Everything there was more organic.

Nodding, the elf withdrew her hand and walked back to the spot she'd been sitting in. The dwarf, chuckling to herself and muttering something about "no spiders", walked back to her own spot.

With that done, Ethan picked up a large stone with <u>Air</u>. Levitating it to the entrance, he placed a stone down on the first tile immediately in front of him. Nothing happened.

"That's weird, nothing..." he started.

SCHLIK! Four-foot-tall metal spikes shot up from the three holes around the tile causing everyone to start. Ethan and the group couldn't help but notice the dried blood on the spikes. Cuthbert's blood.

A moment later, the spikes retracted quickly back into the floor. The group looked at Ethan, who shrugged. "One down. Ninety-nine more to go."

To better keep track of the tiles, Ethan numbered them in his mind. He numbered them from 1 to 10, starting at the leftmost tile and going to the rightmost tile. Ten tiles per row and ten rows.

The two doors spanned the middle six tiles, or tiles 3-8. If it weren't for the thickness of the doors themselves, 2 and 9 would be directly accessible. As it was, they'd have to hug the door and step diagonally if they wanted to get to either of those tiles.

With his numbering scheme decided, Ethan began to systematically repeat the process several more times before finding that the tile just to the left of the door, tile number 2, did not cause any spikes to shoot forth.

"I think we found the first safe tile," Ethan told them. The group, crowded around him, gave mutters of agreement.

"Listen," he told them. "This could take a while. Why don't you all go into the cave and relax while I figure the safe tiles."

The others exchanged looks and then collectively shook their heads.

"I will stay with you," Nia said.

The kobold bobbed his head. "Par'karr want to watch!"

Ainslee and Yuliana nodded along with the kobold. "We're staying too."

Shrugging, Ethan turned back into the room. He guessed watching someone playing around with a trapped room was more interesting than sitting around in the dark, waiting. It wasn't like they could watch TV or play with their smartphones.

Going on the assumption that the safe path was meant to be traversed by someone roughly human, he began testing the tiles around the safe tile. Each one caused spikes to appear. He then moved one tile further out. After all, a person could easily step over a single tile with no problem.

All of those tiles caused spikes as well. He was about to try the tiles even further out, when he remembered some of the MMORPG puzzles. Some of them reset whenever you chose a bad tile.

"Ainslee," he said, turning to the dwarf. She had a faraway look in her good eye but blinked and looked up at him. "Do they make tiles that would reset if you chose the wrong combination?"

"Huh?" the dwarf muttered.

"If I find the first tile in the sequence," he clarified, "but then chose the next tile wrong, could that reset the sequence? Meaning, I'd have to start all over from the first tile?"

Ainslee rubbed the unscarred part of her chin for a moment and then nodded. "Possibly. It would make it much harder to figure out the correct sequence."

Ethan groaned. He'd come to the same conclusion. If he had to reset the first tile each time he tried a new secondary tile, and then reset the first two when he tried to figure out the next tile in the sequence, this was going to take a very long time.

He checked his *Mana* levels.

Mana: 45

How far would he get before he ran out of *Mana*? He felt a smile creep across his face as he remembered how he could quickly recharge his *Mana*. Unfortunately, with everyone nearby, that made it impossible - or at least, indecent.

Since he still had *Mana*, he continued the process. He lifted the stone and let the tiles reset before trying it again.

Place the first stone on the first tile, try the next tile, place the stone back on the first tile and repeat.

He found the second tile fifteen minutes later. It was the tile two diagonally to the left, or row 2, tile 1. It was flush against the wall which could mean that one of the tiles on the wall might be part of the door unlocking sequence. He sighed. Safe path first, door sequence later.

Over the next thirty minutes, Ethan found two more tiles: row 3, tile 1 and row 4, tile 2. By then, he was mentally exhausted and nearly out of *Mana*. Constantly using his *Air* magic while maintaining the balls of light was taxing, though he had received several skill updates in both *Air* and *Fire*.

Stepping back, Ethan wiped the sweat from his forehead. "I need a break."

Nia gave him a quizzical look. "You are out of mana?"

Tired, he nodded.

"I will help you to get your mana back," she said, reaching for his pants.

Flushing furiously, Ethan grabbed her hands. "We can't do that here!"

The foxgirl looked around the cavern and then back to him. She cocked her head. "Why not? We can lay down the blankets."

Ethan opened his mouth but no words came out. There was no shame or embarrassment on Nia's face. She might have just asked him to sit down for a picnic for as much concern as her face betrayed.

His eyes darted to his other companions. Like him, Yuliana was flushing furiously but there was something in her eyes that didn't quite mesh with her red face. Was it...

curiosity? Ainslee just rolled her one eye and turned her back to them.

Par'karr on the other hand looked around at the faces of the other companions, clearly not understanding what was going on. He scratched his scaly head. "We... help Ethan?"

"No," snapped Nia. "I will help Ethan recharge his mana. We have found that mating recharges it quickly. It is pleasurable to help him recharge."

"Uh...I... ah..." Ethan sputtered. He felt his face growing even hotter at the foxgirl's open admission. He was pretty sure his companions already knew about it but Nia's blunt words left no question.

Ainslee snorted and looked up at him. "Did you think we didn't know? Well, maybe not about it recharging your mana. But we knew you two were shacking up. The elf heard you two the first time you did it back in the wasteland." The dwarf chuckled. "You should have seen her turn all sorts of shades of red."

Ethan felt his temples throbbing with all the blood rushing to his face. He looked at Yuliana. "You heard us?"

The elf, her own face as red as his, nodded.

Nia was completely unfazed. She cocked her head at him again. "This bothers you?"

Unsure what to say Ethan just nodded. Then he took a deep breath and let it out. "It's just that... uh... people on my world don't really... uh... talk that openly about sex... er... mating."

"Really?" the foxgirl asked.

"Can't say dwarves do either," Ainslee admitted. "Well, not in mixed company and not without a few meads."

"We... do not talk about it at all," Yuliana admitted, her face still bright red. "It is usually only discussed by the mother to her daughter just before the joining. Though, sometimes... friends do share some... secrets."

"Par'karr know all about mating." The kobold shrugged. "Par'karr been mating rabbits for years. Kobolds pretty much same way."

Everyone turned to look at Par'karr and the kobold just grinned back. "Par'karr happy to share experiences."

There was a chorus of "no thank you's" and "maybe another time's". The kobold just shrugged. "Par'karr good breeder."

"I'm... uh..." Ethan cleared his throat. "Sure you are."

"You two do what you need to do," the dwarf told them, looking between the two of them with her good eye. "Trust me when I tell you, it won't be the worst I've seen or heard."

Ainslee looked at Yuliana, who looked mortified. The dwarf gestured down the tunnel. "Maybe just take it down the tunnel."

Thinking about the elf hearing them, Ethan felt embarrassed. He'd never been any sort of exhibitionist and facing his companions after having sex with Nia seemed like it would be difficult. That was doubly true if he knew the elf could hear every little thing.

An idea came to him and he reached down and grabbed his backpack. He untied the front pocket and reached inside to retrieve the Necklace of Silence he had made. It would block out all sound - including the sound of their lovemaking.

When he reached in, his hand felt the necklace but also felt something square and hard. He pulled out both.

"Merlin's Journal!" he exclaimed as he recognized the book.

"What?" Nia asked.

"This is Merlin's Journal," he repeated. "Remember, I found it in the library in Patheos. With the ambush right after we got out of the library, I forgot all about it!"

"What book do?" Par'karr asked with interest.

"I don't really know," he said. "I didn't read it yet. I forgot about it until just now. I haven't even been in that pocket of my backpack. I wouldn't even have found it if I hadn't dropped the necklace in the same pocket."

He thumbed through the pages of the journal as he held out the necklace to Yuliana. "This is the necklace that dampens all sound. Maybe this will help."

Recognizing the necklace, she took it from him and flashed him a little smile. But Ethan wasn't paying attention to the elf anymore. Out of the corner of his eye, he had spotted something in the pages he'd been flipping through.

Turning to the book, he flipped through the pages again, Ethan spotted what had caught his eye. He opened the book to the page he'd spotted and then turned back to the symbols carved into the archway.

Ethan looked back and forth between the symbols on the page and the symbols on the archway. He couldn't be completely sure, but the symbols appeared to match. Ethan swore loud enough that everyone looked at him.

"What is it?" Nia asked, tensing with concern.

Excitedly, he held up the book, Ethan showing the group the page in the journal he'd found. "These are the same symbols as the doorway!"

17

———

"What does that mean?" Yuliana asked, squinting at the symbols.

Ethan turned the book around and looked at it. Then he shrugged. "I have no clue."

Ainslee rolled her good eye. She growled, the misshapen skin on her left side making her look sinister. "You have no clue? You made us think you'd found something important!"

"Sorry," he apologized. "But I think this is important. I just don't know how yet."

The dwarf turned and walked back to the side of the archway and sat heavily on the ground with her arms crossed. "You and foxy go do your thing so you can get us past the traps and we can get back to town."

He'd almost forgotten what they'd been discussing a moment ago but he felt his cheeks color. Ethan looked over at Nia. The foxgirl stood there looking at him impatiently.

Ethan cleared his throat. "Uh, right."

He pulled out some candles from his backpack, thankful he'd remembered to pack them. Even if he were close enough to the others, there was no way he could maintain balls of light when he was... distracted.

"You need tips from Par'karr?" the kobold asked helpfully as Ethan lit the candles with a touch of *Fire*.

"Uh, no, Par'karr," he replied. "But thank you."

The kobold grinned in reply.

"Come," Nia said with an impatient smile. She grabbed her backpack with one hand and his arm with the other. As the foxgirl led him down the tunnel, back to the intersection, he caught sight of a red-faced Yuliana putting the Necklace of Silence on.

Twenty minutes later, Ethan and Nia were both smiling as they walked back to the others. His *Stamina* was down a bit, but his *Mana* was full. Completely full.

When they walked back into the tomb chamber, they found the others lying around near the archway. Ainslee caught sight of them and snorted. "About time."

Ethan suppressed a smile. Since they had entered the mine, the dwarf had seemed more like her old self. Was it because she found the underground area more like her home? Or was their reliance on her knowledge of stonework and mechanical things helping? He didn't know, but despite her gruffness, he liked having more of the old Ainslee back.

Yuliana took off the Necklace of Silence and set it near his backpack. She didn't look him in the eye as she did and he guessed that just knowing what they were doing had been enough to embarrass her.

"Pouch have more food?" Par'karr asked as Ethan got closer. "Par'karr hungry."

At the mention of food, Ethan realized he was feeling hungry too. There was no way to mark the passage of time in the lightless tunnel. Was it lunch time already?

"Let me check," he said and reached into the pouch. He pulled out the water bottles and after checking to make sure they were full again, he handed them out.

Like before, one of them had mead and he gave that one to the dwarf. Ainslee snatched it away and took a long sip from it. Ethan suppressed a smile. The dwarf was definitely more like her old self.

Also inside the pouch were some bowls with roasted potatoes, onions and chunks of peppered beef. It looked like Elspeth had taken the meat from Yuliana's serving and put it into Nia's, so her bowl was only the meat and Yuliana's serving had only the potatoes and onions.

Upon smelling the food, Ethan realized he was famished. Maybe it was because it was lunch time, or maybe his recent "exertions" had given him an appetite. Either way, he devoured the food quickly and then set about the rest of his task.

It took him several more hours before he had figured out the remaining tiles. He also gained rank 4 in *Air* and *Fire* magic, which gave him 2 additional points of *Intellect*. That put his maximum *Mana* at 66.

Wiping the sweat from his forehead, Ethan turned to the others. "I think I found them all!"

The group, most of whom had been lounging around on their bedrolls, looked up at him. Ainslee squinted her good eye at him. "What about the other door?"

Ethan sighed. "I need to... refresh my mana before I try that."

Nia, who had been practicing some sort of kata or

weapon form with her scimitars, slid the blades into their scabbards in a fluid motion and looked over at him with a slight smile. Ethan shook his head with a grin. Where was this girl back in his college days?

"Fine... fine," the dwarf growled and then leaned back against the archway with crossed arms. "Hurry up about it so we can get back to town."

Nia motioned for him impatiently as she scooped up her backpack. Ethan walked over to the foxgirl and took her outstretched hand, and the two of them walked back down the tunnel again.

WHEN THEY RETURNED, Ethan immediately set to figuring out the tiles needed to unlock the door. He guessed that the tiles would be on the wall, within arm's reach of the safe tiles. Unfortunately, that meant checking about thirty tiles for each safe tile.

Luckily, upon hitting the first "trigger" tile with his stone, Yuliana perked up. Coming to stand by him, she put her hand on his shoulder. "Can you do whatever you just did?"

"Why?" he asked curiously.

"I heard a... clicking sound just now," she told him.

Ethan grinned. "A clicking sound?"

"Yes," she replied, tilting her head. "It was something I hadn't heard before."

"That's probably it!" Ainslee exclaimed, obviously having overheard them talking. "The trigger tiles will probably make some sort of clicking sound as they lock in place. Tap the same tile again."

Doing so earned a nod from the elf. "There it is again. The same clicking."

"And none of the other tiles did that?" he asked.

"No." The elf shook her head.

"Can you stay here while I test the others?" he asked.

"Of course," she said.

The other two quickly moved over to see what Ethan, Yuliana and Ainslee were talking about. As Nia approached, Yuliana removed her hand from his shoulder and took a step away.

"You have figured out the opening tiles?" Nia asked.

"We think Yuliana is able to hear the clicking of the correct tiles," he replied. He gave the elf a smile. "She's like a safe-cracker!"

"Safe cracker?" Nia, Yuliana and Par'karr gave him curious looks but the dwarf nodded.

"Aye," the dwarf chuckled. "With ears like that, she'd make a lot of safe makers back home more than a wee bit nervous."

"I'm about to try some other ones," he told them. "Tell me if you hear a click."

The elf nodded and Ethan began to quickly move the rock from tile to tile. Within a few minutes, they'd found the next tile. Both opening tiles were on the wall adjacent to the safe floor tiles. But the next few tiles were not adjacent to any walls.

He tested the nearby wall plates with no success until he got to the later safe tiles, which once again were adjacent to walls. Then he found another one near the 8th safe floor tile and the final one on the wall over the last safe floor plate.

When nothing happened when he tapped the fourth

wall tile, he looked at Ainslee. "That's all of them within arm's reach. Do you think there are more somewhere else?"

Ainslee screwed up her face, an action that was a bit disconcerting with the ruined half of her face and her milky-white eye. "There's probably a reset mechanism. You have to do them within so many seconds of each other or it resets."

"Geez," Ethan groaned. "Without you and Yuliana, I don't think we would have figured this out."

The elf flashed him a smile and looked away but the dwarf just grunted in acknowledgement. "You might be a wizard, but you ain't no dwarf."

"Okay," he told them, looking back at his companions. "Everyone back away from the door. I'm going to test Ainslee's theory and if the door opens and something like poison darts or whatever fly out of there, I need you to all be out of the line of sight."

"What about you?" Nia demanded.

"I can protect myself with an air shield," he replied with a smile. "But I'm a bit low on mana, so I don't want to try and extend it over the entire doorway."

Nodding, Nia and the others moved to either side of the doorway, making sure they were not in the line of sight.

Ethan checked his *Mana*.

Mana: 13

It was more than enough to keep up his light balls, tap the lock tiles with his stone and raise an Air shield to deflect any darts, spears or anything else that came flying out of the far door. But before they actually crossed the floor using the safe path, he'd have to recharge his Mana. He smiled at that thought, glancing briefly at the foxgirl to the side.

"Okay," he said. "Here goes nothing."

"Nothing?" Par'karr asked with a perplexed look.

Ethan chuckled. "It's an expression where I'm from. It means, I'm about to try it."

"Okay! Here's go nothing!" the kobold repeated, bobbing his head.

Ethan picked up the stone he'd been using and moved it to the first lock tile on the wall. Then, manipulating the rock with *Air*, he tapped the first tile and then moved the stone and tapped the second tile next to it. Quickly, he moved it to the middle of the room and tapped the third tile before moving the rock next to the far door and tapping the final tile.

"Something is happening," the elf said from his left. "A different sound. A grinding."

Ethan heard it too then, and saw movement from the door. Slowly, the door began to slide down, just as Ainslee had said it would. The grinding sound intensified as it moved slowly, but another sound emerged too. It was a strange clicking and chittering sound.

And that was when the giant spiders began pouring out of the far door.

18

Giant spiders began pouring out of the opening door, scrambling over each other to get through the door, even as it continued to lower into the floor. The spiders' bodies alone were the size of small dogs. The creatures were a dark gray with a lighter-gray tiger-striped pattern over their bodies. They would blend in perfectly with the cavern walls.

Unlike the spiders of Earth, these didn't appear to have eight eyes. At least, not from where Ethan stood. They had three large black bulbous eyes set just above large, sharp-looking mandibles, or were they called fangs.

The spiders' bodies might be only a foot wide and a couple feet long, but with their legs, they appeared enormous. Each of their eight legs had to be at least four feet long if stretched out, making them seem larger than they actually were.

From next to him, he heard a high-pitched scream and saw Ainslee scrambling backwards, eyes wide. He swore.

He'd forgotten the dwarf had said something about hating spiders. It didn't appear she'd be any good in the impending fight.

"Spiders! Spiders! Spiders!" the dwarf gasped in horror as she fled the doorway.

Ethan looked back into the room as he heard the sound of spikes thrusting from the floor, impaling some of the lead spiders. The impaled spiders twitched, spasmed and convulsed on the spikes but that didn't stop their brethren from trying to get by them.

As the spiders hit the next row of tiles, more became impaled. Again, this did not dissuade the host of spiders behind them. They continued to swarm forward, dodging some spikes and getting impaled on others.

As more and more spiders became impaled, the other spiders began to crawl atop their kin's corpses, coming closer to Ethan and his group.

"Ethan!" A voice snapped him out of his trance-like fascination with the spiders and he turned towards Nia. She was looking at him with wide eyes.

"What?!" he answered back.

"There are too many of them!" she yelled. "We must flee!"

Ethan knew they'd never outrun the spiders. Not in the caves. They were too fast. He looked around at the doorway. "The doors! Shut the doors!"

Stepping back, he used *Air* to move the stone beam he'd put between the doors, even as he moved to the side to help her push it. A wide-eyed Par'karr ran to the other door but alone, the little kobold couldn't budge the door.

Together, Ethan and Nia struggled to push the door shut but it was slow going. Too slow. Whatever hinges or mechanism that allowed the door to open and close had been corroded or worn. They weren't going to close it before the spiders got to them.

Pulling up his HUD, Ethan checked his *Mana* level.

Mana: 10

He cursed. He didn't think he had enough *Mana* to close both the doors. Still, he knew he had to try. If he didn't, the spiders would make it through the door and keep on coming. He glanced into the room. There had to be dozens of them dead on the spikes and yet more kept coming.

Taking a deep breath, Ethan backed away and raised both his hands. Raising his hands wasn't necessary, of course, but it helped him focus on what he needed to do. He couldn't touch the doors with his magic directly. But he could touch something that touched the doors. A hack of sorts.

Reaching down with tendrils of *Air*, he picked up two nearby stones and pushed them against the doors. And pushed.

Slowly, the two large, stone doors began to swing shut. His HUD was still up and he watched as his *Mana* began dropping.

Mana: 9

Despite his steadily dwindling *Mana*, Ethan kept pushing the stone doors together. He tried to ignore the swarm of spiders getting closer, climbing over the bodies of their fallen to reach his group.

Mana: 7

The two stone doors groaned and creaked as Ethan exerted more force on them, closing them further.

Mana: 4

Ethan felt the energy draining out of him. He knew he couldn't keep this up. If his *Mana* dropped to zero, he'd collapse and wouldn't even be able to help fight off the spiders.

Mana: 1

In a Herculean effort of will, Ethan switched from *Mana* to *Stamina*, burning his reserves to keep pushing the door.

Stamina: 13

Unfortunately, his *Stamina* was still low from his time with Nia and he wasn't sure he could get the doors before he ran out of *Stamina* too.

Stamina: 10

A spider leaped through the closing doors, landing near him. Nia quickly sliced at it, driving it back. Then two more slipped through. Ethan couldn't move. All of his concentration was on pushing the doors together.

Stamina: 6

With one final force of will, Ethan pushed the two doors together with a crash, sealing the rest of the spiders inside. He staggered back and nearly tripped over a spider as it scurried after Par'karr.

Ethan stretched out his hand and shot a bolt of *Fire* into the middle of the spider's eyes, causing it to chitter and squirm as its eyes boiled and popped. Par'karr spun and lunged forward, burying his spear into its eye cluster. The thing spasmed and collapsed.

```
Stamina: 4
   Tunnel Spider dies.
   You gain 30 experience. Experience
to next level 2445.
```

Taking a moment to move around, Ethan saw that one spider was trying to get to a screaming Yuliana, while Luna struck out repeatedly with her large paws to keep the spider away.

"Help Yuliana and Luna," Ethan told the kobold. Par'karr nodded and rushed over to join the fray.

The little kobold sprang up behind the spider and jabbed at the thing with his spear. The spider chittered as the spear punctured the back of the creature's abdomen, bringing forth a splash of yellow ichor.

The spider started to turn towards the new attacker. That was when Luna's claws sliced across one of the creature's eyes, ruining it. The spider tried to back up, but Par'karr was still there. The kobold pulled out his spear and jabbed the thing again.

This time, the spider spun, taking a glancing blow from

Luna as it did. The spider snapped its fangs at Par'karr, who backed away. Then it charged. At least, Ethan guessed that's what its intention had been before two hundred pounds of mountain lion pounced on it.

The force of the blow drove its thorax and abdomen into the ground. The lion dug her front claws into the spider's thorax and began raking with her back claws. So strong was the cat's rear legs, that the spider was torn in half between the thorax and abdomen, spilling yellow ichor all over the cavern floor.

A pained shout alerted Ethan and he saw Nia on the ground with one of the spiders atop her. She was keeping the fangs at bay with crossed scimitars but the spider was pushing down on her, using its eight legs to drive it closer and closer to her face.

Overcome with a sudden rage, Ethan lashed out at the arachnid with heat. He didn't use fire. He was afraid Nia might get burned. Instead, he heated up the creature's body from the inside out.

The spider began to spasm. The skin on its thorax and abdomen began to blister. Smoke or steam came from the creature's legs as it twitched and spasmed, not understanding what the pain was or where it was coming from.

One by one, the spider's eyes popped, spraying disgusting pieces of its eyeball all over the floor and across Nia. The creature gave out a final spasm and then collapsed on top of the foxgirl in a smoking heap.

Tunnel Spider dies.
      You gain 30 experience. Experience to next level 2415.

Darkness began to crawl in at the edges of Ethan's vision as he struggled to catch his breath. He felt like he'd just run a marathon. Maybe he had - a magical marathon. He saw his *Stamina* score in his HUD.

Stamina: 1

He nearly used all of his *Stamina*. He literally had nothing left. He was dizzy and dropped to his knees to prevent himself from falling over onto the hard stone floor.

Behind him, he heard the spiders throwing themselves at the door. They were relentless. Then he heard the doors groan and he slowly turned towards the doors. The spiders were starting to push the doors open!

"We... have... to... block... the door," he gasped, trying to take deep breaths.

Crawling over the large stone beam he'd used to prop the doors open, he struggled to push the thing in front of the doors. Unfortunately, he was too weak and exhausted to budge it. Then Nia appeared next to him on his right while Par'karr appeared on his left.

He grinned weakly, feeling his strength ebbing. "On three, let's..."

He heard heavy footsteps and he saw a wild-eyed, pale-faced Ainslee come running up next to Par'karr. She didn't look at anyone, but kept her eyes straight. Yuliana bent over next to Nia, hands on the stone beam.

Nodding, he took a deep breath. "On three... one... two... three!"

Ethan pushed with the last of his strength, grunting loudly. He heard similar noises from the others as they slowly moved the beam a few inches, then a foot and finally against the doors.

Blackness invaded from all sides as he felt himself slipping away. Ethan collapsed and knew no more.

19

He was drowning. Ethan felt the cold water closing in on him and he choked and sputtered as it filled his lungs. His eyes shot open as he coughed up water. Wide-eyed, he clutched at his throat and the hard object in his mouth. The water stopped flowing into his mouth and he gasped for air as his eyes darted around.

Everything was black and he still felt wet. He flailed his arms around, hitting something soft and hard at the same time. Whatever it was made a noise and then a growl. Then he felt a sharp stinging against his left cheek, along with the loud smacking of skin on skin. Had someone just slapped him?

"Calm down, Ethan," Nia said. "Wake up!"

Ethan knew his eyes were open but he couldn't see the speaker. But he did recognize the voice. It was Nia. Was he blind? What couldn't he see?!

"Drink more water," Nia's voice said as a hard, cold shape was pressed against his lips.

A bottle. It was one of the stone bottles he'd made.

Ethan relaxed and stopped struggling. He wasn't drowning. They were pouring water down his throat to restore his *Stamina.*

He remembered collapsing and everything going dark. He must have used the last bit of his *Stamina* pushing that stone beam in front of the doors. Coughing again, he brought up his HUD.

```
Stamina: 1
  Mana:  5
```

Both *Mana* and *Stamina* were low. He must have pushed himself too hard and gotten his *Stamina* into the negative. Given how much *Mana* he had recovered, he had probably been out close to five minutes.

Ethan looked around but there was only blackness. Fighting down panic, he turned towards where he had heard Nia's voice come from. "Why can't I see?"

"The candles went out in the fight," the foxgirl shot back. "When you fell unconscious, your balls of light went out too."

He nodded but then realized no one could see him. He sighed and created two glowing balls of light near his head. Ethan heard groans and complaints as he caught sight of his companions shielding their eyes from the sudden brightness. He blinked his own eyes several times as they grew used to the new level of illumination.

"Bout time!" grumbled Ainslee, shielding her eyes with her beefy hand. "Was hopin' you weren't dead."

A scaly face loomed over him and suddenly little kobold arms were thrown around his neck. "Ethan okay! Par'karr worried Ethan bit by spider!"

"I'm fine, Par'karr," he chuckled but then looked around. "Is everyone okay?"

Ethan struggled to a full sitting position and made a quick inventory of faces. Nia was next to him on the left, her strong arm still against his back from helping him sit up. Her other hand held one of their water bottles.

Opposite him was Ainslee. The dwarf's ruined face with her one good eye stared back at him. The facial muscles of her ruined right side didn't quite work correctly, so judging her expression was difficult.

Backing away from him on the right was Par'karr. The little kobold was still grinning, happy to see that his friend was alive and, for the most part, well.

Just beyond Par'karr he saw the green hair and tanned face of Yuliana. She was sitting with Luna draped over her legs, petting the mountain lion's head. The elf and big cat looked back at him, blinking against the light.

Ethan sighed in relief. It appeared everyone was still alive. Nia thrust the water bottle into his hand. "Everyone is fine. You must drink more."

Noises broke through the silence then and he turned towards their source: the double stone doors. Ethan had heard the noise since he had awakened but his own safety and the safety of his friends had been the first thing on his mind.

"They are still trying to get through the door," the dwarf shuddered, purposefully not looking at the door. Ainslee fixed him with her good left eye. "I hate spiders. I... I can't think rationally around them. And giant spiders.... Well... I mean, I just... ran. I'm sorry."

"We call it a phobia," Ethan said sympathetically. His dad had been plagued with claustrophobia in his later years. It had gradually gotten to the point where he could no longer get an MRI or go on a plane without taking some sort of anti-anxiety pill. Even long elevator rides were a struggle for him. "It's an irrational fear. It's nothing to be ashamed about."

Ainslee said nothing but lowered her eyes, looking down into her lap. "Wasn't right to leave my friends."

Ethan grinned. "Any fight you can walk away from is a good fight. And it looks like we walked away."

The dwarf muttered something he couldn't make out but didn't look up.

"Drink!" Nia commanded. "You must restore your stamina so we can mate and restore your mana!"

Ethan, who had just put the water bottle up to his lips and taken a swig, suddenly sprayed out the water as he coughed. "What?!"

Nia frowned and wiped the droplets of water off her face. She gave Ethan a disapproving look.

"Sorry," he said sheepishly. Ethan was really not used to a woman being so forward with him and so completely open about sex. None of the women he'd dated on Earth had ever been that way. They hadn't been that vocal about sex, let alone as enthusiastic about it.

Of course, he wasn't the same person he'd been back on Earth. Here, he was a wizard. He had real power. He had magic and could create fireballs and move objects with *Air* - as long as his *Mana* held out. He could create portals to other worlds!

Was that it? Was that why she was attracted to him and had declared him her mate? Because he was powerful? Because here, Ethan was an alpha? He smirked. Did he really care? She was gorgeous, fierce and completely unlike any other woman he'd been with - physically and personality-wise. Sometimes, it was best not to look gift horses - or foxgirls - in the mouth.

He brought up his water bottle and took a long swig to hide his smirk. He took several more long draws from the bottle, emptying it. He checked his stats again.

Stamina: 15
Mana: 7

The water had restored a quarter of his *Stamina* and his *Mana* was regenerating slowly. Nia took the empty bottle and handed him another full one.

Ethan frowned and shook his head. "This is someone else's."

"It is mine," the foxgirl chided him. "And I want you to drink it. I have plenty of stamina. You need more. Drink!"

"Do it, wizard-boy," Ainslee ordered, looking back up at him and gesturing around the cavern. "If you pass out again, we're all in the dark. And that ain't no fun."

He nodded grimly. It hadn't been fun when he'd first awakened in absolute darkness. He wasn't sure how long they'd been in darkness, but he was sure it hadn't been a fun experience.

Taking the offered bottle, Ethan drank it down as well. As he did, he knew he needed to make sure that the group wasn't left in the dark - literally and figuratively - if he passed out again. His mind began to come up with ideas on how to craft a magical token that shed light.

He also scolded himself. During the spider attack, he hadn't even thought of his magical shotgun in his backpack. He could have conserved some *Mana* had he used it. But things had happened so fast and his backpack had been twenty yards from the door. He needed to be cognizant of his weapons and keep them on him at all times.

When he was about a quarter of the way through the water, he checked his stats again.

Stamina: 30
  Mana: 9

He smiled and handed the water bottle back to Nia. She shook her head and instead handed him the stopper. She flashed him a sly smile. "Keep it. You will need it soon."

She stood up and reached down a hand to help him up. As she did Ethan caught Ainslee rolling her good eye at them. "Before you two run off and breed like rabbits in heat, what are we going to do about the... spiders. We can't get through that many - even if I could make myself."

Ethan had been thinking about the spiders as he had been drinking water. The only possible thing he could think of was to burn them. Burn them all. If he could open the doors just half a foot, he could pour fire into the room and incinerate them.

Depending on how many there were, he may have to do that several times. Ethan could technically do it as many times as he could restore his *Mana*, but that could take days. If they kept coming after that, he might have to rethink this quest.

He looked at the dwarf. "We burn them. We burn them with fire!"

His attempt at humor fell on deaf ears and he sighed as he stood up. "We'll be back in a bit but this might take longer than usual."

Nia looked at him with a raised eyebrow. "Longer than usual?"

Ethan smiled and shrugged. "I have an idea about some light-generating magical items but I need to charge some crystals."

The foxgirl nodded approvingly and smiled. She reached down and grabbed her bedroll. "I can accommodate you."

"Uh," the dwarf said from behind him. "Before you start all of your accommodating... you think you could light us a few candles so we're not sitting here in the dark while you two start acting like rabbits?"

"Rabbits?" Par'karr perked up.

20

Two hours later, Ethan and Nia returned to the group. The two of them had to recharge his *Mana* several times in order for him to charge up some Chymera crystals. Ethan had certainly enjoyed it and judging from the foxgirl's smile, she had too.

Now, Ethan was ready to try and take care of the spiders. His *Mana* was full and he'd been thinking of ideas in between making love and charging crystals. He'd thought about fireballs, a wall of fire and several other things but in the end, he went with a flamethrower.

Ethan had to test his idea and found that he could generate steady streams of fire from his hands. It was very cool and he felt like some mutant or a superhero, stopping just short of yelling "Flame on!"

He'd also created several magical stones. He wished he had a few lanterns to enchant, especially a hooded lantern, but he worked with what he could. At the moment, there was plenty of stone and he could shape it with his *Earth* magic.

The results were five magic rocks with two embedded crystals: the spell crystal and the battery crystal. And they did one thing. They created light equal to one of his light spheres, about the same as a torch.

"About time!" Ainslee huffed as they walked into the cavern. "I thought we'd have to find you and pull you two apart!"

Nia shrugged but Ethan felt a little heat in his cheeks. He really wasn't used to having sex within earshot of someone, let alone have all of his friends know exactly what he and Nia were doing. It was weird to his Earthly sensibilities, despite Nia's much more cavalier attitude towards it.

Ignoring the awkwardness he felt, Ethan put a grin on his face. "But I come bearing gifts."

Opening his hand and letting his balls of light dissipate, the cavern was suddenly illuminated in bright light from the stones. The sudden change in light levels caused his companions to blink and shield their eyes.

"Was is it?" Par'karr asked, wide-eyed.

"Magical stones that created light," Ethan told them. "I enchanted one for each of us."

"Good!" Ainslee snorted. "At least the next time you decide to take a nap, we won't all be in the dark until you decide to get up."

Ethan smirked at the dwarf. She was sounding more and more like her old self all the time. Still, there was something different in Ainslee's good eye. Not the same spark of life there had been.

He couldn't blame her. Ethan knew he'd be devastated if he'd suffered the same sort of disfigurement that the dwarf had. Not that he'd been the best-looking guy, but the scarring Ainslee had suffered was next-level stuff. It wasn't something he or anyone looking at her could ignore.

Quickly handing them out to Ainslee, Par'karr and Yuliana, he gave them a minute or two to examine and play with the enchanted stones.

"The enchantment is very simple," he told them. "So it should recharge itself continually and provide light forever."

"Par'karr like magic!" the kobold said, waving the stone around in his hand.

"Good," Ethan said and slid off his backpack. "Because I'm going to let you use this until we stop whatever is making the sound."

He handed over his enchanted stone shotgun to the kobold, whose eyes grew as large as saucers. Par'karr took the shotgun reverently, staring at it open mouthed. "For... Par'karr?!"

"For now," Ethan said. He remembered the initial spider attack and how he hadn't been able to get to the shotgun in time. "I can't work my magic and use it effectively. But it will give you something else to use besides the spear. If you like it, you can keep it and I will make another one when we get back."

Ethan spent the next ten minutes explaining how the shotgun worked, demonstrating it and then letting Par'karr try it out. They then waited a few more minutes as the kobold fired it off several times.

"Remember," he told Par'karr, "it takes almost a full minute to recharge, so be careful when using it. You may need to...."

Looking at it, Ethan got a sudden idea and grinned. The shotgun took a minute to recharge. His original idea had been to alternate between the shotgun and his own magic.

Giving it to Par'karr presented a dilemma. The kobold's magic didn't work the same as Ethan's.

Par'karr's summoning magic was similar to Ethan's ability to summon an elemental. Unlike Ethan, it was the only magic the kobold had. And for now, the kobold couldn't even do that. The demon rabbits he summoned immediately went berserk from the sound as soon as they showed up.

His friend would need something to defend himself while he waited for the shotgun to recharge and Ethan's idea might solve that issue. Grabbing a stone the size of his fists, Ethan brought it to the barrel of the shotgun and took a spare dagger from his backpack.

Using a little Earth magic, he shaped the stone around the blade and merged it just under the double barrels of the shotgun. This world's first bayonet, like the old muskets from the American Revolutionary and Civil Wars.

"There you go," Ethan said. "When you're not able to fire the shotgun, you can stab things with it."

Par'karr grinned wickedly, admiring the weapon. "Ethan best wizard ever!"

Ethan chuckled and looked at the doors to the trapped room. He let out a breath. "We're about to find out just how good I am."

"What are you planning, wizard-boy?" Ainslee asked with a narrowed eye.

"We're going to open those doors a bit..." he started but his companions erupted into pandemonium.

"We're going to what?!" the dwarf sputtered, her good eye gone wide. Ainslee took an involuntary step away from the door. "You want to open the door to those things?! Did you see how many of them there were?"

"I did," he replied. "But we're going to open the door a bit and I'm going to burn them."

"Burn them?" Yuliana asked.

Ethan caused torrents of flame to shoot up into the air from his hands, showing them his magical flame throwing ability.

Only Nia didn't flinch, having seen it before. The others gasped or scrambled away. They'd seen him create small fire or fireballs, but fifteen-feet cones of fire was something completely different.

"Thor's Hammer!" the dwarf muttered as she looked at where the flames had just been. She blinked several times before the left side of her face broke into a grin. "Now that's what I'm talking about! Burn those eight-legged freaks!"

"I will," Ethan told her but then put a grim expression on his face. "But I need you at the door to help me close it if I can't keep up with the spiders. You're the strongest one here. I need you up there or I don't think this will work."

Ainslee shuddered and stared at the door for a long moment before slowly nodding. Ethan caught the glint of perspiration on her forehead and knew he was asking a lot of the dwarf. Unfortunately, it couldn't be helped.

He hadn't been lying; Nia was strong but Ainslee was the strongest one in the group. He needed her there to close the doors if he overexerted himself again. Without her there, the doors may stay open too long and more of those spiders would get into the cavern. Ethan didn't want a repeat of their last battle.

After explaining the full plan to everyone and having them agree, the group gathered around the doors. Even after hours had gone by, the spiders were still banging on the doors with a single-minded determination.

"If any manage to get through," he told them. "Just keep them off me. I need to keep a steady stream of fire to prevent an all-out assault on the door."

"We will protect you," Nia said confidently as she tightened her grip on her scimitars.

Par'karr flashed him an almost maniacal grin as the kobold brandished the shotgun. "Par'karr blast anything that get through."

Yuliana just nodded. Ainslee, who was white-faced, said nothing. She just stared at the doors and swallowed hard.

"Here we go," Ethan said and took a deep breath and wiped his sweaty palms on his pants. It was showtime.

Then, using *Air*, Ethan pulled the two stone beams that were holding the doors shut a foot apart. As he did, he saw the three-eyed spiders pushing and shoving to get through the gap. That's when he unleashed his flame-throwing spells.

Immediately, he heard the crackling and popping of burning spiders, along with a high-pitched squealing. Then the smoke and acrid odor of burning spider hit his nose and he almost gagged. He began breathing through his mouth and kept the flames pouring into the gap, moving them up and down to prevent any spiders from trying to squeeze through.

"Die, spiders!" screamed Ainslee, her face a mask of rage and hate.

Looking at his HUD, he began to see experience messages on his HUD.

Tunnel Spider dies.

  You gain 60 experience. Experience to next level 2355.

Tunnel Spider dies.
You gain 60 experience. Experience
to next level 2295.

The messages began to scroll by too quickly for him to count but he didn't let up the fire. He did keep an eye on his *Mana*.

Mana: 34

He was almost down to half of his *Mana*. He had no idea how many he'd burned but the air was thick with smoke and the smell of burning spiders. Still, the spiders kept coming.

"Burn those spiders!" screamed the dwarf, nearly hysterical. "Burn them all!"

Taking the dwarf's suggestion, Ethan kept pouring more and more fire into the opening, hearing the squealing and the crackling and popping.

He didn't understand why the spiders kept coming. Most creatures would run away from fire. The intense heat alone was usually enough to keep most creatures away if not send them running.

These spiders were throwing themselves at the fire as if they had no concern for their lives. It was as if they were obsessed with getting to and killing his group. But why? It didn't seem like normal spider behavior. Then again, these three-eyed, giant spiders were not Earth spiders. Who knew how their instincts worked.

Ethan kept spraying fire into the room beyond until his Mana got low and then used *Air* and pushed the two stone beams against the doors, slamming them shut with a thud that echoed through the chamber.

When he was done, Ethan stepped back and listened. The others did the same. There was no thudding on the door this time.

"Did we... get them all?" the dwarf asked, her good eye full of hope.

"I don't know," Ethan said. "Let's give it some time and see if they come back."

He quickly scrolled through the backlog of system messages until he found the last one.

```
Tunnel Spider dies.
   You gain 30 experience. Experience
to next level 915.
```

His spider burning escapade had earned him nearly 2,000 experience. Just under 1,000 more and he'd gain another level.

"In the meantime," Nia said matter of factly, "we should recharge your Mana."

Next to Ethan, he heard a snort. "Hah. You deserve it, wizard-boy. If you didn't have Nia, I'd offer to do it myself for you killing those spiders!"

Then the dwarf looked embarrassed, her right hand coming up to her ruined face. "I mean... you know.. Before..."

Ainslee stopped talking, her eyes going to the floor. Ethan wanted to say something but wasn't sure what to say. Instead, he reached out and gripped the dwarf's shoulder and gave it a squeeze.

21

Ethan and Nia recharged his *Mana* and returned to the cavern. This time, they could tell they were getting near by the stench of burned spiders. Ethan hadn't remembered it being so bad but apparently, a little time away and he realized how bad it was. He saw Nia's nose twitched and knew the smell must be much worse to her sensitive nose.

The others were waiting for them and didn't seem to be bothered by the smell. When Par'karr saw them, he hopped up and ran up excitedly.

"Spiders not knocking at door!" the kobold exclaimed, gesturing wildly at the stone doors.

Ethan raised an eyebrow. "They're gone?"

"The elf says she don't hear them nearby," Ainslee confirmed and Ethan couldn't help but notice the look of relief on her face. "Says they've moved away."

"When did that happen?" Ethan asked. He didn't understand why the spiders, who had shown single-minded determination to get out the doors, had suddenly given up.

"Shortly after Ethan and Nia leave," Par'karr chimed in happily. "Spiders gone!"

"She'll tell ya," the dwarf said, nodding to Yuliana.

The green-haired elf looked up from petting Luna. "They are right. I heard the spiders leave. I now know that it is they who made the sounds I heard earlier. There weren't many left inside the room but shortly after you left, I heard them crawling away."

"You don't hear them at all now?" Ethan asked. He wondered if they had gone far or perhaps were lying in ambush. Perhaps some of them hadn't even left but were just staying still, trying to lure them into a false sense of security.

Was he ascribing too much intelligence to them? They were only spiders after all. Or were they? Their three eyes meant they were different from any spiders on Earth. Could they be intelligent? He didn't know. It was best to assume that they were intelligent instead of assuming they weren't and being unpleasantly surprised.

Yuliana cocked her head right then left, her long tapered ears twitching slightly. Turning back to Ethan she shook her head. "I do not hear them at all now."

"That just means they are not moving," Nia said, putting words to Ethan's thoughts. "Like hunters hiding in the bushes, they may be trying to lure us in."

"Lure us into what?" Ainslee asked, squinting at them with her good eye.

"An ambush," replied Nia before Ethan could say the same thing.

Ethan was thinking of the Earth spiders who waited in holes for their prey like the wolf spider or the trapdoor spider. He silently thanked the nature channels he'd watch sometimes while chilling out.

But was that why these spiders had retreated? They certainly hadn't been dissuaded by the fire, though he had expected them to flee in terror. Were they falling back because of the losses? Or were they falling back to lure them in?

A third possibility loomed in his mind. Was there some sort of "queen spider" or something else controlling them? Could it be whatever was creating the sound that was causing all of the mammals to flee?

But why now? They'd heard the sounds of, what they now knew as spiders, the first time they'd been in the mine. Obviously, they'd been in the mine before Ethan and his companions entered - probably even before the old mayor had met his untimely death in the tomb entrance.

Ethan had too many questions and not enough answers. Unfortunately, the only place he would get answers was inside the tomb.

"We'll have to be careful," Ethan told his companions. "Nia's right. On my world, there were spiders who set traps and waited for their prey to get close enough for them to fall into a trap or close enough for the spider to jump out at them."

He saw the dwarf shiver at the mention of falling into spider traps and spiders jumping out at prey. Ainslee glanced to the tunnel entrance that led back out of the mine. And he didn't blame her.

The idea of spiders lying in wait for them was terrifying to him too. If something like that happened and his reflexes weren't quick enough, he could very quickly find himself dead - assuming these spiders had venom.

He suddenly had flashbacks to that movie about an alien aboard a spaceship. He remembered how they searched for it in the air ducts and rooms, only to get taken out one by one. And that was just one alien. Who knew how many spiders there might be left.

Ethan involuntarily glanced back at the tunnel out. Maybe this quest wasn't worth it. Maybe they should just go back and tell the villagers to abandon the village. He swore silently. No, he couldn't just abandon them to starvation or death along the road to the next village. Especially not the children. He couldn't live with himself.

"We'll be careful," he repeated, partially to reassure himself. He looked around at the group. "But if anyone wants to stay here or go back to the village, I understand."

He purposely didn't look at the dwarf. Ethan didn't want to call out the dwarf because of her arachnophobia.

Emotions played over the good side of the dwarf's face. Unfortunately, the strange mix of her scarred right side and her good left side made it impossible for Ethan to guess what Ainslee was thinking.

Finally, she let out a breath and looked at Ethan. "I'm coming along with you. Ain't got no other friends on this world. And lookin' like this, I never will."

Ethan walked over to the dwarf and bent down to look her eye to eye. He looked into her good eye, struggling to find the words when he remembered something from Norse mythology. "We're your friends and we'll stick by you no matter what. As for your looks, remember, Odin only had one good eye. You have battle scars from saving your friends. I can't think of a better way to earn them."

The dwarf's good eye moistened and she bit her lip but then nodded before stepping away and turning to get her pack. Ethan didn't miss that she wiped her sleeve across her good eye.

"Alright," he told them. "Let's get ready and we'll make our way in."

As soon as he finished speaking, his companions began to pack up their gear and get ready. Ethan went over to his own pack and gathered up his items. As he did, his eyes fell on Merlin's journal.

He really wanted to read it but he just didn't have the time at the moment. He flipped through a few pages of the regular text and found more of the symbols interspersed through the pages. Maybe once they found out whatever was causing the sound and stopped it, he would have time to read the journal.

When Ethan had finished packing his stuff, he shouldered his backpack and walked over to the doors. The others were done and came to stand behind him.

"You still don't hear anything?" he asked Yuliana.

The elf pulled her hair away from her ears and listened for half a minute before shaking her head. "I do not hear them at all."

Ethan blew out a breath. "Let's be ready for anything. They could just be staying really still. If things go bad, we retreat back here and I shut the doors. If I can't... Nia, you and Ainslee do it."

His companions nodded, grunted or spoke their agreement and Ethan turned towards the doors. He mentally readied himself to begin shooting jets of flame the moment he saw anything. Thus prepared, he reached out with Air and moved the stone pillar in front of the doors. Then, slowing, he pulled the doors apart.

He immediately regretted it as a wave of stench and the smoke of charred bodies rolled over them. Ethan had to back up as the smoke stung his eyes and the odor made him want to vomit. He stopped himself, but just barely. His experience living out in the country, surrounded by farmers who liked to use manure as fertilizer, had given him a tolerance to strong odors.

Blinking away the tears and backing up, he tried to watch for any spiders that might be moving. Somewhere in the smoke, he heard the others coughing and he thought he heard at least one of them losing their lunch.

Remembering he had magic at his command, he created a gust of wind and pushed the smoke and stench back into the room and out the opposite doorway. The blast of *Air* also caused the pile of scorched spider bodies to crumble into ash, which further obscured the air until he pushed it out as well.

It took five minutes of continual *Air* and nearly half his *Mana* to clear the room to a point where they could actually see the tiled floor.

Ethan's eyes were still stinging and he was still coughing, as were his companions. With the smoke clear, he could see that both Yuliana and Par'karr had been sickened by the fumes had lost their lunches.

"Everyone okay?" he said with a cough.

"That may be the most wretched thing I've ever smelled," Ainslee complained. "I thought they smelled bad on the outside!"

He couldn't help but agree. Of all of them, Nia seemed the least affected despite her enhanced sense of smell. Was she simply more used to strong scents?

Watching the opposite doorway, he waited for his companions to get over the lingering effects of the smoke inhalation and the stench. It took several minutes but eventually they had all recovered enough to advance.

Once they were all assembled at the doorway, Ethan used some more *Air* to clear the safe tiles of spider debris and bodies. He pointed out the safe tiles. "Remember, whatever you do, stay on the path. Don't stray off it or... well... you know what happens."

They nodded or gave muttered agreements and Ethan took one last look through the opposite doorway. Then he stepped onto the first of the safe tiles and began to cross the trapped room.

22

Ethan made it across with no issues, other than some additional coughing from the smoke and foul stench that still lingered in the room. Once he was across, Nia came, followed by Par'karr with light stones illuminating their way. That's when things got interesting.

Ainslee tried to come next, but her wide large feet made it difficult for her to stay completely on the path. For the dwarf, it was almost like balancing on a tightrope. Luckily, in most places the wall was nearby for her to brace against.

When the dwarf got to the 4th through 7th tiles, Ethan was forced to create barriers of *Air* to help her balance herself while Par'karr and Nia watched the tunnel doorway. This allowed Ainslee to make it through the remaining tiles without any mishap.

Finally, it was Yuliana's turn. As Yuliana looked across to Ethan, they both seemed to come to the realization at the same time. No one had thought of the elf's animal companion, Luna. Luna might be magically bound to the druid, but she didn't have any special intelligence.

While the two shared some sort of magical bond that allowed them to communicate simple commands, navigating the maze of correct tiles was beyond the scope of the animal's normal intelligence and the communication bond they shared.

"We can't leave her here," Yuliana pleaded, looking between the mountain lion and Ethan. "But I do not know how to tell Luna how to cross."

Ethan sighed. He had hoped not to use a lot of *Mana* and save it for any fights against the spiders. He was down to almost half from clearing out the smoke but it looked like he'd need to use more to levitate the big cat across the expanse.

"I'll lift her over," he called to the elf and saw the woman visibly relax. "Just explain to her as best you can what I'm going to do. The less she struggles, the less mana I'll have to use."

Yuliana nodded and whispered some words to the cat in a soothing tone before looking over at Ethan. "I think she's ready."

Ethan wasn't so sure, but he nodded back and reached out a hand. Suddenly, he felt like the space wizard trying to lift his star-fighter out of a swamp. Ethan snorted. Hopefully, he'd do better than Luke had. If he remembered correctly, Luke had failed and the star-fighter had sunk further into the swamp.

Pushing the memories of old movies out of his mind, Ethan willed the *Air* to embrace the big cat. Luna felt the air around her but seemed more curious than anything else, sniffing to her left and right. And then, Ethan picked her up.

Immediately, the cat let out a hiss and a high-pitched whine and began to windmill her front and back paws, trying to find purchase. The moving cat became more difficult to hold but Ethan wrapped her in more <u>Air</u> and quickly brought her across the room and set her down next to Nia.

"Hold her," he told Nia. "Don't let her run back across the room!"

Par'karr and Nia crouched down and immediately began stroking the cat's fur and cooing to the mountain lion. Ethan turned to the elf. "Come on across, quickly if you can."

The elf did. Her light steps and dexterous movements made it look no more difficult than skipping down a forest trail. When she got to the other side, Ethan reached down and pulled her up.

She immediately wrapped her arms around him, squeezing him in a big hug. "Thank you for bringing her across. I couldn't bear to leave her behind."

Ethan felt the crush of the elf's firm body and ample chest against him, reminding him once again how attractive the elf was. His body reacted to the attractive elf's embrace but he also remembered that he was spoken for by Nia.

"You'd better make sure she's okay. We don't want her trying to run back across," Ethan said, disengaging from the elf. He gestured to the cat nervously. As he did, he caught Nia watching him. The foxgirl didn't look angry or jealous, just curious - perhaps even thoughtful.

Clearing his throat, Ethan stepped around the group and peered through the doorway and into the tunnel beyond. He sent his balls of light down the tunnel for thirty feet. He craned his head to see any holes, pits or places that spiders could be hiding.

The corridor leading away from the spike room was about six feet wide by nine feet tall and stretched into the darkness. The walls, ceiling and floors were smooth, worked stone formed into 3x3-feet stone blocks.

There was no real mortar between the stone blocks like he would have expected. It had probably been carved out of the very stone of the mountain by either magic or very skilled stonesmiths. Experimentally, he reached out with *Earth* and tried to shape the stone. Like the stone tiles in the spike room, his magic slipped off the stone blocks.

Someone had gone through a ton of work to make all of this stone anti-magic. But why? And who had done it? His thoughts went to Merlin, the journal and the strange writing on both the journal and the outside of the tomb. He really needed to take some time and read the journal!

Despite his curiosity about the journal, Ethan knew that now was not the right time. People in horror movies who stopped to do mundane things like read books, tended to have something sneak up on them and stab them.

Frowning, he remembered another trope of horror movies. He glanced at Nia. Didn't the couple who had sex in a horror movie always die. Or, at least, didn't one of them die? It was best not to think of that. After all, maybe this was an adventure movie - or an action thriller.

For now, they needed to find the source of the noise and stop it. He glanced back. "See anything?"

"I see no spiders," Nia said. She had the best eyesight of any of them with her almost cat-like night vision. She could probably see twice as far as Ethan in the dark.

"Alright," Ethan told the group. "Keep your weapons ready. They could literally be anywhere. And Par'karr, remember friendly fire isn't friendly."

The kobold looked at him in confusion. "Fire?"

Ethan sighed. "Watch where you're shooting the boom-stick. Make sure you don't hit one of us with it."

Par'karr looked down to the shotgun in his hands and nodded enthusiastically. "Par'karr careful!"

Taking a step into the corridor, Ethan remembered some of the alien movies. He looked up at the ceiling. Spiders could climb and cling to surfaces. Could these spiders? "Keep an eye out above us too. We don't know what these things are capable of."

He began to take another step but then looked down at the floor. Would there be more spike traps? He didn't want to be using *Air* to test every single step down the corridor. He needed something to probe the ground in front of him. He grinned. He needed a 10-foot pole.

The 10-foot pole was a staple of pen and paper role-playing games, especially at low levels before players had access to any sort of divination magic or a detect traps spell. It should work in real life. He hoped.

They had no long poles with them and no tree branches to use a pole without going all the way back out. He couldn't form one out of the stones around him. He looked back at the stone beam holding the two doors open.

Reaching out with *Earth*, Ethan carved off a ten-foot-long section of the beam. He knew stone would be heavy, so he kept it only about an inch thick. Then, using *Air*, he levitated the pole back to him.

The others were looking at him curiously as he grinned. He gestured to the pole. "It's a 10-foot pole!"

Eying the pole, the group looked at him confused. He sighed again and let the grin fade. "It will help us discover traps without me having to use magic all the time."

"Ah," came a collective acknowledgement and once again

Ethan wished some of his roleplaying buddies were with him.

Ethan moved to the front of the group again and began prodding the floor with his new pole like a blind man probing the ground in front of him with a cane.

Slowly, he and the group began to move down the corridor. They were all tense and alert, watching every direction for spiders. Once they had moved about a hundred yards, Ethan suddenly went pale as he heard the grating of stone on stone behind them.

Spinning, his worst fear was realized as the door into the spike room was starting to raise up out of the floor. "The door!"

As one, the group spun and ran for the door. By the time they got to it, the door was already half way up. Ethan reached out with *Air* and tried to stop the door but the magic rolled off the door. He swore loudly.

Nia and Ainslee threw themselves against the door, desperately trying to stop the door from rising but they might as well have been children trying to stop a car. The stone doorway continued to rise.

He cursed. He didn't have enough time to get all of them through, especially without throwing them onto one of the trapped tiles in the room. And that meant certain death.

Ethan wracked his brain for an idea but nothing came. Par'karr joined in with Nia and Ainslee trying to prevent the door from going up but it was futile.

Watching his companions struggle against the door, Ethan stood impotently as it rose further and further.

The door was now too high for his companions to grab onto and they backed away. Standing in a line across the corridor, they collectively watched the door as it raised the last couple of feet. When it reached the top, it stopped with a deep, resounding thud of stone on stone.

The five of them looked at each other. They all knew the truth of the situation. There were no special tiles on this side. There was no opening mechanism that they could see, and no way to lower that door from this side.

Par'karr squeaked what they all realized. "We is trapped!"

23

The sound of the closing door still echoed down the corridor behind them as they stared helplessly at the stone door.

"What caused door to close?" Par'karr demanded in a shrill voice.

"Maybe I triggered some switch," Ethan admitted. He hadn't heard any clicks or sensed any depressions from a plate being triggered but the 10-foot pole was much more unyielding than he had imagined in his pen and paper role-playing games.

"Probably some sort of timer." Ainslee shrugged. "We did have it open for a long time."

"Or the spiders somehow forced it to close," Nia offered.

Ethan was taken back by her suggestion. Could the spiders really have triggered some sort of mechanism that closed the door? If so, then they had much more intelligence than he'd given them credit for. And yet, it didn't reconcile with the creatures that were just throwing themselves into a spiked room and into his fire.

Could he have been right before? Were these three-eyed spiders just drones of some sort being controlled by a queen? If so, where was the queen and would she wade into the fight? Or would she keep sending her drones? He wasn't in any hurry to find out.

"Can you break it down with your hammer?" Ethan asked the dwarf.

Ainslee looked at him and then burst out laughing. "Sure, wizard-boy. In about a month or two. I don't know if you noticed as we went over it, but that door's a foot-thick granite." She held up her hammer. "This thing ain't going to do anything against it."

Ethan swore. Knowing what he'd find, he nonetheless reached out with *Earth*. As before, the magic fell away as soon as he touched the door. He swore again. "Enchanted! I can't do anything with it."

"What we do?" Par'karr asked, wide-eyed.

Ethan turned and looked down the corridor and then back to the door. He already knew what the options were. "I can charge up some crystals..."

"More sex..." Ainslee snorted.

"...and..." Ethan cleared his throat and tried not to blush. He wasn't even sure why he was embarrassed. It wasn't like everyone didn't already know he and Nia were having sex or that the sex recharged his *Mana*. Remnants of his old life maybe?

"And I create a portal to the town," he continued. Ethan wasn't 100% certain he could, since the only runes he'd created had been in the chest he used for the portal pouch. He was familiar enough with his house that he thought he could still create a portal back there.

"The other option," he told them, gesturing down the

corridor, "is to follow the corridor to wherever it leads and, one, see if there's another way out. And two, see if we can find the source of the noise."

The group was quiet as they considered their options. Both had merits, as well as drawbacks. If they used a portal to get back to town, they could regroup and come back but then they faced the same problem when they got to this point unless Ethan somehow wedged a piece of stone from the cavern between the door and ceiling. That risked letting the spiders out of this area.

If they stayed and went forward, they no longer had an avenue of retreat. They were effectively trapped unless they found a way out. Trapped with who knew how many more spiders.

Ethan's instincts told him to press forward. Or maybe it wasn't just instincts. Something had been drawing him further in since the noise started. It was just a strange nagging in the back of his mind, but now, inside the corridor, it was more palpable. Something wanted him to continue.

"I go where you go," Nia said without a hint of fear. Ethan gave the foxgirl a smile. He appreciated the foxgirl's support.

"Par'karr follow Ethan too," the kobold said, though with slightly less determination than Nia.

"If we can't find a way out," the dwarf started, eying him. "You can still open a portal, right?"

"Theoretically." He shrugged.

"Theoretically?!" Ainslee repeated loudly. "What in Thor's hammer does that mean?

"I mean," he clarified. "I can open a portal if we charge up the crystals. But I can't do it in combat. It takes too much focus."

Ainslee bit her lip. The dwarf looked from the door to

the corridor and then back to Ethan. "Fine, I'm in... for now. But this place is really getting on my nerves."

"Mine too," Ethan agreed. He looked over at Yuliana, who had sat down against the wall. She stared down at Luna as she stroked the big cat. "You?"

"I would prefer to be back," the elf replied without looking up at him. "But I know we must find the source of the sound that is scaring away the animals. The town will not survive if we do not and the entire area is in disharmony."

"So it's agreed," he said and looked down the corridor. "We keep going."

"Like lambs to the slaughter," Ainslee muttered.

Their decision made, the group resumed their marching order. Ethan took up his position in the front with his 10-foot pole. He still wasn't sure if he had inadvertently activated some sort of switch that shut the door but this time he tried to be very aware of the different feeling and sound the pole made as it tapped the floor in front of them.

When he reached the area where they'd been when the door began closing, he searched around for any plates or anything that might have activated the door but found nothing. He asked Ainslee to look around too but the dwarf came up equally empty-handed.

"Must have been a timer," the dwarf said and then looked the walls up and down. "Or magic, I guess."

Ethan considered that possibility. There was still so much he didn't understand about how magic worked - especially enchanting. He hadn't thought it was possible to make things "anti-magic" and yet everything in this place seemed to be enchanted that way.

Could they have placed some other enchantment, along

with the anti-magic on the stones? He didn't understand how that would be possible, but that didn't mean some wizard couldn't have figured it out.

Experimentally, he reached for the crystals he knew were inside the rocks. He felt them, felt the battery crystals and the spell crystals. The magic in the spell crystal was too complicated for him to get a grasp on but he probed the 10 spell crystals and they all felt the same to him. It only felt like one enchantment.

"I guess it could be magic," he said. "But I only sense one enchantment and I'm pretty sure that's the anti-magic one."

Ainslee nodded and the others did likewise. He had come to realize that talking "magic" to non-wizards was like talking "computers" to laymen back home. You got blank stares and glassy-eyed nods.

Ethan grinned despite the situation. He'd gone from being a computer geek to being a magic geek. Overall, not a bad change considering he could now make magic items, shoot fireballs and move things with *Air*.

"Let's keep going," he said and the five of them continued down the corridor.

They traveled another two hundred or so yards down the corridor before they came to a cave-in. Part of the roof and the left side of the passage had caved in, almost completely blocking the corridor ahead. It also revealed a jagged hole in the wall that seemed to open into a natural stone cavern or passage.

Sending his balls of light into the new area, he stopped just inside the passage. The walls of the new passage were lined with spiderwebs.

"I think we just found where the spiders came from," he

told them. He saw Ainslee take an involuntary step back, eyes wide and hand tightening on her hammer.

"So the spiders are not guardians of the tomb?" Nia asked, sniffing the air. Her scimitars were out, but tilted downward.

Ethan shrugged. "I can't say for certain. But the area in this new passage is webbed, these corridors aren't. It seems like a safe bet."

"Did they dig their way in?" Yuliana asked curiously. "Like Burrow Beetles?"

"I don't know." He shrugged. Ethan had no idea what burrow beetles were and whether these creatures were tunnelers or not. Were there tunneling spiders? Where was that nature discovery channel when you needed it.

"No," Ainslee answered. She pointed to the debris blocking the corridor. "This rock collapsed. Maybe a minor quake, a flaw in the stone or maybe unstable rock above." The dwarf shook her head. "This was definitely not dug out or tunneled into. No marks."

Ethan looked again at the debris. He saw nothing but a bunch of rocks on top of each other.

"It does not matter how it happened," Nia said. "We must clear it away and this will take some time."

The foxgirl slid her weapons into their scabbards and started forward but Ethan held out a hand. "One second."

Reaching out with *Earth*, he tried to affect the rocks. It worked! This time, the magic didn't roll off but instead he knew he could manipulate them. These must have been part of the natural rock outside of the wall.

"I can use magic on these stones," he told them triumphantly. "I can clear this away in a..."

"Woah! Woah! Wizard-boy!" Ainslee cried, warding him off with a gesture. "Hold on there. Don't do anything yet."

Ethan gave her a confused look. "Why not?"

The dwarf rolled her eyes and gestured around the area with her hammer. "You want to bring this entire area down on us?"

He looked around and swallowed. "What do you mean?"

"The area collapsed because it was made unstable by something," she explained. "You start shifting things around and you might just bring more of the corridor on us."

"So we can't move the debris," he asked.

"I didn't say that." The dwarf grinned. "We just have to do it the right way and shore things up as we go."

Ethan remembered the mine and how the miners had used timbers to shore up the walls of the mine. He nodded to the dwarf, trying not to think about what he might have just done. The idea of being buried by thousands of tons of rock held no appeal whatsoever. "Tell me what to do."

24

—————

Under Ainslee's careful eye, Ethan was able to shape the debris into stone supports to hold up the ceiling. It was slow, nerve-wracking work as the debris shifted and rumbled whenever he reshaped a large piece.

Halfway through, Ethan received a welcome message in his HUD.

```
You have reached Rank 4 in Earth
Magic.
   +1 Intellect.
```

The point of *Intellect* gave him a few more points of *Mana* but he still wasn't sure what, if anything, the ranks in the various skills did. So far, the only benefit was the increased *Intellect*.

Ethan continued to reinforce the roof of the corridor by shaping the unenchanted stones. He was nearly done when

Yuliana stood up suddenly, face white. Beside her, Luna growled, sensing her master's unease.

"What is it?" he asked, glancing up and down the corridor. He also brought up his *Mana* reserves.

Mana: 15

He cursed as he saw how low it had gotten. Even though shaping stone was easy for him and didn't seem to take much *Mana*, he realized the sheer volume of the stone must be draining him faster than he thought.

"Spiders!" Yuliana squealed. She pointed to the hole in the corridor that led to the spiderwebbed area. "They are far off, but they are getting close. Quickly!"

Ethan saw Ainslee shudder but then pulled out her hammer and slapped it into her hand. "How many?"

The elf cocked her head. "Many! Very many!"

Swearing again, Ethan glanced around the corridor and into the stone passage. He didn't have enough *Mana* to fry another horde of spiders and they couldn't fight dozens of the creatures. He needed to prevent the spiders from getting to them.

He glanced at the remaining rubble. There wasn't enough to make a wall. Scratching his head, he realized he didn't need to seal them off completely. He just needed to keep them at bay. An idea came to him and he began manipulating the remaining rubble.

Using *Earth* and *Air* to shape and move the stone from the corridor to the inside of the passage. He began to form stone bars from the top of the passage to the floor, merging the stone together to form a sort of jail cell. Or was a spider zoo more appropriate?

He kept a wary eye on his *Mana* and was only halfway done when he ran out. He cursed and switched to *Stamina*. He remembered the old wizard's warning about the consequences of using *Stamina* but at the moment, the consequences of letting dozens of spiders get to him were more dire.

"How much time?" He grimaced with exertion. Handling so much *Air* and *Earth* so quickly was taxing and the lower his *Stamina* got, the more taxing it became.

The green-haired elf looked terrified. "A minute at most! They are very loud!"

Ethan nodded and realized he could hear chittering and the clicking sounds of insect legs on stone. Swearing, he struggled to get the last bars in place.

"I see them!" Nia shouted and brought up her scimitars in a fearsome-looking stance. Beside the foxgirl, Ainslee was ashen and had a death-grip on her hammer but stood strong. Ethan knew it couldn't be easy for the dwarf given her phobia.

Pushing himself even more, Ethan quickly put the last stone bars into place just as the first of the spiders threw themselves at the stone prison. There was some shaking, but the bars held.

Ethan looked at Ainslee, whose good eye had gone wide. "Will the bars hold?"

The dwarf just stared, slack jawed and white-faced at the dozens of spiders pressing against the stone bars.

"Ainslee!" he cried out and the dwarf started. She blinked and looked at him in confusion.

He sighed and lowered his voice. "Ainslee, will the bars hold?"

The dwarf blinked again but then seemed to finally

understand what he was saying and looked from Ethan to the bars. The dwarf shuddered and then swallowed, gritting her teeth as she forced herself to look at the spiders and bars.

"I'm not sure," she said finally. "That's granite, same as the doors back there. But it's only three inches, so I'm not sure. I'm just not sure."

"It's okay," Ethan told her, trying to keep his voice calm and reassuring. He turned back towards the spiders. They were sticking legs and even their mandibles through the bars as they hissed and spit at them. But the bars held - for now.

Ethan checked his *Stamina* and *Mana*.

```
Mana: 2
  Stamina: 3
```

He grimaced at the low numbers. Until he recovered, he was effectively useless. He briefly considered asking Par'karr for the shotgun back. Unfortunately, the little kobold was in the same situation until they figured out a way to stop the sound.

"We should go," Ainslee said, already starting to edge down the corridor.

Ethan bit his lip. He too wanted to continue down the corridor. Whatever was causing the sound was most likely coming from something inside the crypt.

At the same time, he was loath to leave an enemy - even a caged enemy - behind him. Tactically, the stone passage was a choke point but he doubted it would make a difference. They might fight the spiders off for a while, but they wouldn't be able to hold them off for any length of time.

There were just too many of them.

No. They needed to find the source of the sound and hope there was an alternate way out of the place. It was really their only hope.

"Ainslee's right," he told the others. "We should go."

"But - " Nia started but he held up a hand. Ethan moved really close to her, his lips brushing her fox-like ear and causing her to shiver. When he spoke, it was the softest whisper he could manage and still hope to be heard. He only hoped Yuliana wouldn't hear. "You and I both know we can't hold them back no matter where we are. Let's try to find a way out and seal these things in here forever."

Nia looked up into his eyes and nodded grimly. He saw in her eyes that she knew the truth too. She didn't think their small group was going to hold off dozens of spiders.

He remembered the 300 Spartans who held off the Persian army for days at a narrow pass. It was a similar situation, though he'd gladly take 295 more people to help him. Then he frowned as he remembered the end of that story. Didn't all the Spartans die at the end?

"You are right." She nodded. "We should leave and find another way out!"

That was all the encouragement the others needed and they were quickly lined up in their marching order. Once again, Ethan led the way with his ten-foot pole in one hand and his light stone in the other hand.

Ethan might be able to maintain balls of light but if he did, he wouldn't regenerate any *Mana* at all. So instead, he used the light stone he'd enchanted earlier. He tapped across the corridor as the group moved down the corridor - this time with slightly more haste. It didn't last long.

He hadn't gone more than ten feet when the smooth

stone floor abruptly became tiled. Looking to the right and left walls, he saw that the walls were also tiled, though in a more elegant pattern than the floor. Ethan stopped cold.

"Ainslee," he hissed, motioning the dwarf to come and stand next to him. With a glance over her shoulder at the caged spiders, she quickly walked up next to him.

"What is it?" she asked and then noticed the tiles. "Oh."

She bent down and looked at the tile, taking her enchanted, light-giving rock in her hand to look over the tiled floor. After a minute, she stood up and looked at the left wall and then the right wall.

"I'm guessin' this is a trap," she told him.

Ethan sighed. Of course it was a trap. "What kind of trap?"

The dwarf pointed to the left side of the corridor walls. "Hold up your light stone and look at those little swirly patterns."

Holding up his light, Ethan squinted at the patterns until he saw what she meant. Each tile had a swirly, whirlwind type pattern carved into. In the middle of every other swirl was a hole. He nodded. "Darts?"

"Or more spikes," the dwarf replied with a frown. She held her light up high and looked down the corridor. The tiles went on for as far as they could see. "I don't suppose you got enough magic to get us all over this area?"

Ethan's frown deepened and he shook his head. "I got nothing."

"I figured," the dwarf said. "That was a lot of stone you moved with your magic."

As he looked across the tiled floor, he saw something lying on the floor. He held up the light to get a better look at it. Squinting, he finally recognized it. It was a stone dart. Near it, he saw another and then another.

He'd been right. Darts would fly out of the holes, probably when someone depressed one of the tiles. The tiles were probably the triggers and would pepper them with darts.

Ethan looked at the tiles again. These tiles were only about six inches each. Unlike the spike room, he didn't think there was a safe path across this one. But if that were the case, how would someone make it across - assuming they didn't have magic?

"What?" the dwarf asked.

"It is darts," he said, pointing out the spikes lying on the floor. "And I don't think we're the first ones down this corridor."

"The spiders," Nia said, coming up on his left side. He and the dwarf both jumped.

"Spiders?" Ainslee muttered. "Are they breaking through?!"

"No." Nia grinned. "The spiders have been down this corridor. I can smell them."

Ethan turned to Nia. "Are you sure?"

Nia nodded and sniffed. "They were here within the last few days."

"So how did they get through?" Ethan asked, mostly to himself.

The dwarf snorted. "Maybe they didn't."

"What do you mean?" he asked.

"Maybe they set off the darts," she suggested.

"What?" he asked, wrinkling his forehead.

"Press down on one of them and see what it does," Ainslee suggested.

"We don't know what it might do," he countered.

"Just do it," she repeated.

Ethan shrugged and backed up as far as he could and motioned the others to do the same. Once everyone was clear, he tapped one of the tiles with the 10-foot pole. Immediately there was a click and then a whoosh of air. But nothing else.

Ethan wrinkled his brow again. "Where are the spikes?"

"Used up," the dwarf smirked. "The spiders must have run across the tiled floor enough times that they used up all of the darts."

"Then where are the spider bodies?" asked Nia.

Lines appeared on the dwarf's forehead as she considered the question. Ainslee looked around the tiled corridor, holding her light stone to illuminate the various parts.

Ethan already knew the answer. He thought back to the way the spiders had thrown themselves into the spiked room and then again into the flames. "There are no bodies."

"No bodies?" Nia asked with a frown.

"The spiders took the bodies." He shuddered. "As food."

The entire group exchanged uneasy looks before, as a group, looking back to the strange arachnids still trying to get through the stone bars.

25

The spiders continued to gnaw and push at the bars while the group discussed their options. Their constant clicking, chittering and hissing made it difficult to focus on the conversation.

Ainslee thought all the darts had been used up but Ethan thought they should play it safe. Even a single dart to the wrong area could kill one of them. The dwarf didn't seem very concerned but eventually Ethan was able to present his case in a way she understood.

"Have it your way, wizard-boy," Ainslee said, rolling her eyes. "We'll pretend there might be darts left."

That decided, next they talked about strategies to avoid or defeat the darts. As they weighed the options, Ethan checked his *Mana* and *Stamina*.

```
Mana: 6
  Stamina: 4
```

The time they'd spent talking had given him a few points

back, but he was still low. Too low. With so little *Stamina* and *Mana*, he was useless.

"What do you think, wizard-boy?" he heard Ainslee's voice say, drawing him back into the conversation. Everyone was looking at him expectantly.

"I'm sorry, " he apologized, realizing he'd lost track of the conversation while looking at his HUD. "What?"

"Do you have enough mana to make shields or do you need fox-girl over there to get down on all fours?" the dwarf huffed.

Ethan felt his face grow warm at the dwarf's crude words and looked over to see that Nia was both embarrassed and upset. The foxgirl narrowed her eyes at Ainslee, who seemed to realize she might have gone too far.

"Get over it, you two." The dwarf shrugged. "If you think I'm staying here until those spiders manage to break through those bars and take me away for a snack, you've got another thing comin to ya!"

Ethan was still blushing but he understood the dwarf's desperation. She looked at him with her hands on her hips, good eye daring him to object. "So can you make two shields out of stone or not?"

He frowned, remembering how low his *Stamina* was. Ethan wasn't sure exactly how much he used during their lovemaking, but he did know it was more than the 3 points he had. It wouldn't help him if he collapsed into unconsciousness in the middle of it.

"I don't think I can..." he started.

"We won't look," the dwarf told him, then she gave him a wink with her good eye. "Much."

Clearing his throat, he shook his head. "No, I mean, I had

to burn some stamina earlier when I ran out of mana. I don't think I have enough to um...uh... "

"Get the job done," the dwarf snickered. "Drink some water."

Ethan shook his head. "I used up all stamina restoration earlier when we were charging the crystals. I can't restore any more stamina from drinking water until we sleep."

Ainslee rolled her good eye at Ethan and Nia. "Well, just sit there and let her do all the work, but let's get to it! Come on!"

The dwarf made a "get on with it" gesture with her hand and stared at the two of them in anticipation. That's when Ethan saw that Yuliana was red faced as well, though he did notice that the elf hadn't turned away.

Par'karr was looking between Nia and Ethan with wide-eyed fascination and interest. The kobold looked as if he was about to watch a movie. He was just missing the popcorn.

"That might work." Ethan cleared his throat again and glanced at Nia for confirmation. The foxgirl nodded. He used his head to gesture meaningfully towards the stone door back down the corridor. Nia shrugged and nodded.

"Fine," he told them. "We'll go back towards the spike room."

"Just get a move on it," Ainslee retorted. "And make it a quickie."

Ethan started walking back towards the stone door to the spiked room. It was as far away as they could get from the others, given their current predicament. He'd never been particularly shy about sex - not that he'd gotten an over-abundance of it. But the dwarf's crude manner and in-your-face speech was somehow embarrassing.

After a few steps, Nia fell in next to him. She looked over

to him. "I do not mind mating in front of the others. It is done all the time back on my world. I have seen hundreds of couplings. They are interesting to learn from."

"Hundreds?" Ethan sputtered. He tried to process her words. She'd literally seen hundreds of couples having sex? He wasn't sure how to handle the piece of information. On the plus side, she hadn't complained about him, so hopefully that meant he was doing something right. "I.. uh... prefer a little privacy."

"That is fine." She shrugged. She gave him a wicked smile. "And do not worry about your stamina. I will do all the work."

Ethan nodded and soon found that the foxgirl lived up to her promise.

TEN MINUTES LATER, they walked back to the group. Nia had done all the work and he had restored half of his *Mana*, not all of it like previous times. He'd also used almost all of his *Stamina*, even just sitting there.

Ethan wasn't sure if that was because he hadn't been a very active participant or if there was some sort of formula that restored a certain ratio of *Mana* for the amount of *Stamina* used. Or perhaps it was something completely different. Whatever the reason, when he looked at his stats, he wasn't completely happy.

```
Mana: 29
   Stamina: 1
```

Nia seemed to misread his scowl. She gave him a hurt look. "You were not... pleased?"

Ethan glanced over to her and took her hand, giving it a gentle squeeze. He flashed her his best smile. "I am always pleased. But for some reason, it didn't restore all of my mana."

"Why not?" The foxgirl's look changed to one of concern.

"I don't know," he said. "It could be anything. It might even be this place."

"Do you have enough mana to do the dwarf's plan?" she asked.

He nodded. "More than enough. Creating stone shields shouldn't be that difficult."

"Good." She smiled but then gave him a mischievous grin and a wink. "But I must confess. I do not prefer the, what did the dwarf call it, the quickie."

Ethan chuckled. "I guess if that's all we have time for, I'll take it. But I agree. I enjoy our longer...ah... mating."

They walked the rest of the way back to the group and were met with interested looks. Ainslee had her arms crossed over her chest and was tapping her foot. "I said a quickie! You know... like a couple of minutes! We could be spider food by now!"

"We mated as quickly as we could," Nia said matter-of-factly. "And if truth be told, I prefer it when he..."

"Okay, okay." Ainslee held up her hands to stop the foxgirl. "I don't need a blow by blow description of what you two do. Let's just get on with it."

Nodding Ethan walked over to some of the remaining debris and shaped the stone into large, tall shields. He modeled them after the old Greek and Roman shields they used to form a phalanx. In tabletop roleplaying game terms, they were tower shields.

Instead of the two the dwarf asked him to create, he created four. Ainslee seemed to think the darts were only coming from the side walls. If that were the case, then one shield on either side would be enough. But if any of the darts were angled, they might slip through the side shields. They needed to be protected on all sides. Better to err on the side of too much shielding than too little.

"You sure we need four?" the dwarf asked him as she stared down at the newly formed shields.

He lifted one of the large, rectangular shields up. Ethan groaned at how heavy it was. He had gained back an additional point of *Stamina* but watched it flash away in his HUD. He cursed.

"What?" Ainslee demanded.

"It's heavy," he told her. "And I don't have enough stamina to hold it."

"Don't worry, you just sit back and relax and us women will do all the work." The dwarf smirked. She shot a glance at Nia. "You should be used to that."

"And Par'karr!" the little kobold chimed in happily.

Ethan sighed but had no defense. His *Stamina* was too low for him to help. If he tried, he'd likely pass out. If that happened, they'd either have to wait for him to come to or carry him and the shields. "Fine."

His four companions each grabbed one of the shields. Nia and Ainslee lifted theirs easily but Yuliana and Par'karr struggled with the large shields.

The group formed up with Ethan and Luna in the middle. To his right was Nia and to his left was Ainslee. Yuliana went in front of him, while Par'karr brought up the rear. Each lined up their shields with the others, creating a cube of stone around them.

"Alright." Ethan let out a breath. "Let's go!"

Slowly, the group began making their way across the tiled floor. With each step, there were clicks and hisses, yet no impacts. It appeared that the darts had been used up.

Then, once they reached fifteen feet onto the tiled floor, a single crack sounded against the left shield. Everyone stopped.

"Huh!" snorted Ainslee. "One dart!"

They took a few more steps and several more cracks sounded against the left and right. A few more steps and even more cracks. Within another twenty feet, multiple cracks were hitting all shields with each step.

"Loki's Balls! I guess they weren't out after all!" shouted the dwarf, glancing up at him.

No one responded as the group kept up their pace. Slowly but steadily they made their way through the tiled passage until they finally reached a stretch of smooth stone floor. One by one, his companions let their shield fall to the ground and looked around.

What they saw was completely unexpected.

26

———

"Is that... a dragon?" Yuliana gasped.

Ethan stared at the ornately carved stone door in front of them. This door was massive, taking up the entire corridor from floor to ceiling. The outside edges of the door were inscribed with the same sort of strange runes he'd seen before. But the runes weren't what held their attention.

In the center of the massive door were raised carvings of men in plate mail armor and tabards. There were twelve of them and they were arranged in a circle around a central raised carving of a circle. A carving of a circle with a dragon in it, one with large Chymera crystals as eyes.

The dragon was coiled in an "S" shape within the circle and in one clawed hand it held a sword and in the other it held a cup of some sort. Looking closer, Ethan saw that there were many horns protruding from the dragon's head.

Squinting, Ethan realized it wasn't horns. It was a crown. Was this some sort of dragon king that men worshipped?

"It looks like a dragon to me," Ainslee replied, breaking

the silence. "Though this one's got a sword and a cup - probably with some good ole mead!"

Something about the picture nagged at Ethan's brain. Dragon. Knights. A sword and a cup. A round circle. Something about it was very familiar.

Ethan's eyes went wide. Not a round circle. A round table! He swore, causing his companions to look at him. He ignored them as his mind tried to wrap around what he had just thought of. Could this be Arthur Pendragon, or as most people knew him... King Arthur?!

The dragon wore a crown. Arthur Pendragon was a king. The dragon held a sword. Could that be Excalibur? And the cup. Was it a chalice? Could it be... the Holy Grail?

"No way," he breathed.

"What? What is it?" came the questioning voices of his companions.

Ethan shook his head. How could this be? How could there be a tomb for King Arthur, a fictional Earth character, on an alien world? It made no sense.

Then again, he remembered, he had a journal belonging to Merlin - another Earth legend. And Michalus had claimed to have known a Merlin a long time ago. Could it be the Merlin from legends?

He shook his head again. No way. It was too fantastical! Or was it? Was it possible King Arthur and his knights had been abducted too, hundreds of years ago? If that were the case, how long had these aliens been abducting people from Earth?

"WIZARD... BOY?!" Ainslee's loud voice broke into his thoughts and he started. He looked over at his companions who were looking at him with concern. All except for

Ainslee who looked more annoyed than anything. "What is going on?!"

Ethan looked at them blankly before shaking his head. The possibility that this carving depicted an ancient Earth legend like King Arthur had really shaken him. It was just too strange to wrap his head around. Not to mention it raised a ton of questions.

Focusing on his group he started to speak but got tongue-tied. He took a deep breath and let it out. "I think this stone carving depicts legends from my world. From hundreds of years ago. Maybe a thousand years ago now."

Ethan gestured to the dragon and the crown. "King Arthur Pendragon. Notice the crown.

"He had twelve knights. Well, actually there were more than twelve, but there were twelve main knights," Ethan continued, pointing out the twelve different knights.

Outlining the circle with his finger, he continued. "And they met at a round table."

He could see some confusion and skepticism among his companions so he continued. He pointed at the sword. "In the legend, Arthur Pendragon had a magical sword named Excalibur.

"And," he continued, pointing out the cup. "He had a magical chalice, or cup, called the Holy Grail. Drinking from it could cure any wound. Some said it granted eternal life."

"And you believe this carving is of this King Arthur?" Nia asked, head cocked.

"It just seems too coincidental not to be," he replied, still excited. After all, people had been trying for decades, maybe even hundreds of years, to prove the existence of King Arthur and the quest for the holy grail was the stuff of legends, books and movies.

"You really think some old king from your world is buried behind these doors?" Ainslee asked. The good side of her face showed nothing but skepticism.

"I don't know," Ethan admitted. "I mean, supposedly King Arthur lived over 1,000 years ago. But no trace of him has ever been found." He gave them a grin. "What if he was abducted like us?"

The dwarf shrugged and looked unconvinced. She scratched her head and then looked back at Ethan. "So you think this dead king guy is making the noise?"

Ethan shrugged. "Something in the tomb must be."

"You know that sounds crazy," the dwarf said. "I mean, what are the odds."

Ethan had already thought of that. "I've seen plants and animals from my world and Yuliana's people have been here for generations - which is thousands of years. These abductions have to have been going on for some time."

Ainslee rubbed her chin. "Suppose this is King Dragon. What does that mean?"

"I don't know," Ethan admitted. And he didn't. He had no idea what any of it meant. If this really was the resting place of King Arthur, what did it mean? Did it mean the aliens had been abducting people for a thousand years? Longer?

There were so many mysteries on Earth that people attributed to aliens. Stonehenge. The Pyramids. The Nazca Lines. Maybe even Easter Island. Could aliens somehow be responsible for all of that - as well as abducting people.

Ethan looked around at his companions. "I don't know what it means, but hopefully answers lie beyond this door."

"That much," Ainslee snorted, "we can agree on. And hopefully a way out too! But I'm not sure how we're going to get through this door. It's like the other door. It'll go down into the floor - if we activate it."

Ethan eyed the door and nodded. It was much larger than the door in the spike room and had to weigh a few tons. Even full of *Mana*, he couldn't hope to lift it. And that was IF it didn't have that anti-magic enchantment.

Experimentally, Ethan reached out with a bit of *Air* and felt it dissolve away as it touched the door. He swore. "It's anti-magic."

The group searched the area for some sort of panels or tiles that might open the door. They searched from the trapped tile area to the door but found nothing that remotely resembled a triggering or locking mechanism. The floor, ceiling and walls were nothing but smooth stone.

A search of the door itself also revealed nothing. None of the ornate carvings moved, slid or depressed.

"If there's a way to open this door," Ainslee said finally. "I don't know what it is. There ain't even any seams in the stone. The door is literally one big piece of granite."

Ethan nodded and looked over the door. The dwarf was right. It was all one piece of granite, except for the two Chymera crystals that made up the eyes. But they'd tried to press, turn and pull the eyes to no effect.

Ethan had probed the eyes with magic to see if there were any spells in them but there were none. They weren't spell crystals. If anything, they were battery crystals only they were empty. Whatever enchantment they had powered was gone.

He tilted his head and looked at the eyes, an idea coming to him. Normally, the battery crystals powered the spell crystals and that created the enchantment. Once the magical "circuit" was created, it somehow recharged itself - sometimes quickly, sometimes slowly depending on the spell and the size and number of batteries.

At least, that's what Michalus had taught him. It was how he'd created all of the magical items he'd made. But what if there were other ways of creating magical items. Ways maybe even Michalus didn't know about.

He probed the crystal eyes again. There wasn't even a trace of magic in them. What if it wasn't a recharging circuit like normal magic items. What if you had to charge up the eyes to activate some magic - like magic that would lift the door. It would ensure that only wizards could get past the door.

Experimentally, he channeled some *Mana* into one of the crystal eyes. It accepted it but then it drained out almost as soon as he stopped. He frowned. Regular crystals didn't drain that quickly.

Ethan tried channeling *Mana* into both eyes and found it much more difficult than he would have expected. He pushed a point of *Mana* into each of them and then stopped. He probed the eyes and this time the magic stayed, but only for a minute before draining away.

He groaned. That was definitely not normal behavior for crystals. It took days for a crystal to drain away if it wasn't used. This was draining almost instantly.

"Are you okay?" Nia asked as she walked over to him. The others stopped and looked at him as well.

"I'm fine," he replied with a forced smile. "I might know how this thing opens."

"You figured it out, wizard-boy?" Ainslee asked, coming to stand next to him.

"Maybe," he replied, still smiling. "I think... I think these crystals power a spell that will lift the door. I think whoever created this door, made it so that only a wizard could open it."

"Par'karr thought you said magic not work," the kobold said.

Ethan nodded. "You're right. The door itself is anti-magic. But those crystals are different. I can actually load mana into them."

"Then do it, wizard-boy," Ainslee demanded, looking over her shoulder. Even several hundred feet away, they could hear the pounding of the spiders against the stone bars echoing down the corridor.

Checking his *Mana*, Ethan saw that it had regenerated during their trek through the tiled area and the time they'd spent searching.

Mana: 47

He'd gained *Mana* back, but he wasn't at full. Would it be enough to charge up both eyes? He stared at the carved drag-on's head and the two Chymera crystal eyes. There was only one way to find out.

27

After explaining what he was about to do, Ethan plunged right in and began charging up the dragon's eyes. He did it the same way he charged up his battery crystals, only splitting the *Mana* across the two eyes.

Normally, when feeding *Mana* into a crystal, Ethan had some sense of how full the crystal was. But doing both crystal eyes at once, it was impossible for him to get a sense. That worried him a bit.

He knew from experience that overcharging a crystal caused it to explode. If Ethan overcharged these crystals, not only would they explode but doing so would end any chance they had of getting through the door. They would be trapped.

If that happened, the only thing he could do was try to open up a portal. He'd done it before, in the library of Patheos, but it had required charging several crystals and even then, he'd barely managed it.

Of course, he had gained a level since that time, as well

as some additional *Mana*. Perhaps it wouldn't be so difficult the next time. He'd have to wait and see if he could get this door open or if they'd have to resort to the portal.

Ethan checked his *Mana* in his HUD.

Mana: 23

He tried getting a feel of the *Mana* in the eyes, but it was too difficult to focus on the amounts at the same time he was splitting his *Mana* between the two eyes. Had whoever created the door intended it to be so difficult?

As he thought about the creator of the tomb, Ethan realized it had to be Merlin. It all fit. Somehow, Merlin, King Arthur and the Knights of the Round Table were all real. Not only had they been real, but they'd been abducted to this planet too.

It was difficult to wrap his brain around. Just a couple of months ago, he hadn't even been sure there was really intelligent life in the universe. Sure, he'd hoped there were some sort of benevolent aliens out there, but he'd never seen any convincing proof.

He snickered to himself. Convincing proof. He had proof now. But of course, if he somehow found a way back to Earth, who would believe him? He wasn't even sure he could convince his friends.

Suddenly all the UFO abduction stories he'd read came back to him. Is that what he would be if he got home and told people about his experience? Just another crackpot with an unbelievable story?

His train of thought almost caused him to falter in channeling *Mana* into the eyes. He quickly pushed the other thoughts out of his mind and focused on the crystals.

Ethan checked his *Mana* again.

Mana: 11

Frowning at his level of *Mana*, Ethan silently prayed it would be enough. If not, he'd have to recharge. That meant sex with Nia. He enjoyed their lovemaking sessions. Enjoyed her more than any other woman he'd been with. That wasn't the problem. The problem was privacy.

There was no privacy. There was nothing but an empty corridor between them and the trapped tiles. That meant there was no hiding their lovemaking from everyone else.

It wasn't that he was particularly prudish. He just wasn't an exhibitionist. He'd only ever had sex with women in the privacy of a bedroom - and occasionally some other rooms of the house. He'd never done it in front of other people. Ethan wasn't even sure he could.

Ethan let out a breath. Why was nothing ever easy! It was like he was in a novel, a movie or a video game with one challenge after another being thrown at him.

He paused. Could that be why everything seemed so hard? Why did they keep running into all of these challenges? Could the aliens be watching them... observing their reactions... testing them? Were they pulling the strings and he was just dancing to their tune like a puppet?

It was a disconcerting thought but as he thought back to their adventures, he didn't feel like he was being manipulated. They'd made their own choices. Or had they? A rat in a maze might think it's making its own choices, turning left or right. But at the end of the day, it didn't have a choice not to be in the maze.

Were they all just rats in some sort of alien maze? If so,

why hadn't the aliens shown themselves or made any attempts to communicate? Were he and his companions too "primitive" to communicate with?

With a start, Ethan caught his *Mana* dropping out of the corner of his eye and immediately stopped the flow.

Mana: 1

He breathed out a sigh of relief. One more point and he would have passed out.

Ethan looked at the door. The eyes were glowing blue but nothing else was happening. He quickly focused on one of the eyes. Probing it for the level of *Mana* in the crystal, he swore loudly.

"I didn't even fill it halfway!" he growled.

"Get busy with the fox-girl and fill up your mana and try again!" the dwarf insisted. "In case you weren't paying attention, there have been some loud cracking noises from the spider prison you created."

Standing up, Ethan whirled to face the corridor. He hadn't heard the cracking but even as he listened, a loud crack reverberated down the corridor from the area where they'd left the spiders. It sounded like the spiders were breaking through.

Ethan swore again and turned back to face his companions. "I can't!"

The dwarf rolled her eyes. "We'll turn our backs. I mean... it's not like everyone here hasn't seen you naked before."

Ethan felt the heat in his cheeks as he remembered the incident in the inn. It was when he'd first discovered portal magic. It wasn't one of his fondest memories of this place.

He'd been taking a bath when a drunk Ainslee had

passed out at the door and he'd helped drag the unconscious dwarf inside. Wearing nothing but his towel. Somehow, his towel had slipped and he'd unconsciously teleported from the room, back into the tub - completely naked.

The power he'd used to teleport had left him unconscious and almost dead. He'd been unconscious for days and during that time, everyone had gotten a look at his naked body. Not exactly his finest hour.

"Just do it before those spiders come scurrying down the hall," Ainslee demanded, casting a wary look down the corridor.

Ethan forced himself to push the embarrassing memory away and focused on what he needed to tell them. "I can't. I don't have enough mana."

"I know!" the dwarf retorted, hands on hips. "I just said... climb on top of the fox-girl and..."

"No!" Ethan growled in frustration. "You don't understand. I only filled it about halfway. Even if I had all of my mana, I couldn't fill both of those eyes. It's impossible."

"Ethan," Nia said softly, coming over to put a hand on his shoulder. "What about using crystals like you did in the library to open the portal?"

"It won't work." He shook his head. "It takes too much focus to pull mana from a crystal. Maybe I could do it with one eye... maybe. But there's no way I can focus on drawing mana from one crystal and putting it into two others at the same time."

"Can you do one at a time?" Yuliana asked. The elf had been quiet for so long, it was easy to forget she was there.

"Unfortunately," he replied with a smile. She spoke up so infrequently, that he didn't want to discourage her. "I think they have to be filled at the same time."

The elf nodded and then went back to stroking Luna. If she was worried about the spiders breaking down the stone bars and rushing down the hall at them, she hid it well.

"So what are you saying?" Ainslee glared at him. "That we're stuck?!"

Ethan let out a breath. "I can't fill them both. I don't have the mana. Either it's meant for a much more powerful wizard than me or two wizards working in concert have to fill it."

He remembered movies where, for security purposes, soldiers or spies had to have two people with keys turn them at the same time to open a vault or secret door. Was that what this was? Some sort of security measure to guarantee that there had to be two wizards?

"Well, we ain't got no other wizards with us!" the dwarf said. The dwarf's eyes were large and bloodshot and her face was pale and sweaty. If Ethan didn't know better, he would think Ainslee was on the verge of hysterics.

"Am I able to fill it with my healing magic?" Yuliana asked, causing everyone to look over at her.

Ethan opened his mouth but then closed it. He was about to tell the elf that it wouldn't work, that only *Mana* would work. But another idea had come to him.

Bringing up his HUD, he paged through his abilities until he found what he was looking for.

```
Mana Siphon
    Type: Wizard
    Cost: Special
    Range: 10 ft
    Duration: Special
    Description: Wizard can pull Mana
```

**from objects or people to channel into
a Chymera crystal.**

It was an ability he'd gained back in the library of Patheos when he'd been unable to regenerate *Mana* normally. The ability allowed him to pull *Mana* from people to charge a Chymera crystal. He grinned.

If he restored his *Mana* to full and then pulled *Mana* from his companions and used it to charge the eyes, he might just have enough. But that was only if it were easier to use other people's *Mana* than it was to pull *Mana* from a crystal.

"I have an idea!" he said, trying not to sound too excited.

"About time!" the dwarf grunted. "I thought I was going to have to think of everything!"

28

Ethan had to explain his idea several times as it seemed difficult to the group to accept that they had *Mana* and that he could siphon it from them. He had each of them check their character sheet in their HUDs. At least, he had each of them except Par'karr. The little kobold had no character sheet.

It was one of those things which nagged at Ethan. When he'd asked Michalus about having a HUD, the old wizard had admitted he didn't have anything like that. In fact, he'd given the impression that no one on this world did. The exception being what Michalus called offworlders. Abductees, like Ethan and his companions.

Why did he and his companions have HUDs and seemingly game-style logic and rules applied to them but others didn't? Shuddering at the memory, he recalled a dream he had about aliens and some sort of surgery.

As scary as the thought was, Ethan guessed that everyone who had been abducted had something surgically implanted in them. Maybe some sort of computer chip, or the alien equivalent, that gave them the HUD.

Maybe to the aliens, it was like the trackers conservationists put on animals to track their movements. Was that what the aliens were doing? Tracking him? Watching him? It was a chilling thought and he involuntarily looked around.

Par'karr was a native to this world. The same as Michalus. They'd been born here and neither had a HUD. To Ethan, that backed up his idea that his group, the abductees, had been somehow surgically altered.

Whatever the case was, Par'karr was the only one who couldn't tell him his exact <u>Mana</u> score. The others gave him the information one by one.

```
Nia
   Mana: 26
   Ainslee Arnbuckle
   Mana: 32
   Yuliana Madeiras
   Mana: 30
```

"So what does all that mean?" Ainslee asked, scratching her head. "How come we got mana but can't cast spells?"

"If it's like the Earth... uh... simulations," Ethan replied. He had barely caught himself before he said 'Earth games' instead of simulations. He still wasn't sure how he'd explain MMORPGs to them, let alone whether they'd trust his advice if they knew it came from games.

"In Earth simulations," he explained. "Your class determines how you can use different stats. For instance, I have karma but I think that is like mana but for some other class.

Or maybe some special ability. But we each have different levels of the stats based on our classes."

The others nodded but their glassy-eye stares told him they had no idea what he was talking about or simply didn't care.

"Anyway." He cleared his throat. "You each have mana, which means I should be able to draw on it to charge the crystals."

"And how exactly are you going to draw on it?" Ainslee asked as she gave him a skeptical look with her good eye.

Ethan paused. That was a good question. He actually had no idea how he was supposed to draw on *Mana*. He shrugged and then smiled. "I have no idea. Guess I'll have to do a little experimenting!"

A loud crack, followed by another crack echoed down the corridor. Ainslee flinched and even Ethan was growing worried. He wasn't sure how long those bars could continue holding the spiders back. They needed to get this door open now!

"You should experiment quickly," Yuliana noted, turning from the corridor to look at him.

"Ya think?!" the dwarf added, once again verging on hysteria.

"Fine," he said. "Let's do this quickly!"

Ethan took the women through some experiments. First he tried to sense the *Mana* in them and found that if he focused hard enough, he could. It seemed like their pool of *Mana* was located near the front of their heads. Was that the prefrontal cortex?

Ethan didn't have the chance to mull over where the *Mana* seemed to reside. If those spiders broke loose, he wasn't sure how long the darts would hold them off. He needed to figure out how this worked quickly.

Once Ethan had found the center of their *Mana*, he tried to draw it from Nia it like he would a Chymera crystal. Unfortunately, that didn't work. He saw Nia crease her forehead. She hugged her arms around herself and shuddered. "That was a very strange and disturbing feeling. Like something was pulling at my very soul."

"Sorry." Ethan gave her an apologetic look. "Maybe if you think about letting me draw on your mana?"

"I will try," she said. "But it is... uncomfortable."

He gave her a reassuring smile. "Don't worry, I won't make a habit out of it."

She allowed him to try again and this time he was able to draw a little out. It was tough. Much tougher than pulling *Mana* from a crystal. It was as if *Mana* in a crystal was neutral and didn't care where it went, but *Mana* in a person wanted to stay with that person. Was it some sort of defense mechanism?

Nia shivered again. "I think I felt it. I felt... something... leaving me."

"Yeah, that was me," he told her. He realized he was breathing a little heavy from the exertion of trying to pull the *Mana* out. "But I can't concentrate on pulling mana from you and feed it into two crystals at once. It's too much."

"Thor's hammer!" Ainslee exclaimed. "You mean we're trapped?!"

Ethan frowned. "I'm sorry. Pulling mana from a person is harder than pulling it from a crystal. I thought it might be easier, but it's not. It's like the mana doesn't want to..."

He trailed off as an idea came to him. "Nia, can you come here and put your hand on me."

Nia walked over obediently and put her hand on his shoulder.

Shaking his head, he picked up her hand and moved it to his face so they were in direct skin to skin contact. "When I first learned how to channel mana through a crystal, I had to hold the crystal. I want you to think about channeling your mana to me, from your head, through your arm and to me."

The foxgirl wrinkled her forehead, giving him a skeptical look. She started to take her hand away but he caught it in his. "I do not channel mana..."

"It doesn't matter," he told her, giving her hand a squeeze. "Just try."

She gave him a slight smile and a nod and placed her hand back on his face. Then she closed her eyes.

Ethan reached out and felt for her *Mana* and tried drawing it in and feeding it to the crystal eyes. And it worked. Her *Mana* flowed to him easily though he saw her shudder as he drew it in. What he guessed was a point of *Mana* flowed into the two crystal eyes.

He stopped and the foxgirl opened up her eyes. His own face split into a grin. "It worked! I was able to draw it out easily! I think I can use it to channel it into the eyes."

Nia shuddered again. "It still feels very odd."

"Thank Odin!" Ainslee said, still watching the tiled corridor. "Let's get this door open."

Ethan quickly tried the same process with the others, making sure he could pull the *Mana* with no problem. Both Ainslee and Yuliana had issues initially but eventually mastered the idea. Par'karr had no problem and was able to feed him *Mana* on the first try.

"Good job, Par'karr," he told the little kobold.

Par'karr gave him a toothy grin in return. "It like when Par'karr summon rabbits."

Nodding, Ethan guessed that whatever ability allowed him to be a summoner, it operated on *Mana* as well.

"Are we ready then?" Ainslee asked.

Ethan checked his *Mana* and felt his face growing warm again. He'd been trying not to think about it, but there was no way to get around it. He needed to recharge his *Mana*. And there was only one way to do that.

"I... uh..." Ethan stuttered and Ainslee chuckled.

"Oh." She smirked, making a gesture with her hands and her hips whose meaning was unmistakable. "That's right. You two need to get busy! Well... go ahead."

Nia gave the dwarf a defiant look and grabbed Ethan by the hand. She pulled him to the far side where she had laid out her bedroll. She started to unbuckle her breeches.

"Wait... what about..." Ethan started, gesturing to the others. They were all watching. Ainslee looked vaguely interested, though he suspected she was more interested in seeing him being embarrassed.

Par'karr had sat down and was staring with wide eyes, unblinking eyes. There was a strange look of interest and fascination on his reptilian face.

The surprising one was Yuliana. The elf hadn't made any move to put her Necklace of Silence on. Instead, she just stood there with her head cocked to the side, watching them with a slight smile on her face.

That was too much for Ethan. He dropped his pack, pulled out one of his blankets and put it around his shoulders. After getting himself ready and lowering Nia down onto her bedroll, he threw the blanket over them so they couldn't be seen - and more importantly, he couldn't see anyone else.

The sound of cracks from the corridor and the soft muttering of his companions beyond the blanket pushed them to finish up as quickly as possible. Whether it was knowing that they were being watched or knowing that there was danger only a couple hundred feet away, their lovemaking was quick and intense.

When it was finally over, they were both gasping. From outside the blanket, they heard someone clapping.

"Not bad, not bad," came Ainslee's voice. "Though the blanket ruined my view of wizard-boy's bottom!"

Ethan hurriedly pulled up his breeches and Nia did like-wise before they threw off the blanket. He knew his face was red but he didn't care. His *Mana* was full and it was time to open this door and get away from these spiders.

29

Ignoring the stares of his companions, Ethan walked over to the door and sat down in front of the two dragon eyes. His face was still warm and he knew he'd only feel more embarrassed if he looked at anyone. So he didn't.

Ethan got into a comfortable sitting position. Once he was sitting he checked his *Mana* before beginning to explain exactly what he was going to do and what he expected of the others.

Mana: 68

"I'm going to channel our mana into the eyes," he started, keeping his eyes on the two large Chymera crystals. "I'm going to start off channeling your mana first..."

He was interrupted by the loudest crack so far, followed by a crashing sound. As one, the group turned to the corridor. The far end bathed in darkness. They couldn't see the spiders coming through, but the chittering and the sound of legs on stone told them all they needed to know. The spiders had broken through.

As if to confirm what they all knew, Luna growled and Yuliana's eyes went wide. "They are coming!"

"WHAT?!" screamed Ainslee, her good eye wide and her voice shrill.

Ethan swore loudly and spun around to face the door. "We need to do this now!"

"Do what?!" the dwarf squeaked, her face completely white.

"We...need... to... open... this... door," Ethan enunciated. His heart thudding in his chest and he felt the sting of adrenaline or fear. "We need to get this door open before they get to us!"

The sound of darts and the squealing of dying spiders filled his ears and Ethan cursed under his breath. They needed to get this started.

"Ainslee!" he ordered in his firmest voice. "Get over here and put your hand on my head."

The dwarf didn't move and he could see she was frozen in fear, her eyes huge and her face drenched in sweat.

"AINSLEE!" he shouted as loud as he could and the dwarf turned. Her movements were mechanical, as if her conscious mind had shut down and she was on automatic pilot. "COME HERE!"

The dwarf moved slowly and stopped in front of him. Her face was a mask of horror, despite that they still couldn't see any spiders. The sound of darts being launched and the screeching of spiders was getting closer.

"PUT YOUR HAND ON MY HEAD!" he shouted. She didn't move. "DO IT! DO IT NOW!"

Ainslee slowly put her hand on his face and he immediately began channeling. He pulled the *Mana* from her as fast as he could. He pushed it into the two eyes, trying to mentally keep track of how much he was pulling but it was impossible.

He had originally planned to have them pull up their HUDs and read off their *Mana* score as he used it up. Unfortunately, Ainslee was in no shape to do anything at the moment. She was literally scared stiff.

It was also more difficult to pull her *Mana* since she wasn't focusing on sending it to him. If she wasn't touching him, he wouldn't be able to do it at all. As it was, it took all of his concentration to keep the flow going from Ainslee into him and then into the Chymera crystals.

Ethan was going by feel and instinct at this point. Without knowing how much *Mana* the dwarf had left, he had no way of knowing exactly how much he'd channeled so far and when to stop. He had to improvise.

It had taken him about a second to channel the equivalent of one *Mana* from Nia. Ainslee had 32 mana, which meant after 30 seconds, she would be close to empty. He quietly counted to thirty as he fed *Mana* from the dwarf to the dragon eyes.

"Done, Ainslee," he called out. He stopped pulling *Mana* from the dwarf but kept the flow going with his own *Mana*. Ainslee didn't move. "Ainslee, you're done!"

The dwarf was still frozen in place, her eyes unfocused and staring into the darkness in horror. Cursing, he pushed her hand off his forehead. "Yuliana! Your turn!"

The green-haired elf moved next to him. She put both her hands on his face. They were cold and clammy and she was pale with fear as well. "What do I do?"

"Think about giving me your mana," he told her but he

was already reaching for her *Mana*. "Bring up your HUD and tell me when your mana reaches 2 or 3."

Yuliana nodded and her eyes became unfocused. "I'm full. Oh!"

The elf's eyes went wide as he tugged at her *Mana*. Her forehead wrinkled and there was a moment of resistance but then it began to flow easily. Ethan took her *Mana* and shoved it into the two crystals as fast as he could.

Behind him, he was dimly aware of the sounds of scurrying feat and chittering mandibles were getting louder and closer. Ethan knew they were running out of time. He just didn't know if they would get the door open in time. He pushed harder.

"3!" rasped Yuliana and Ethan switched from her to his own *Mana*.

"Par'karr!" he yelled and the little kobold ran over to him and put his clawed hand on Ethan's head.

"Par'karr ready!" the kobold nodded.

Ethan reached in and tugged at the kobold's *Mana*. It came easily and Par'karr didn't even flinch. He smiled at the kobold and Par'karr gave him a toothy grin.

Counting the ticks in his head as he pulled the *Mana* from Par'karr, Ethan was careful to watch the little kobold. Without a HUD, he had no way of knowing exactly how much *Mana* Par'karr had. He could have as little as Nia or as much as Ethan himself. Considering the consequences of going over, Ethan wanted to err on the side of caution.

After mentally counting to 24, he called out to Nia. The foxgirl was in front of him in a second. She bent down and put her hands on either side of his face and pressed her forehead against his.

"Take what you need, my alpha," she said softly and closed her eyes. "But be quick! They are almost to us!"

Suppressing the need to turn around and see how close the spiders were, Ethan reached into the foxgirl's head and pulled at her *Mana*. It came quickly and easily. It was almost as easy as channeling his own *Mana*.

Ethan pushed the *Mana* into the two eyes as quickly as he could, seeing them glow brighter and brighter as he did. They had to be close to getting full but he couldn't spare the concentration to check.

In less than half a minute, Nia's *Mana* was down to only two points and he stopped. He switched back to his own *Mana*. It only took a few points of his *Mana* before the eyes flashed and he heard a resounding click from somewhere below them. There was the sound of stone grating on stone and the door began to lower. He spun and looked down the corridor.

The spiders had made it into the illumination of their light stones as they leaped and ran towards the group. Darts continued to fly from all directions, hitting and killing spiders. But still more came.

"Get ready to go through the door!" he shouted. "Don't wait for it to get all the way down. Just climb over it as soon as it gets low enough!"

One of the spiders managed to get in a good leap and might have made it to them but a double barrel shot of stone balls hit it in the eyes, dropping it back.

"Good shot!" he told Par'karr. The kobold didn't respond. Instead, Par'karr busied himself with reloading the magical shotgun. It would still be just under a minute before the thing recharged itself, but at least he'd be ready.

"It's down enough!" Nia cried from behind him. Ethan

glanced over his shoulder to see that the door was far enough down for them to scramble over it. That was when an ear-piercing shriek assaulted his senses.

He didn't recognize it at first since the sound echoed around the corridor but he quickly realized it was Ainslee. The dwarf was standing there frozen in a look of absolute terror, hand outstretched and finger pointed down the corridor.

"I know!" he said, rolling his eyes. "Spiders! But the door is down! Let's go...."

Ethan's voice caught in his throat as he looked down the corridor. There were still spiders trying to get through the darts and dozens, if not hundreds of dead spider bodies, lining the corridor. But then he caught sight of something that made his own heart skip a beat.

Just on the periphery of their light was a spider. But this spider was not like any of the others. It was enormous. With its legs, the monstrous arachnid was easily as tall as the corridor and Ethan thought it might be hunching down.

Three, large glistening eyes glinted in the dim illumination as the creature seemed to stare right into Ethan's very soul. This was no stupid drone. This was an intelligent, calculating spider. This was the queen.

Surrounding the queen were a half dozen spiders that were twice as large as the small ones they'd seen so far. These were sleeker and had long, sharp scythe-like forelegs. Ethan guessed they were some sort of guardian or soldier spiders. He swore.

"Holy - " Ethan started but his words were drowned out by a renewed screech from Ainslee.

Glancing back, he saw the others were through the door,

which was just under halfway down now. He stepped over to Ainslee and shook her. "COME ON! WE HAVE TO GO!"

It did no good. The dwarf was paralyzed with fear, unable to take her eyes off the approaching giant spider.

Cursing, Ethan ran over and hopped up and over the descending door. Spinning, he grabbed the dwarf with *Air* and yanked her through the doorway.

"How do we stop the door and make it go back up?" Nia shouted.

"I don't..." Ethan started but had to drop the dwarf on the floor and shoot out a long gout of flame at two of the smaller spiders. They had made it through the darts and were leaping over the wall.

```
Tunnel Spider dies.
   You gain 30 experience. Experience
to next level 885.
   Tunnel Spider dies.
   You gain 30 experience. Experience
to next level 855.
```

More spiders were coming. He needed to close this door. But how? If filling the crystals up opened it, would ripping the *Mana* from them close it? Or was it a onetime trigger? There was only one way to find out.

Reaching down where he knew the dragon eyes were, he felt around with his magical sense until he felt the two pulsating Chymera crystals. Using all of his will, he ripped *Mana* out of them.

Two things happened at once. The first thing that happened was the door ground to a halt. After a moment, the door began to ascend.

The second thing that happened was Ethan screamed. It felt like his entire body was on fire. He fell to his knees and barely managed to bring up his HUD.

Mana: 118

Despite the pain, or maybe because of it, he swore. He'd meant to pull the *Mana* out of the crystals but somehow, this time, he'd pulled it INTO himself. Now, he had too much *Mana* and it felt like it was burning him from the inside out. He had to get rid of it and quickly or it was going to kill him.

Stretching out his hands, he channeled as much *Mana* as possible into the gouts of flame in front of him. The flames roared around, incinerating the smaller spiders that came near him.

The queen spider and her escort stopped, staying just out of range of the flames. The giant spider's three large eyes fixed on him. In those eyes, Ethan saw anger and death. The spider knew he was the one who had killed all her brood in the spike room. He could tell it wanted revenge.

By now, the door was almost up. Ethan continued to spray fire across the opening until the door slammed shut. Only then did he manage to see the messages in his HUD and check his *Mana*. There were a ton of kill messages, but the latest one told him he was only 75 experience away from leveling.

Mana: 61
    Tunnel Spider dies.
    You gain 30 experience. Experience to next level 75.

He also saw that he had received some sort of damage.

```
You take 4 points of undefined damage.
You take 3 points of undefined damage.
You take 3 points of undefined damage.
You take 2 points of undefined damage.
You take 2 points of undefined damage.
You take 1 point of undefined damage.
```

Ethan swore as he saw his *Health* was down to half. Had he not used up his *Mana* when he did, he'd probably have died. It was a scary thought of how close he'd come. Definitely not something he wanted to repeat.

Looking around in the illumination of the light stones, he saw all of his companions except Ainslee seemed to be okay. The dwarf was lying on the floor with Yuliana hovering over.

Alarmed, Ethan strode over to them. Having seen the terror on the woman's face, he hoped the poor dwarf hadn't given herself a heart attack. "Is she okay?"

Yuliana looked up and smiled. "I think she just passed out. She's sleeping now."

As if to punctuate the elf's statement, a loud snore erupted from the unconscious dwarf.

30

———

Ethan let the sleeping dwarf lie. He stood up and looked back at the door. He half expected to hear the spiders thudding against the door. Straining his ears, he heard nothing. Was the door too thick?

"Are they trying to get in?" Ethan asked Yuliana.

The elf pulled her long green hair away from her right ear and cocked her head. She moved her head slightly, as if trying to zero in on a sound. Frowning, she straightened her head. "I think I hear them retreating. I'm not sure though. The door is very thick."

Nodding, Ethan remembered that the door had been about a foot thick when he jumped over it. The spiders might have broken through the bars he'd hastily constructed, but there was no way they'd be able to get through a foot of solid granite. For now, they were safe.

Ethan looked around the room they had entered. It wasn't so much a room as a corridor, much the same as the one they'd just been in. He followed the corridor with his eyes to where it turned into a staircase leading down. Walking to the edge of the steps, he looked down the staircase.

The staircase was carved from the same stone as the corridor around him. In fact, it was the same width and relatively the same height. The stairs were smooth stone with no discernible markings.

Ethan cursed as he realized he'd lost his 10-foot pole. Looking around, he also realized they'd left the shields on the other side of the door as well. He sighed but knew losing the stone shields and stone pole were a small price to pay for not becoming spider food.

"We go down?" Par'karr asked, stepping up next to Ethan.

Ethan surveyed the corridor they were in. There were no signs of any other passages or exits from the area, other than the staircase. He nodded. "It looks like we have no choice."

"What do you think is down there?" Nia asked. She moved up next to him on the opposite side, resting her hand on his shoulder.

Ethan frowned. "Probably more traps."

"Maybe no more spiders?" Par'karr asked hopefully, looking up at Ethan.

"They can't get through that door." Ethan grinned at the kobold. He purposely didn't add "hopefully" to the end of the sentence.

He was fairly certain the spiders couldn't get through. If they could have, they could have gotten through the door out of the spike room. Of course, that wasn't real evidence but the fact that they weren't even trying to get through the door reinforced his theory.

"Do we go down the stairs now?" Nia asked.

Ethan shook his head. "No. Let's rest a bit. We can check the portal pouch and see if there's any more food or drink. Maybe even get a few hours sleep."

Par'karr glanced back at another loud snore from the dwarf. "Ainslee already asleep!"

Chuckling, Ethan turned to look at the dwarf lying on the stone floor. Yuliana and Luna sat nearby, silently watching Ainslee.

"True," Ethan replied. "I think we can let her sleep for a while. She had quite a fright."

Nia snorted dismissively. "She is a coward."

Ethan looked at the sleeping dwarf and then to the foxgirl. "Nia, none of us were warriors before coming to this world except you. We aren't used to facing down foes. Before this, Ainslee said she was a blacksmith. I was a... computer wizard and Yuliana tended a grove of trees."

The foxgirl furrowed her brow and scoffed. "That is no excuse. She..."

"She is terrified of spiders," Ethan interrupted. "I don't understand it but it's an irrational fear she can't control. Other than spiders, she's never run from a fight. Has she?"

Nia looked thoughtful for a moment. "No."

Gripping Nia by the shoulders, he looked into her eyes. "You are a fearsome warrior. I doubt there is anything you're afraid of."

Nia smiled and lifted her chin slightly. "I am not afraid."

"I know." He smiled at her. "I'm thankful you aren't afraid of anything. Just bear with her." Ethan looked at the prone dwarf with her ruined face. "Given what she's been through lately, spiders could have just been the last straw."

Nia looked at the dwarf and bit her lip. Finally, she nodded. "Very well. I will withhold judgement... for now."

"Fair enough." Ethan smiled. "Now, let's set up camp and see if everyone can get a little rest before we go on."

Ethan had them all set up camp near the door. He was confident that the spiders couldn't get through it and it was as far away from the steps as they could get. That would at least give them some time to react if anything came up the stairs.

He asked for Par'karr's light stone and used <u>Air</u> to float it down the stairs about 30 steps, before gently setting it down. He still couldn't see the bottom of the stairs, but they'd be able to see anything coming up the stairs.

"The light will give away our position up here," Nia pointed out.

"True, but it will also give a little warning if something does come up those stairs. Besides," he grinned, "the dwarf's snoring will give us away if it hasn't already."

They shared a chuckle for a moment but then Ethan doubled over in pain. "Argh!"

"Ethan!" Nia cried out, grabbing him before he collapsed.

Ethan gritted his teeth as his eyes teared. Spasms of sharp pain wracked his body. He struggled to activate his HUD but the pain shot through his brain like electricity, making coherent thought impossible.

His muscles spasmed and Ethan felt like his bones were going to snap as his arms and legs twitched uncontrollably. The pain wracking his brain and his body made it impossible to hear or see anything.

He was unsure how long it went on. Just when he thought he might snap in half, he felt an icy-hot energy surge through him and saw a green glow through his lidded eyes. Yuliana. Yuliana was healing him.

As the icy-hot healing magic surged through him, Ethan

felt his muscles relax. They still twitched and his head felt like it was on fire but he could force his eyes open.

Nia, Par'karr and Yuliana were knelt down around him and the elf's hands were on his chest and his head.

"Are you okay, Ethan?!" Nia asked, her voice cracking. "What is wrong? Are you injured?"

Ethan blinked away the tears and tried to sit up.

"No!" Nia and Yuliana said at the same time, pushing him back down gently but firmly.

"What is wrong?" Yuliana asked, her voice full of concern. Par'karr poked his head over Ethan and looked worried as well.

"I... I don't... know," Ethan gasped. Everything hurt. Every muscle in his body felt like he'd just overworked them. "I... I just... started hurting."

Nia began checking him out, moving her hands over his body, pulling at his clothes and then sniffing at him. Ethan just lay there since it was easier than arguing with the girls. When the foxgirl was done checking his front, she and the others rolled him over and checked his backside.

After several minutes of prodding and sniffing, they rolled him over again. Ethan was actually starting to feel better, though he was still sore.

"I see no injury," Nia said and Yuliana nodded. "I thought perhaps one of the spiders had bitten you."

Ethan nodded. Poison might have caused that but no spiders had gotten close to him and he was pretty sure he would have noticed a huge, freaking spider biting him.

He remembered the pain and the messages after he had pulled the *Mana* from the eyes. Too much *Mana*. He swallowed. What had it done to him?

Squinting, he nodded. "I think... I think it was... from pulling in... the mana... from the dragon eyes."

The two women exchanged confused glances and Ethan brought up his HUD to check his *Health*.

```
Health: 30
  Mana: 61
  Stamina: 2
```

His *Stamina* was almost gone but Yuliana had healed him back to full *Health*. So what had caused the pain? Even though the HUD hurt him to look at it at the moment, he forced himself to scroll up through his messages.

```
You take 1 point of undefined damage.
   You    take    1    point    of    undefined
damage.
   You    take    1    point    of    undefined
damage.
   You    take    1    point    of    undefined
damage.
   You    take    1    point    of    undefined
damage.
   You    take    1    point    of    undefined
damage.
   Yuliana    Madeiras    heals    you    for    9
health.
   Yuliana    Madeiras    heals    you    for    11
health.
   Yuliana    Madeiras    heals    you    for    1
health.
```

There was that undefined damage again. He bit his lip. What did that mean? The messages had started right after he'd pulled the *Mana* from the eyes. It had damaged him in some way. Some way that even the HUD was not able to interpret - or wasn't programmed to interpret. Was it fixed now that he'd been healed?

The undefined damage worried him. In a game, undefined usually referred to an error in the game code itself: a missing variable, a bad pointer or something along those lines. What did it mean in this context? Had he done something the aliens really hadn't accounted for? If so, how bad was it?

"You must rest," Nia insisted and Par'karr and Yuliana agreed.

Ethan wanted to object but everything ached and he suddenly realized how tired he felt. He nodded and accepted their help to the corner where they took his pack and laid out his bedroll.

Sitting down on his bedroll, he took off his belt and handed the portal pouch to Nia. "Take this... and see.. if there is any food. I'm not sure... if I can... eat anything."

"You should at least drink something," Nia insisted.

He shook his head. "I can't restore any more stamina until I sleep."

The foxgirl rolled her eyes. "You still need water!" She reached into the portal pouch and pulled out one of the water bottles.

She uncorked it and then held it up for him to drink from. "Drink!"

Too tired to argue, Ethan did. He drank half of the bottle and then waved it away. "Thanks."

He was finding it more and more difficult to keep his eyes awake. He lowered himself to the bedroll. "I'm... pretty... tired..."

That was the last thing he remembered before darkness closed around him and he knew no more.

31

E than woke to excruciating pain. Every muscle in his body felt like it was being torn apart and his brain felt like molten lead had been poured into it. He thought he screamed but wasn't sure. He felt his body convulsing and his heart racing but other than that, everything was pain. Pure pain.

Through the pain, a green glow appeared and gradually the pain subsided until it was gone and he lay sweating on the hard stone. With an effort, he forced his eyes open. Blinking against the sudden light, he saw his companions hovering over him with concerned looks.

"Ethan okay?" the reptilian face of Par'karr asked.

He blinked again, trying to comprehend what the little kobold had said, his brain still addled from the intense pain. When Ethan tried to reply, he found his mouth was dry. "Water..."

Immediately, a water bottle was pushed against his lips and someone tilted his head so he could drink. Ethan was parched and greedily drank down the cool water until he coughed. The water bottle was pulled away from him and he tried to sit up.

"No," Nia said, gently pushing him back down onto his bedroll. "Not yet."

"What... what happened?" he asked hoarsely. Despite drinking the water, his throat still felt parched.

"You had a fit, wizard-boy," Ainslee said. The dwarf's voice held more concern than he'd heard from her before and that worried him.

"Fit?" He coughed and motioned for more water.

"Your body was all... contorted," Nia explained, pushing the water bottle to his lips. "And you were screaming."

"We didn't know what was wrong with you," Yuliana said. "But when I healed you, you stopped having the fit."

Pushing the water bottle from his lips, he forced himself to bring up his HUD.

```
Health: 30
  Mana: 68
  Stamina: 17
  You   take   3   points   of   undefined
damage.
  You   take   1   point   of   undefined
damage.
  You   take   2   points   of   undefined
damage.
  You   take   3   points   of   undefined
damage.
  You   take   3   points   of   undefined
damage.
  You   take   1   point   of   undefined
damage.
```

```
     Yuliana   Madeiras   heals   you   for   7
health.
     Yuliana   Madeiras   heals   you   for   6
health.
```

There it was. More undefined damage. There was no doubt any longer. He had done something to himself when he'd drawn in all of the *Mana*. Ethan swore silently.

Ethan needed to talk to Michalus. He needed to find out if the old wizard knew anything about what was happening to him. More importantly, he needed to know how to stop it. If Yuliana's healing didn't fix him, what would?

"Same thing," he rasped, "as before. Some sort of undefined damage."

"Why is my healing not making you better?" Yuliana asked with a furrowed brow.

Ethan shook his head. "Don't know. Might not be something... that can be healed."

Nia blanched. "What does that mean?"

Forcing a smile, Ethan looked from the elf to the foxgirl. "It means we might need to start sleeping with Yuliana."

"What?!" both women said at the same time.

He chuckled, though it hurt his sore muscles to do so. Everything was sore. He felt like he had just run a marathon, did an insanely intense workout in the gym and did a billion sit-ups. All at once. "I mean... she might need to... sleep near us in case... I have more fits. I have a feeling... it won't stop... without healing."

"What are you sayin', wizard-boy?" demanded Ainslee. "That it will kill you?"

Ethan nodded weakly. "Unless... we can find... some way to heal it. Or... I naturally... recover from it."

His companions were silent for a long time and Ethan slowly tried to sit up. Once again, Nia put a hand on his chest. "Just lie still for a bit."

"What about the honey?" Yuliana asked. "The honey we got from the giant bees. It has healing properties."

Ethan had forgotten about the honey. Not that it mattered. It was in a small chest back in his house in Hawkshead. He shook his head weakly. "Back... in village."

"Tell Elspeth to get it and put it in your portal-thingy," Ainslee suggested.

He blinked and looked at the dwarf. That was a good idea. The honey they'd taken from the giant bees on their way to the library at Patheos had remarkable healing properties. He'd stashed it away in a chest when they'd returned to Hawkshead and hadn't remembered to bring it with them.

The problem was how to communicate it to the innkeeper's wife. He smiled. "Napkins?"

"Napkins?" Yuliana asked, cocking her head.

"Is there any cloth... in the portal pouch?" he clarified.

"Nah," Ainslee said, holding up a small wooden bowl. "Just bowls."

He frowned but then motioned to his bedroll. "Cut a piece off. A one-foot-by-one-foot piece will do."

His voice was getting better, but his entire body still ached. Still, he was starting to feel better and pushed himself up. This time, Nia watched him but didn't push him back down.

Ainslee grabbed one of his blankets and, using her dagger, cut a piece from it. She held it up. "Now what? You got something to write with?"

Ethan grinned. He focused a tiny bit of *Fire* and scorched a message into the cloth. When he was done, he read it.

Elspeth, get vial in small chest in back closet. Put in portal chest.

"You think that will explain it well enough?" Nia asked.

"I hope so." He shrugged. "Help me stand up. Place this in the portal pouch."

"You should..." Yuliana started but Ethan held up his hand.

"I think I need to walk around," he said. "Moving my muscles might help."

Yuliana looked at Nia, who nodded, and the women helped him to his feet. Ethan was already near the wall, so he braced himself against it with one hand.

"It's in the portal pouch," Ainslee said, holding the pouch out in front of her. "Let's hope she sees it soon."

Ethan nodded and tried taking a step. Using his muscles was painful but he forced himself to walk around the room. First, he braced himself against the wall as he walked. After walking around the room once and not collapsing, he tried walking without the support.

The more he walked, the easier it became and the better his muscles felt. He circled the room several times before starting to walk around normally. At least, as normally as he could.

"Did anyone go down the steps?" he asked as he stopped in front of the stone staircase. Looking down, he still saw the light stone where he had left it.

"No," Nia said, coming to stand next to him. She reached over and took his hand in hers, giving it a gentle squeeze. He squeezed back and flashed her a smile.

"We were waiting for you and Ainslee to wake up," Yuliana said.

"Ainslee and Ethan sleep long time." Par'karr bobbed his head.

"We were keeping watch on the stairs," Nia told him. "There was no movement."

Ethan nodded and looked around, as if he could somehow tell the time by looking at the room. "How long was I out?"

Nia shrugged and gestured around the room. "Several hours at least. Hard to know exactly without the sun."

He had no sense of how long he had been out. He also didn't remember dreaming. Ethan wasn't sure if that was a good thing or a bad thing.

"At least I went several hours without an... episode," he commented.

"Hopefully, the honey will fix you," Nia remarked.

"While we wait," he said. "I'm going to scout out what's down there."

"You can't..." Nia started but Ethan squeezed her hand and flashed her a smile.

"With my air elemental." He grinned.

Nia rolled her eyes at him, let go of his hand and slapped his bottom. "That is fine, but you will stay up here!"

The foxgirl's tone left no room for argument. Not that Ethan was about to argue. He felt better, but in the back of his mind, he was worried about another episode.

"Deal," he said and lowered himself to the floor, near the stairway. Focusing on his *Summon Minor Elemental* ability, he summoned the air elemental he'd conjured before.

The elemental formed in front of him, a semi-transparent bird that resembled a raven or hawk. The thing had appeared in midair and immediately began flapping its wings.

Ethan took a few deep breaths and used his clairvoyance ability to take control of the elemental. Immediately, his perception shifted and suddenly he was looking at Nia and himself.

He frowned inwardly. He looked haggard. From the eyes of the air elemental, he could see his own eyes were blood-shot and had large bags under them. He looked sickly. No wonder the women were concerned for him.

Once again, Ethan wondered what he'd done to himself. More importantly, he hoped that whatever he'd done could be undone.

Pushing those thoughts to the back of his mind, Ethan willed the air elemental to look down the steps. The air elemental's eyes were sharp, but still needed light to see - much like Nia.

He commanded the elemental to fly down and pick up the light stone on the step. Once it had the light stone, it flew to the bottom of the stairs. There it hovered, surveying the next room.

The stairs opened into a long chamber, 50 feet wide by 20 feet long. Opposite the stairs was a 10x10 door. The door was tiled with three columns and four rows of tiles, each of which had a rune symbol on it. But that wasn't the most intriguing part.

The walls of the room had the stone reliefs of twelve knights carved into the walls of the chamber. The stone reliefs had amazing detail. There were runes carved into the walls near each knight as well, but Ethan had no idea what they meant.

Placed evenly around the room, about 10 feet from the corners, were four metal pillars. At the top of the pillars were clear spheres that resembled plasma ball lamps. Electricity coursed inside the spheres, emanating from the center of the sphere to the edges of the sphere. Were those some sort of magical Tesla coils?

Ethan got a bad feeling in the pit of his stomach and forced the elemental to look at the floor. It was smooth and at first glance looked like the same gray stone that made up the rest of the tomb. Then he saw the seams and recognized it for what it was. The floor wasn't stone. It was steel. Steel plates. A nice conductor for electricity.

The trap seemed obvious, but he knew he needed to test it out. Before he did, he took another fly-by around the room, looking for anything that might give him any other clues about the room.

When he found none, he said a silent "I'm sorry" to the elemental and had it land in the middle of the room. He'd expected it, but the speed at which electricity shot from the spheres to the elemental was almost too quick for the eye to follow.

Your minor elemental (air) has been dismissed.

Ethan's awareness snapped back to his body and he frowned. Nia and the others were looking down the stairs.

"What in Odin's beard was that zapping sound and that flash of light?" Ainslee swore.

"Was that lightning?" Nia gasped.

"It's a trap!" Ethan replied.

32

———

"I t does what?!" boomed Ainslee, staring at Ethan incredulously.

Ethan had tried explaining how the trap worked in more scientific terms but finally gave up and just told them it shot lightning at anyone stepping on the floor. While not exactly accurate, that was for all intents and purposes the effect.

"So if we step on the floor... ZAP... Lightning hits us?!" the dwarf bellowed. "How in Odin's One-Eye are we supposed to get past that?"

"Can you use magic to move us across the floor like you did with Ainslee when she was unmoving?" Yuliana asked.

Ethan nodded. "I could. But the entire floor is metal. Anywhere we step will complete a circuit... er... will get us struck by lightning."

"Then we cannot go forward?" Nia asked.

"I think there's a way to deactivate the trap," he answered. It had been fifteen or twenty minutes since he'd had his attack - if that was the name for it. He was feeling better and his mind was clearer now. He thought back to his view of the room.

There had been the twelve knights carved into the wall. The steel plasma ball lamp things and the door. But the door had been tiled. Broken up in twelve tiles. Was that a coincidence? Twelve knights. Twelve tiles on the door? He didn't think so.

It was probably some sort of lock, like the passcode on a cellphone. Type, or press the runes in this case, the right runes in the right order and the door would open. But twelve runes meant an insane number of combinations. And he didn't even know how big the "passcode" might be. It could be one rune or twelve runes in a specific order.

He didn't even know what the runes meant, which made trying to figure out the code nearly impossible. It would just be random guessing on his part.

Thinking of the runes reminded him of Merlin's journal. He remembered seeing the runes when he'd thumbed through the book. He just hadn't had time to sit down and actually read the book. Things had been a bit chaotic. Maybe now was the time.

"I think I need to read Merlin's journal," he told them. "Or at least skim through it."

"The book you found in the library?" Nia asked.

"Yes," he replied. "It has some runes. If I can figure out what the runes mean, maybe I can figure out what the right sequence is."

"I guess we ain't got anything else to do," the dwarf grumbled. Then she looked up at him hopefully. "Unless you want to portal us back to town."

"We still haven't found anything that might be creating the sound," Ethan pointed out.

The dwarf threw her hands up. "And we might never! For all we know, that big-arse spider is causing the sound!"

Ethan nodded. He'd considered that possibility too but it didn't feel right. He felt like there was something else. Something further inside this tomb. He wasn't sure why he felt that way, but he did.

Maybe it was the gamer in him. After all, wasn't the best treasure at the very end? He frowned inwardly. Wasn't there always some big boss at the end too?

Pushing thoughts of treasure and bosses out of his head, Ethan sat down and pulled out Merlin's journal. He began thumbing through it, scanning it for anything that might be helpful.

Most of the journal was written in English. At least, it appeared to be English to Ethan. He still thought there might be some sort of translation going on - just like the way all of his companions seem to speak English despite being from different planets.

Flipping through the pages, he did see runes scribed in the margins. He also found several lines of runes scribbled in between paragraphs of English text. There were also several pages scattered through the book with nothing but runes. Unfortunately, there didn't seem to be any sort of translation matrix or anything hinting at the meaning of the runes.

Ethan sighed and turned back to the first instance of runes he found and read the passage. He read the area near the rune. It was a description of a battle involving Arthur and the knights against a group of giants. During the battle, one of the knights fell. It was Sir Gareth.

In the margin, next to the sentence that mentioned Gareth, was a rune. Ethan raised an eyebrow. Could it be that runes were names? Or at least, perhaps they were symbols for people.

Flipping to another page with a single rune, Ethan found a passage describing how Sir Gawain had reported that he had helped a village put down a goblin uprising. In the margin, was another rune. Coincidence? Or was he on to something?

Quickly flipping through the journal, he found mention of other knights along the way. Just like the others, each of them had a rune next to their name. At least, the first time they were mentioned they had a rune.

Just from skimming through the book, Ethan started to grasp that the journal was like a chronicle of the knight's deeds. It included a few things about Arthur, mostly large battles, but for the most part, it was more about the knights themselves.

Then again, he was only reading the passages that had runes on them. Ethan wanted to read the entire journal but his primary concern was getting them past those Tesla coils. He could go back and read the entire journal when they got back to Hawkshead.

Going on the assumption that the runes were symbols for the various knights, Ethan spent the next half hour skimming to different parts of the book. He specifically took note of any knights and their associated runes. He ended up finding ten different knights mentioned, along with their associated runes.

Once he knew some of the runes, he searched the pages and longer passages of runes for any patterns of the knight runes. He was examining the second full page of runes when pain exploded inside him.

The book fell from his hands as his body convulsed, pain wracking his muscles. He thought he might have screamed but the fire inside his brain made it impossible to concentrate. The world glowed green to his shut eyes and the pain subsided and finally left.

Gasping, he blinked open his eyes. He was on the ground with Yuliana's hands on his head. He forced a weak smile. "Thanks."

He didn't need to bring up his HUD to know what it would say. More undefined damage. Ethan cursed silently. This was getting old. He remembered the honey and turned to Nia. "Check the pouch. See if the honey is there."

Nia nodded, but she was already pulling out a water bottle. The foxgirl handed it to Ainslee and dug her hand back into the portal pouch.

Ainslee reached down and cupped his head and put the water bottle up to his lips. In her one good eye Ethan saw concern and worry. He remembered how haggard he looked when he'd seen himself from the elemental's eyes. He probably looked even worse now.

"Thanks," he said when she withdrew the water bottle.

"No honey yet," Nia reported. "Maybe it is night time."

"Maybe," Ethan agreed and tried to sit up. His muscles were sore but he forced himself to sit up despite the women's protests.

"You should rest," Yuliana insisted.

Groaning, Ethan sat all the way up and leaned himself against the wall. "I'll be okay. I need to finish figuring out the puzzle."

Par'karr and the women exchanged glances and then backed away to give him space. Nia picked up the journal and handed it to him. "You should rest. You do not smell well."

Ethan forced himself to smile. "I'll be fine."

The foxgirl narrowed her eyes at him but nodded and went to watch the staircase.

Alone, Ethan opened the book. He didn't look at the words or the symbols, but just stared down at it. Something was wrong with him. Very wrong. He had thought he could feel it before but Nia's comment about him not smelling well made him certain he wasn't imagining it.

Once again he wished Michalus or another wizard was here that he could ask. Even if he was dying, he'd rather know than live with the uncertainty.

Despite his morbid thought, one thing was clear to him. He needed to get them through the door before it became more serious. Maybe he was dying. Maybe he wasn't. But if he did die or wasn't able to function, the rest of the group would be trapped in here forever.

He wondered if he should just portal them out at this point. Even if he died in the effort, at least they'd get out alive.

Unfortunately, he didn't have any crystals charged. Even if he wanted to charge some up at this point, he wasn't up to any sort of "recharging" with Nia. He cursed silently. He needed to get them past that door and hope there was another way out beyond it.

Ethan looked around at his companions. They were his friends now. His only friends. He had to figure it out so they would make it - even if it meant he didn't make it.

He snorted. Ethan had always wondered if he would

really be the self-sacrificing type when the chips were down. He smiled to himself. Turns out, maybe he was.

Opening up the journal, he turned to the page he'd been looking at before his episode and scanned the runes. Ethan just hoped that he would last long enough to actually be able to get them out.

33

———

E than had another fit about twenty minutes after the last one. This time, he coughed up a little blood but quickly hid it. He didn't know how long he had left but he wasn't going to spend his last hours or minutes being the object of pity.

When he recovered, he continued to look through the journal. After another fifteen minutes, he found a page that contained a column of runes which included the knight runes. It was on one of the pages of nothing but runes and there was a pattern of thirteen runes with the ten runes for the knights among them.

When he'd found the list, he'd marked the page and kept looking. He'd found another page, further in the book with the same list in the same order. Could that be the list of knights? But if so, then why were there thirteen symbols?

Then it hit him, Arthur. He hadn't been looking for the symbol for Arthur since he assumed it was one of the twelve knights he was trying to find. Twelve knights carved into the walls and twelve symbols on the door.

If he assumed that King Arthur was the thirteenth symbol and assumed it was at the top, then the bottom twelve should be the knights. He'd found them in the same order twice in the book. Could that be the order of the runes for the door?

He skimmed through the rest of the pages with runes but no other patterns emerged. There were some pages with three or four of the runes, but none with the ten he thought were knights plus the three others he couldn't identify. It was time to test it.

"I think I have the order," Ethan said aloud.

His companions looked over at him. Nia came and squatted down next to him. "You know how to get past the door?"

"I think so," he said. "I think I found the order of the runes."

"Assumin' you can actually press the runes on the door," Ainslee chimed.

"Yes," he smirked, "assuming I can actually press the runes on the door."

"How will you get across the floor?" Nia asked him.

"I'll use the air elemental again," he answered.

"Better than walking down there and getting zapped!" Ainslee agreed.

Ethan had asked none of them to go down the steps. He didn't trust them. In his devious gamemaster mind, those steps would flatten into a slide and dump them all onto the metal floor below where they'd be fried. He was fairly certain the builders hadn't thought to add that little trap, but he wasn't about to risk it.

Handing the journal to Nia, Ethan once more

summoned his air elemental and took control of it with clairvoyance.

He glided down the staircase and into the room. The light stone was still lying on the floor in the center of the room just where it had been when the previous elemental was zapped. He briefly toyed with trying to pick it up but dismissed the idea. Most likely it would just get this elemental electrocuted as well.

Commanding the elemental to fly around the room, he took a more careful look at the stone reliefs of the knights. They all looked similar with their bucket-style helmets on but there were subtle differences. Sword and shield on one, two-handed sword on another, others with cloaks while yet others with wings or designs on their helmets.

Ethan also examined the runes next to each knight. Now that he had an idea of what to look for, he easily found each knight's rune in with the others. The knight's name rune, as he began thinking of it, appeared at the very end of a column of runes in each instance.

He confirmed the ten runes he knew, then mentally ticked them off his list. He found Lancelot, Gawain, Geraint, Percival, Bors, Gareth, Bedivere, Gaheris, Galahad, and Tristan. That left two others unaccounted for but knowing where to look he identified the other two knights' runes. They were the same runes that appeared in the list he'd found the journal. Almost.

He hadn't figured out what the first rune was or the last two on the list. He'd assumed that Arthur had been the first rune, but that rune matched one of the runes on the wall. And the second to last rune matched the other unknown knight. That meant Arthur was on the bottom. Or was rune style written from bottom to top?

Ethan remembered the concept of the round table from his Arthurian lore. Arthur created the round table so that all knights were equal. That was the act of a humble king. A humble king might have put himself at the bottom of the list.

Either way, he had found all twelve of the knight runes! Excitedly, Ethan smiled. Now to make sure they were the same ones on the door.

Flying over to the door, Ethan scanned the runes carved into the door. After a moment, he grinned even more. They matched. The runes on the door corresponded to the runes of the knights!

Now, Ethan just had to tap them in the right order! He had memorized the order from the book. He just had to see if he could tap them with the elemental and if that was how the door even worked. Given the way they'd opened the spike room, he'd never even thought of any other possibility.

Flying close to the door, Ethan had the elemental strike out with its talons at the first rune from the memorized list. There was a slight clicking sound and Ethan felt a shiver of excitement. He'd been right!

He quickly navigated the bird around the door, clicking the runes in the sequence he'd memorized. When he got to the last one, he clicked it with the elemental's talons and then backed off a few feet.

Nothing happened. Ethan waited. Still nothing happened. He cursed. The order from the journal wasn't correct. He felt his hopes slipping away. Without the right order, he would be trying combinations until whatever was wrong with him finally killed him.

Ethan cursed again. He started to turn and fly back up but stopped as he looked at the stone reliefs of the knights.

Could the reliefs be the order? It seemed too simple. Twelve knights on the walls, twelve symbols. It could be.

He wanted to scratch his head, but he couldn't while in control of the elemental. Instead, he cocked his head. There were twelve knights on the walls. But where was the start of the order?

He tried starting the order from the first knight to the left of the entrance doorway and going around the room clockwise. That didn't work. Next he tried the knight to the right of the entrance doorway and went counter clockwise. Still nothing.

Frustrated, he tried the knight to the left of the actual door and went counter clockwise. Nothing. He tried the knight to the left and went clockwise. Nothing. He cursed.

He looked around the room. Maybe it didn't start next to the doors, which would be the middle of the room. Maybe it started in one of the corners. But which corner? And which direction?

He spent five minutes trying the runes in different corners and going clockwise and then counter clockwise until he finally heard the sound he'd been hoping for.

CLICK!

There was a rumbling and the sound of machinery and the door began to lower. He had done it! He'd figured it out.

Ethan hovered in the air staring excitedly, while the door came down. It hadn't gotten far until he felt his blood go icy.

As the door continued to come down, it revealed a ten-feet-by-ten-feet corridor just beyond. But that wasn't what made him go cold. It was what lined the walls of the corridor. Spider webs. Very large spider webs.

Ethan swore.

He could make out the shapes of cocoons lining the

walls, leaving only a small area to move through. There were no spiders that he could see, but he couldn't imagine the webs were the handiwork of anything else.

There must be another cave in the tomb, further in. And judging by the webs, it must be older than the previous one they'd found. If this area was older, maybe it was abandoned. Maybe they'd moved on to a different area.

It was wishful thinking and he knew it. And after a moment, his hopes were dashed as he heard chittering down the tunnel. The chittering of spiders. And it was getting closer.

Cursing, Ethan dismissed the elemental and his awareness snapped back into this body. No sooner had it done so than his body was once again wracked with pain and he found it impossible to do or say anything.

Green light quickly spread over him and he knew Yuliana was healing him, stopping the pain - for now. Gasping, he tried to speak but couldn't.

"Are you okay, Ethan?" Nia asked, concerned. She reached to his mouth and he felt her finger brush across his lips. It came away bloody. She furrowed her brow in concern. "You are not okay!"

"Ethan..." Yuliana started but he held up a hand.

"Spi..." he tried but his throat ached and burned. He swallowed painfully and lifted his hand to point at the stairs. "Spid... SPIDERS!"

34

"I can hear them coming!" Yuliana shouted, pointing down the stairs. Ainslee's eyes went wide and her face went white but she didn't run. Where could she run? There was no place to go.

Nia stood quickly and drew her scimitars. "How many?!"

"Lots," Ethan rasped.

"Many!" Yuliana said at the same time.

The foxgirl looked around and then set her jaw. "We will go down fighting!"

Par'karr rushed over with the shotgun. The little kobold grabbed two ammo stones and dropped them down the barrel. Like Nia, he looked like he was ready to die fighting. Yuliana and Luna stayed by Ethan, ready to defend him.

Ethan had other plans. He struggled to his hands and knees, coughing a bit of blood as he did. Yuliana gave him a stern look. "You should stay still."

"If we're going to... die anyway," Ethan croaked, wiping the blood from his lips. "I'll die fighting too!"

Nia looked over at him. Emotions played across the foxgirl's face but she nodded before looking back to the stairs. "Yuliana! Ainslee! Help him! They are almost up the stairs!"

As the elf and the dwarf helped him up, Ethan could hear the spiders now. The sound of their spider legs slapping against the stone steps and the chittering of their mandibles as they got close was unmistakable.

The double thud of the enchanted shotgun went off and Par'karr immediately began reloading it. Nia tensed, ready to strike at the spiders as they got within range.

Suddenly, there was a strange sound and both Nia and Par'karr started in surprise.

"What?!" Ethan asked and coughed up a little more blood. "What is it?"

"The steps," Nia said, cocking her head as she looked down the stairs. "They... flattened. The spiders are sliding down."

"Ha!" Ethan shouted and immediately burst into a coughing fit. He'd been right about the steps. Apparently, the builder of the tomb had a devious mind too. But while a stair-slide might slow them, the spiders wouldn't have much trouble climbing up it. They were spiders. Climbing up walls was their thing.

The stair-slide would only buy them a minute, maybe two. Ethan urged Yuliana and Ainslee to move faster. "Get me to the stairs."

His companions helped him to the stairs and sat him at the base. He could see down the stairs now, though not very well. The light from the light stone could barely be seen. Most likely, there were spiders obscuring it.

Ethan could see that he'd been right about the steps.

They had been trapped and they flattened, forming a slide that would have dropped him and his companions onto the metal floor where they would have been electrocuted.

Something was off though. The spiders were trying to come up but they were having a difficult time. He frowned but then reached out a finger and ran it across the stair-slide. The builder had greased it! Nice touch. Ethan approved.

He wouldn't have thought of that in his own tabletop campaigns. It was only a game and if the game master said the slide was slippery, it was slippery. There wasn't an in-depth discussion of friction and physics.

"It's greased," he told his companions. "That'll... buy us some time."

"Time for what?" Ainslee ranted sourly. "We got no place to go."

"Maybe I can... thin the herd a bit," Ethan said and with a thought, he sent a fireball hurling down the steps. It flew down the stone staircase and hit a spider at the bottom before exploding in a brilliant ball of fire.

The explosion scorched all of the spiders he could see and the concussion blasted most of them out of sight. Before the smoke had even cleared, more spiders were coming to take their place.

Looking at his HUD, he saw he'd gained a level from the spiders.

```
Congratulations!
  You have reached level 6.
  +1 Attribute Point.
  New      ability:    Summon    Elemental
(Lesser).
```

He quickly pulled the stat tab open and assigned the attribute point to *Hardiness*. It gave him another 2 points of *Heath* and 4 points of *Stamina*. That wasn't much, but if it helped him stay alive a bit longer, he'd take it.

"More of them are trying to climb up!" Ainslee screeched, pointing down the staircase with a trembling finger.

Ethan looked down at the spiders struggling to climb up the greased stair slide. He smirked and then shrugged. If they wanted to die, he was happy to oblige them.

"Bat'er up!" he chuckled and sent another fireball down the staircase. He was able to send another eight fireballs before his *Mana* was too low to risk sending another one.

After sending the last fireball, Ethan looked down the smoke-filled stairway; he could barely make out any movement. Some of the smoke and the smell of charred spider had wafted up the staircase and he coughed. "See anything?"

Nia blinked her eyes against the pungent smoke and shook her head. "The smoke is too thick at the bottom."

"Can you hear anything?" Ethan asked Yuliana.

The elf cocked her head, ears twitching. She moved her head, brow furrowed. "There is something down there, but it does not sound like the normal sound the spiders make."

"Maybe injured spiders," Par'karr offered helpfully.

Ethan shrugged. "That could be."

Yuliana's face suddenly grew alarmed. "Whatever the sound is, it's coming up the staircase!"

Everyone's head snapped back around to stare down the stone stairway. There was still too much smoke to see clearly, but Ethan thought he heard something too. Yes, he definitely heard a weird, almost metallic scraping sound.

Straining his eyes, Ethan caught movement in the smoke. Then more movement. A moment later, a large, scythe-like foreleg cut through the smoke. It buried itself into the edge of the staircase against the wall, somehow finding purchase. Then, another leg came out of the smoke and did the same with the other side of the staircase. A second later, the two forelegs pulled the body of a large spider into view.

This wasn't one of the smaller spiders they'd been killing. This was one of the larger spiders he'd seen earlier with the spider queen. These were the soldier spiders. At least, that's what he was calling them in his mind. He brought it up in his HUD.

```
Queen's Guardian
   Triple-eyed Spider
   Warrior
   Level 7
```

Queen's Guardian. He guessed that it was basically a soldier spider. But why was the queen sending her soldier spiders? Had she lost too many drones? Or did she just think they'd fare better against them. Ethan hoped it was the former.

He'd burned a ton of the spiders earlier and then even more at the door where he'd pulled in too much *Mana*. How many of them could there be? After all, they all had to eat, right? How much food was in this old mine and the passages the spiders had come from?

Then again, these were some sort of weird, alien spiders. Who knew what they ate or if they even ate at all. They could have some other way of ingesting nutrients for all he knew.

The double thud of the shotgun going off broke the silence. Two stone bullets hit the large spider. One hit it with a glancing blow on the head while the other shot hit the body, just behind the head. Immediately, the little kobold began reloading.

"How many?" Ethan turned and asked Yuliana. "How many do you hear?"

The elf pulled her green hair away from her ears and strained to listen. Her brow furrowed and her ears twitched as she cocked her head, first one way then another. Finally she looked up and bit her lip.

Ethan sighed, knowing it was bad news. Still, they needed to know. "How many, Yuliana?"

"Six," the elf said quietly. "There are six of them."

Ethan swore. He'd only seen six around the queen. Unless she had others, this was her entire guard. Why was she sending her guards to them and not keeping the spiders around her?

He didn't know and it didn't really matter. There was really no way they could handle six of the large spiders. Not with those scythe-like foreclaws. Ethan didn't know how sharp they were but he doubted any of their armor would be able to stand up to the bladed appendages.

Being skewered by giant spiders and then turned into spider food was not the way he had imagined he would die. Not that he sat around imagining ways to die, but if he had, being eaten by spiders would have been nowhere on the list.

Swearing, Ethan looked around the room. There was nothing he could use as a weapon. If he just had a large stone or something he could use as a battering ram, he could crush the spiders with it or even form it into a giant spike and run them through.

All of the stone in these rooms were the enchanted variety. It was immune to his stone shaping ability. He swore again and cursed.

They were going to be spider food and there was nothing he could do to save them. He was still thinking that when his body began to convulse and he slipped to the floor.

35

Even through his closed eyes, Ethan saw the glow of Yuliana's magic. Struggling to open his eyes, he saw the elf over his prone form along with the large feline head of Luna. The big cat sniffed at him and whined. Great. Even the cat knew he was dying.

Bringing up his HUD, he checked his stats:

```
Health: 32
  Mana: 7
  Stamina: 2
```

"Water," he rasped, his voice cracking. The convulsions had left him not only parched, but almost completely depleted of *Stamina*.

"They're coming again!" Ainslee cried. The dwarf was in the stairwell, looking down the stair-slide. Next to her was Par'karr and Nia.

Par'karr let loose with the magical shotgun but then growled in frustration. "Par'karr miss!"

Yuliana pushed one of the stone water bottles to his lips and he drank greedily. He needed to restore as much *Stamina* as possible. If he couldn't burn *Mana*, he'd burn *Stamina*.

He drank down the rest of the water and let the water bottle fall to the floor. He was about to ask the elf for some more water when realization struck him like a thunderbolt. Ethan stared down at the stone water bottle.

The water bottles! He'd shaped them from stone back in the village. He'd been wracking his brain for something he could shape into a weapon and all along, it'd been right under his nose. He swore.

"The other water bottles," he told Yuliana excitedly. "Get all of them!"

The elf looked confused but shrugged and did as he asked. She had the portal pouch next to her and reached in and began removing the bottles.

"Anyone who needs to drink," Ethan groaned, pushing himself upright. "Grab all you can drink right now!"

"We cannot..." Nia started but Ethan waved her words away weakly.

"They're stone! I can shape the stone. So drink what you can before I do! Get any stamina you can!" he told them.

The others had seen him use stone to devastating effect before. They looked at each other and then quickly grabbed one of the bottles and began to chug down the contents.

"Mm!" Par'karr grinned. "Par'karr get mead!"

"Hey," objected Ainslee. "That's mine!"

Yuliana took a few sips and then handed Ethan her bottle. "I do not need any more. You drink the rest."

While he might normally have objected, this time he

didn't. He was really parched and he needed all the *Stamina* he could get.

He drank nearly all the water before his *Stamina* was as high as it was going to get. Thankfully, his short sleep had allowed him to once again replenish his *Stamina* with water, otherwise he'd be useless.

Stamina: 32

Once he was done, he had everyone pour any remaining water into his container and then corked it. Assuming he survived long enough, he might need more water. If he didn't survive, one of the others might.

Taking the other water bottles, Ethan dipped into his *Stamina* and warped and merged the water bottles until they formed a large spike. When he was done, he had a razor-sharp two-foot-long stone spike, ready for him to send down after the spiders.

"They're almost up to the top," the dwarf screeched. Ethan could see the dwarf was nearly hysterical but was somehow managing to keep herself together.

"Get me to the edge," Ethan croaked. His throat muscles were still extremely sore from the convulsions. Actually, everything was sore, but there was nothing he could do about that now. "I need to see them."

Par'karr set down his shotgun and rushed over to Ethan. The little kobold grabbed him by the arm. The kobold strug-gled to move him, but Par'karr was just too small and Ethan too heavy.

Luckily, Ainslee came over and assisted. With barely any effort, she grabbed him by the back of his collar and dragged him to the edge. She gently put him down and then stepped away from the edge, eyes wide.

He saw why. The closest of the large spiders was less than a dozen feet away. Ethan swallowed. This close, those scythe-like forelegs looked much bigger and much more deadly. No doubt, they would make short work of anyone who got close to them. All the more reason not to let them get close.

Focusing his attention, Ethan picked up the newly fashioned stone spike with *Air* and sent it hurtling at the closest spider.

The three-eyed spider, perhaps because it did have three eyes, seemed to see the spike coming for it. It started to move its head but the spike was fast. Too fast. Before the spider could move enough, the spike buried itself into the thing's center eye.

The spider let out a high-pitch squeal and its legs convulsed. Whether it was some reflex action or whether it was trying to reach the spike in its head, Ethan didn't know. And he didn't care. He pushed the spike harder with <u>Air</u> and the sharp piece of stone burst out of the creature's head.

He thought back. Did spiders have heads or were they called something else? He didn't know and right now, he didn't care.

```
You critically hit Queen's Guardian
for 59 piercing damage.
   Queen's Guardian dies.
   You gain 70 experience. Experience
to next level 5,725.
```

The thing's legs went rigid and its other two eyes went dull. The dead spider collapsed onto the greased stone slide and began slipping back towards the one behind it.

The next spider in line tried to stop the dead spider's descent but before it could, Ethan's gore-splattered stone spike buried itself into the second spider's center eye. Like the first one, it squealed and windmilled its forelegs before Ethan forced the spike out of its head. Then it shuddered and went limp, also sliding back.

```
You  critically  hit  Queen's  Guardian
for 57 piercing damage.
   Queen's Guardian dies.
   You gain 70 experience. Experience
to next level 5,655.
```

The third spider was equally surprised, but only for a second as the spike pierced its middle eye and then was pushed through its head, leaving it a twitching corpse.

```
You  critically  hit  Queen's  Guardian
for 61 piercing damage.
   Queen's Guardian dies.
   You gain 70 experience. Experience
to next level 5,585.
```

Ethan wanted to take out the next soldier spider but he couldn't quite see it with the three bodies in his way. Growling in frustration, he brought the spike back. He set the gore and ichor-coated spike next to him.

"I am never drinking out of those bottles again," Ainslee

declared. Ethan turned his head and saw that the dwarf looked a little green. He tried to think of something clever to say but he was just too tired.

Turning back around, Ethan watched the spider corpses slide slowly down the stairs. He cursed. Due to the size of the bodies, he wasn't able to see the other spiders. "I can't see the others!"

"Just wait," Nia said. "They'll start up the steps once the bodies get to the bottom."

He nodded and waited. The bodies did reach the bottom but he didn't see the other spiders. Ethan waited some more but there was no sign of them. Were they purposely avoiding the stairs now? Did they understand what he'd done to the others?

"Why aren't they coming up?" Ethan wondered aloud.

"They see what Ethan do to other spiders!" Par'karr grinned. "Now spiders afraid."

Ethan frowned. Maybe a person would understand what Ethan had done, and that was only if they understood magic. But these were just spiders. Or were they?

Were the Queen's Guardians more intelligent? Did they understand what Ethan had done, using magic to impale their fellow spiders? The queen certainly had looked at him with intelligence. Was it really so unbelievable that the guardians had human-like reasoning skills? The concept was extremely disturbing.

"Why aren't they coming?" Ainslee asked. "They should come."

"But that's good that they're not coming?" Yuliana asked, looking from face to face. "Right?"

"Not really. I could have killed them all just now if I could have seen them." Ethan grimaced. "I don't have much time left..."

"Don't say that!" Nia demanded sharply. The foxgirl's face was pained. Maybe the foxgirl really did like him, maybe even love him. They'd never really talked about their feelings towards each other. For all he knew, she was having sex with him so he would be the alpha and let her fight.

But the sex was so good and, in so many instances, necessary, that he hadn't wanted to ask too many questions. He'd learned from previous experience that sometimes, ignorance really was bliss.

He gave the foxgirl a weak smile. "It's true. I think we all know it's true. Whatever I did back there, pulling in that mana, it hurt me. I don't know exactly how but it's killing me from the inside."

His companions' faces went grim, some of them looking down. It was true then. They had known, or at least guessed, that he was dying.

"We need to get me down there before I do die," he told them. "If I can kill these spiders, then you only have the queen to deal with."

"The really big one?" squeaked Ainslee.

"She's big." Ethan nodded. "But I didn't see wicked claws like those guardians. You should be able to take her."

"Ethan..." Nia started but then shut her mouth.

He looked at the foxgirl. "You know I'm right. Those forelegs are wicked. If I can take them out, you all have a chance."

Nia bit her lip and stared at him. Finally, she nodded.

"Wait?!" Ainslee objected. "We're going down there?! With the big mean spiders with swords as legs?"

"I should be able to take care of them," he said. "But we need to do it now, before I have an attack."

The companions looked at each other and then one by one, they nodded.

"Pack up our stuff and then let's ride this slide to the bottom." Ethan grinned.

36

They quickly packed up their bedrolls and the few other items they'd taken out of their packs. Par'karr packed Ethan's things, telling him to rest. Ethan tried to object but all of his companions insisted.

Propping himself up against the wall, Ethan watched the others get ready. He busied himself with drinking water to get his *Stamina* as high as he could. He knew he'd need it in the upcoming fight. He didn't have much *Mana*, but he could still use *Stamina*.

Ethan had gotten lucky with the three soldier spiders earlier. They'd been lined up with no real way to avoid his spike. He knew the next fight wouldn't be so easy. Not if they had any sort of human reasoning skills.

The spiders were undoubtedly waiting for them and Ethan would need to be quick if he wanted to kill them before they could do serious damage to his companions. Ethan smirked. No pressure.

In a few minutes, the group was ready. Ainslee looked

pale and Yuliana looked both afraid and unsure, but she and Luna were lined up and ready to go.

"I will go first!" Nia said in a voice that brokered no argument. Even if Ethan had wanted to argue, he didn't have the energy. Despite his *Stamina* now being at half, he felt both exhausted and feverish. He felt his head. It felt hot.

He cursed silently. His whole body felt... wrong. It was hard to explain but Ethan knew it wasn't good. He just needed to hang on for a little bit longer.

"I'll go next," Ethan told them, gripping the stone spike. He was in pain, but he tried not to let it show. He just needed to last long enough to kill these soldiers. Then he could rest. Then he could die.

Part of him was afraid of dying but another part of him was just so tired and in so much pain, he just wanted it to be over. Then there was another part of him that wondered if - no, hoped - he would just respawn somewhere or wake up in his bed at home. Either option seemed extremely unlikely, but a guy can wish.

"Me next, I guess," Ainslee muttered. The dwarf's face was pale and sweaty, but she looked down at Ethan with her good eye and set her jaw.

"Par'karr next!" the kobold said cheerfully, raising up his magical shotgun. He looked at the shotgun and then frowned. "But Par'karr only have 4 stones left."

Ethan bit his lip and nodded grimly. "Hopefully, that will be enough."

"Luna and I will come last," Yuliana said, scratching the head of the great cat. Luna looked around indifferently, probably not understanding what was about to happen.

"Alright." Ethan forced a smile. "Let's get this party started!"

"Party?!" Par'karr asked, perking up.

Ethan chuckled. "It's a figure of speech on my world. It means, let's get this over with."

The kobold gave him a toothy grin. "Start party!"

Nia shrugged and moved into position. She paused briefly and looked at Ethan. "Let us go to the party!"

Then the foxgirl leaped onto the stairs, moving quickly down the greased slide.

"Close enough." Ethan grinned and moved in front of the stairs. He pushed himself off from the top of the stairs and down the slide. Behind him, he heard Ainslee grunt as she hopped on.

The wind whipped past Ethan's ears as he accelerated down the slide. In front of him, he saw Nia slide out onto the floor and was immediately beset by spiders. Ethan released his grip on the stone spike and went to pick it up with Air when he was suddenly seized by pain as his body convulsed. He tried to scream "Not now!" but all that came out was a gurgled cry.

He thought he hit the bottom and felt a stabbing pain in his shoulder and then more pain against his back. Ethan heard screaming and other sounds but couldn't quite comprehend what was going on. Something hard hit him and then something else but he was powerless to do anything.

He struggled to force his eyes open but it was no good. His body was wracked by pain and his insides and brain were on fire. Everything was pain.

At one point, Ethan thought he saw the green glow of Yuliana's healing but it cut off abruptly. He continued to be wracked by pain. He felt like his insides were being ripped and twisted as his body continued to convulse.

Part of his mind, the part that was still semi-lucid, knew that this was probably the end. This pain would go on until he died. He didn't even care. Ethan just wanted it to be over.

Green light flared again and he gasped as his body stopped convulsing. Then a huge shape leapt over him and collided with something else. Ethan struggled to see what was happening, having to blink away tears.

Luna was attempting to fend off one of the spiders who had almost gotten close enough to run Ethan through with its sharp forelegs. Even as he watched through blinking eyes, the soldier spider sliced a long jagged gash across Luna's front.

Luna slapped at the spider with her large paw, but the soldier spider backed away with unnatural speed. The spider darted forward, both scythe-like forelegs raised to impale the big cat.

The cat didn't back away or try to dodge. She was protecting Yuliana and Ethan. She wouldn't move and leave an opening. And because the mountain lion was defending her friends, Luna was going to die.

Yuliana screamed, helpless to prevent it. She could only watch the two scythe-like legs come for Luna.

But Ethan was not helpless. He knew his *Stamina* would be low from the convulsions but he still had a little *Mana* left. He didn't know where the stone spike was so instead, he just grabbed the spider's two forelegs in *Air* and held the creature immobile.

"Tell her to kill it!" he hissed through gritted teeth. He didn't have much *Mana* and he couldn't hold the creature for long. He needed Luna to finish it off before he was out of *Mana*.

Luna seemed to understand though, or perhaps it was

just instinct at seeing a helpless prey. The cat leapt on the spider, raking it with her front and back claws.

The soldier spider let out a high-pitch squealing as the cat's huge paws slashed the thing's three eyes, causing them to burst in a spray of ichor. This caused the spider to struggle even more and Ethan was forced to expend more *Mana* to hold it in place.

The mountain lion had slipped under the spider and with her paws tearing into the creature, began wrenching the thing's head left, then right. At first nothing happened, except the spider continued to struggle but then there was a crack of spider carapace. Another crack and the head of the spider twisted off and the thing collapsed atop of the cat.

```
Queen's Guardian dies.
    You gain 35 experience. Experience
to next level 5,550.
```

Luna scrambled from underneath it, bleeding from not only the gash in the front but several other deep gashes Ethan hadn't seen before. The cat limped, favoring her left hind leg where she had one of the deep gashes.

"Luna," Yuliana sobbed as the cat limped towards them.

Ethan heard other sounds of battle and struggled to turn himself. As he faced the other side of the room, he saw Par'karr lying in a pool of blood while the remaining two spiders slashed their forelegs at Nia and Ainslee.

Both women had numerous wounds, their clothes and armor soaked with blood. Yet both fought on with ichor-stained weapons. The spiders were smeared in blood and ichor but seemed unfazed by whatever injuries they had sustained.

Nia was deflecting the scythe-like legs with her scimitars and trying to get in strikes when able but Ethan could see that the foxgirl was injured and not moving as fast as he knew she could.

Ainslee was just screaming and slapping the legs away with her shield and her hammer. She wasn't even trying to be offensive.

Still unsure where the stone spike was, Ethan reached out with <u>Air</u> and simultaneously pulled all of the legs of the spider facing Nia. Unbalanced, the creature fell to the stone floor and Nia sprang forward and buried both scimitars in the creature's eyes.

The foxgirl didn't stop. She withdrew her scimitars and slammed them in, over and over again until the creature stopped moving.

Queen's Guardian dies.
You gain 35 experience. Experience to next level 5,515.

While she was stabbing the spider, Ethan did the same with Ainslee's spider. Unfortunately, he could only grab the legs momentarily before he started seeing black spots before his eyes. He checked his stats.

Health: 19
Mana: 1
Stamina: 3

He cursed but then saw Ainslee take advantage in the momentary distraction to rush forward and slam her hammer into the spider's eyes. The dwarf screamed inarticulately as she pummeled the spider's eyes over and over again until finally, it too stopped moving.

```
Queen's Guardian dies.
   You gain 35 experience. Experience
to next level 5,480.
```

Even then, Ainslee continued to scream and slam her hammer down on the ruined head of the spider until Nia walked over and gently stopped the dwarf.

"You killed it," Nia told Ainslee. "It's dead."

Ainslee looked at the foxgirl uncomprehendingly and then glanced down at what was left of the spider's head. The dwarf blinked, staring down at the spider's body.

"Dead?" Ainslee muttered.

"It's dead," Nia nodded.

"Par'karr," Ethan groaned, pointing to the fallen kobold. "Is he alive?"

Yuliana, who Ethan saw was also bloody, limped over to Par'karr. Placing her hands on Par'karr, they glowed green for a moment.

Nothing happened for a moment but then the kobold stirred. "Par'karr.... Dead?"

"You're not dead yet," Ethan chuckled at Par'karr. "You're getting better..."

37

J ust then, a chittering from the doorway grabbed Ethan's attention. He turned and his heart skipped a beat as the head of the queen spider poked its way into the room. The thing was massive. Much larger than it had appeared from a distance.

He checked it out with his *Analyze* skill.

```
Triple-eyed Spider Queen
   Triple-eyed Spider
   Warrior
   Level 12
```

Par'karr and Yuliana, the closest to the door, scrambled back towards the stair-slide. Luna growled at the queen, ears back but made no move to attack the gigantic spider.

The soldiers had done their work well. While none of them were dead, Ethan and every single one of his companions was wounded. None of them were in decent enough shape to fight off the mammoth spider. Especially not in close quarters.

When he had imagined his companions fighting the queen, he'd thought their smaller size and maneuverability would be their main advantage. Now, they were all injured. Some of them could barely stand, let alone fight an opponent like the queen.

He pulled up his stats.

```
Health: 19
  Mana: 1
  Stamina: 3
```

Ethan swore. He had no *Mana* and no *Stamina*. He had used everything he had on the soldiers. He had nothing left.

"What do we do?!" cried Ainslee. The dwarf looked terrified but held her shield and hammer ready.

"We fight until we have no breath left in us!" Nia hissed. The foxgirl was bloody, the wound across her front still bleeding.

"Can you heal them?" Ethan asked Yuliana, nodding to Ainslee and Nia.

A pained look came across Yuliana's face. "I cannot. I used the last of my healing on Par'karr."

The kobold looked embarrassed, though it was clear from the two jagged puncture wounds in his chest and shoulder that he wouldn't have lasted much longer without the healing.

The spider continued to push itself in through the doorway, squeezing more of its bulk into the room.

Ethan swore again. He was tired, sore and in pain. And he was out of ideas. He knew he didn't have long before another fit and without Yuliana's healing, he probably wouldn't make it.

He chuckled to himself. This was it then. The end. Provided he could do anything at all, whatever he did would probably be the last thing he ever did. The thought was both sobering and liberating.

If he could come up with some idea to help his friends, maybe he could at least die a hero. He liked the sound of that. Ethan the hero.

The problem was, he was all out of ideas. He had nothing left. No *Mana*. No *Stamina*. Nothing.

"It's getting closer!" Ainslee shouted hysterically. "Tell me you have a plan, wizard-boy!"

He looked at the monstrosity of a spider that was slowly pushing itself into the room. No, Ethan didn't have a plan. He had no idea what he could possibly do to give his friends a fighting chance against this thing.

He brought up his HUD again and scanned his abilities. He didn't have enough *Stamina* or *Mana* for *Elemental Armor* or to summon a minor or lesser elemental. Even if he did, he wasn't sure how much damage an elemental would even do to the giant spider.

There was his *Enchantment* ability, but he didn't have the time nor *Mana* to try to enchant anything - even if he could think of something clever to create. Which he couldn't. He needed a rocket launcher or a kilo of C-4 explosive.

Thinking of enchanting, he looked around the room. The four Tesla coils stood dormant. They were powerful enchanted items but they had been turned off by him entering the correct sequence of runes.

If he could figure out a way to reactivate them, they would fry the giant spider. Of course, since they were in the room, he and his companions would also be electrocuted. But if he could figure out a way to get his companions out first, it might be a possibility.

The spider pushed itself even further in, now only a few feet from his companions as they huddled against the far wall.

"Can we go up the stairs?" Yuliana asked, voice breaking as she looked at the enormous spider so close.

"They're greased," Ainslee snorted. "We'd never make it in time."

Nia growled. "Come! We must fight it while it's bottled up!"

The foxgirl limped forward, scimitars out. She'd only taken two steps before one of the queen's large legs lashed out and hit Nia across the torso, tossing her into the wall like a rag doll. The foxgirl grunted as she hit the wall and the scimitars flew from her fingers.

Ainslee screamed. It was a loud, blood-curdling scream born of pain and terror. Then she charged the queen, shield first.

The giant spider tried the same trick on the dwarf but the dwarf was moving faster than the spider must have anticipated and its large foreleg only struck the dwarf a glancing blow. It was enough to arrest her momentum slightly, but not stop it altogether.

Unfortunately, it was enough that the dwarf didn't hit the spider's face with her full force. This was enough that the queen was able to get its mandibles around the dwarf's shield and hold her in position.

The queen moved another leg forward and struck the dwarf on the side. The blow knocked the dwarf away, ripping the shield from her arm and sending her hammer spinning away.

Ethan swore. Their two best fighters had just been smacked around and disarmed in seconds. They were simply no match for the huge creature in such close quarters. It was too big and too strong.

Feeling helpless, he glanced back at his list of abilities. There was only one more ability he hadn't looked at. *Over-channel.* He looked at the description in his HUD.

```
Over-channel
   Type: Wizard
   Cost: Special
   Range: Self
   Duration: Special
   Description: The caster channels his
physical and mental fortitude into raw
magical energy.
   Warning: May cause permanent loss of
ability scores.
```

Over-channel was the ability he'd gained when he'd used too much *Mana* the first time he'd used too much magic. The ability converted his stats into raw energy, or *Mana*. It had also kicked in when he'd inadvertently discovered portal magic the first time.

He winced as he remembered the incident. It had taken a heavy toll on him and he'd needed weeks before he fully recovered from all of the stat damage. The hit to his *Hardiness* had been especially hard since he'd had severely reduced *Health* and *Stamina* for over a week.

Of course, none of that mattered right now. The spider was seconds from reaching them and killing them all. And he was probably only minutes from another fit that would kill him. He literally had nothing to lose. Either way he was going to die.

Steeling himself for what he had to do, he looked around to his companions. He couldn't save himself, but maybe, just maybe, he could save them.

Maybe his friends would remember him as a hero and tell stories about him. Ethan smiled. He'd like to be remembered as a hero.

"Move away from the stairs!" he shouted, getting confused stares from his companions. "Get ready to run through the far door."

"There's a big honkin' spider in the way," Ainslee retorted, as she climbed to her feet.

"Not in a moment, there won't be," he muttered and then willed *Over-channel* on. Surprisingly, it worked.

Over-channel Active.

He reached out with *Air*, feeling the power come from his very essence. It was a singularly uncomfortable feeling, one that had happened so fast last time that he hadn't really felt it before he'd passed out. Now, slowly channeling his life away, he felt it tearing at his very soul. His insides twisted up but he was already in so much pain, he barely noticed.

Ethan grit his teeth and grabbed the queen with everything he could muster. Using the tendrils of *Air*, he yanked the spider forward. The spider jerked and lashed out at the invisible bonds that grabbed it but it was literally like swatting air.

He didn't stop yanking and pulled the spider through the

room and jammed it into the staircase. At least, that's what he attempted to do. The spider was quick and got its legs up on either side of the staircase, trying to pull itself out.

Ethan continued to push, feeling more of his essence burn away. He grimaced as he pushed harder and managed to shout out to his friends. "Go! Get out!"

Yuliana and Ainslee made a run for the doorway, followed by Luna. Par'karr and Nia looked from the door to Ethan and back.

"Go!" he cried out. "I can't hold her much longer!"

The foxgirl and kobold exchanged looks, some silent agreement passing between them. Then, they ran over and grabbed Ethan by the arms and dragged him towards the doorway.

"Leave me!" he pleaded, feeling his strength waning. He didn't have much left. It was taking enormous energy to hold the giant spider back. But his companions didn't listen and dragged him out of the room into a small corridor.

As Ethan passed through the doorway, he did sense the enchantments that had operated the door and the rune puzzle. He'd also sensed the battery that kept the door down. He felt the *Mana* pulsing in it. An idea flashed through his head. One last thing to do. One last thing to be the hero.

Letting go of the *Air* holding the queen, he reached down into the battery and yanked the magic out of it, just like he had with the dragon eyes.

He felt his body burning, but he didn't care. Rumbling from the floor told him he'd done his job and the door began to slide up.

The queen, who'd spun around with amazing agility, threw herself at the doorway as it tried to escape. The three bulbous eyes stared at Ethan with undisguised hatred.

Coughing up blood, he flipped off the spider and then slammed it back with a burst of *Air* as the door continued to close. Blackness swam in the edges of his vision and he knew he was getting close to the end. So be it.

Ethan kept pushing the queen back as it glared at him and struggling against his *Air*, glaring back at the great spider. It became a contest of wills: The queen trying to break free and get through the door and Ethan struggling to hold onto the spider while holding onto consciousness.

Just when Ethan couldn't take it any longer, he heard the sweetest sound he could imagine. The sound of a Tesla coil discharging. There was a bright flash as an arc of electricity slammed into the queen, causing it to twitch and convulse. The giant spider emitted a high-pitched screech, like a cry.

Another zapping sound as a second coil discharged, causing the spider's limbs to twitch in a strange sort of dance. Then another bolt slammed into it and Ethan dropped his channeling as the door continued to rise and the spider continued to screech until finally the door slammed shut.

The last thing Ethan saw before he fell into the inky blackness was a system message. Through the pain, he smiled.

Triple-eyed Spider Queen dies.
    You gain 120 experience. Experience to next level 5,360.

38

Ethan's eyes shot open as he felt like he was drowning. He coughed and sputtered as he coughed up water. He continued to hack up water for several seconds, unable to focus or do anything else but try to breathe. Finally, he got the coughing under control and took in a deep breath of air.

He blinked and tried to focus on his surroundings. In front of him was Nia, holding a large, golden chalice encrusted with glowing blue crystals. Chymera crystals, he knew. She smiled at him.

"It worked," she said with relief. "The water restored some of his stamina and he is awake."

He was still trying to wrap his head around why he was alive at all. Ethan had used up all of his *Mana*, *Stamina* and even burned his stat points on the queen. He literally had nothing left when he blacked out. So why was he alive?

Ethan's body felt warm and tingly, causing him to shiver involuntarily. He also felt a strong itching sensation from his back. He tried to sit up but Nia put a restraining hand on his chest. "Rest, Ethan."

The strange thing was, Ethan didn't feel like he needed to rest. In fact, the longer he was awake, the better he felt. Had Yuliana already healed him?

"Is it me, or does wizard-boy look a lot better all of a sudden?" Ainslee asked.

He looked past Nia and saw the rest of his companions nearby. They were standing, but none of them looked good. Each of them were covered in blood and bore various wounds from the fight with the spiders.

Looking past his companions, he saw that they were in a large chamber. From his vantage point, lying down, he couldn't see exactly how large. Ethan could see that the walls and floors were covered in spiderwebs.

"What is this place?" Ethan asked.

Ainslee shrugged. "Don't really know. But there's a pool in the middle of it with a stone coffin surrounded by a pool of water. Sparkly water. That's where we got the gold cup. At the bottom of the pool."

Ethan's eyes went wide as her words sank in. There was a sarcophagus and the golden cup had been on top of it? If that was Arthur's sarcophagus, then that made the golden cup...

"The Holy Grail," Ethan muttered, staring at the chalice still in Nia's hand.

"What?" Nia asked, following his gaze to the Grail in her hand.

Ethan swore. "The cup. It's got to be the Holy Grail."

"The holy what?" Ainslee asked, brow furrowed.

"The Holy Grail," Ethan said. "The magical cup that King

Arthur and his knights were searching for in the stories. It's said to be able to heal any wound."

Excitement flooding him, Ethan popped open his HUD. There were dozens of messages waiting for him. Most were from the fight and he saw he had indeed burned up a ton of his stats in his final conflict with the queen. He'd also gotten a skill up in *Air* magic, giving him another point in *Intellect*. Then he scrolled down to the newer messages.

There he saw it.

```
You   have   drunk   the   water   of   the
Fountain of Youth.
    You have been Healed.
    New ability: Immortality.
```

Ethan's heart skipped a beat as he read the new ability. He went back and read it again, just to make sure he hadn't read it wrong. He had a new ability called *Immortality*. He quickly brought up the description of the new ability.

```
Immortality
    Type: Special
    Cost: N/A
    Range: N/A
    Duration: N/A
    Description:  Arrests   the   natural
physical aging of any living creature.
The  creature  remains  the  same  age  as
when they first received the ability.
```

Ethan whistled. If he understood the description

correctly, he would no longer age. He'd stay 29 forever. Or was he 30 now? He'd lost track of the days and weeks he'd been on this world. His birthday had only been three months away when he'd arrived. Not that it mattered anymore.

It appeared that the *Immortality* he now had would stop him from aging or dying from old age, but he wasn't immortal in the god-like sense of being unable to die. He might not die of old age, but he could still die of an arrow to the chest.

He wasn't sure how he felt about living forever. He was still trying to process everything that had happened. It was too much to wrap his head around at the moment.

"I'm... immortal," Ethan muttered, looking around at his companions.

"I think maybe he's still loopy," Ainslee snorted. "He's delusional."

He quickly checked his stats.

```
Strength: 10
  Agility: 13
  Hardiness: 16
  Intellect: 30
  Intuition: 15
  Charisma: 12
  Health: 32
  Energy: 70
  Stamina: 64
```

He was completely healed. His *Health*, *Stamina* and *Mana* were all at maximum and whatever stat damage he'd incurred was completely healed as well. He grinned.

"I'm not delusional." Ethan grinned and gently removed

Nia's hand before getting to his feet. "The Holy Grail. It healed me. And according to the system message, the water is the Fountain of Youth."

"What is the fountain of youth?" Yuliana asked.

"It's a legend from my world," he replied excitedly. "It gives the drinker eternal youth."

"Eternal youth?" Ainslee made a face. "Did you hit your head or something?"

"No!" Ethan grinned. "I'm completely healed and all of my mana and stamina are restored. The Grail did it... or the combination of the Grail and the water did it. Look at me. I'm completely better."

His companions regarded him skeptically but Nia walked around him and ran a finger down a spot on his shoulder blade. "His wound is completely gone. There is not even a scar."

"What wound?" Ethan asked. He vaguely remembered a pain in his back, but he had been in so much pain, it was hard to remember a specific pain. Ignoring him, Yuliana, Ainslee and Par'karr rushed over and examined his back.

While they stared and prodded his back, Nia came around to face him. She was still bloody, with scrapes and cuts littering her body. Her left hand clutched a bloody cloth over her abdomen.

"You should drink from the Grail," he told her. As he spoke, he scrutinized the Holy Grail in his HUD and *Appraised* it.

```
The Holy Grail
   Type: Cup
   Range: Special
   Damage: Special
```

Durability: Special

Special: A drink from the Holy Grail performs a Complete Heal. A Complete Heal cures all ailments, restores all ability damage and heals all wounds to a living creature. A creature can only use it once per day.

Skill increase: Appraise +1%.

It was the Holy Grail. The magical cup that King Arthur and the Knights of Camelot had quested for. Obviously, the knights had found it. Or was that just a story in his world? Was it just a powerful magic item in this world?

Ethan looked over the chalice in Nia's hand. It had dozens of Chymera crystals embedded in it. Probing them, he found that he couldn't make heads or tails of the enchantments. Whoever had created the Grail was light-years beyond Ethan's meager skill.

He glanced at the stone coffin. It looked more like a sarcophagus than a coffin with carvings along the sides. Was this the final resting place of King Arthur? And if so, why had they buried the Grail with him? Was Excalibur here as well?!

"We all should." Nia nodded. The foxgirl turned and, taking the chalice, began walking towards a raised dais with a large sarcophagus. As she did, Ethan took a better look around the large circular chamber.

The chamber was huge, easily two hundred feet in diameter. It was also covered in spiderwebs. Lots of spiderwebs. There were webs all over the walls, on the floors and across the ceilings. Scattered throughout the webs were cocoons. Were the cocoons previous victims? But from where?

As Ethan glanced over the walls, he saw that part of the wall had collapsed inward, revealing a tunnel not unlike the one they'd seen back in the corridor near the spike room. Had the spiders tunneled in? Or had some sort of tremor caused it to collapse?

Nia had reached the pool. Bending down, the foxgirl filled the golden chalice with water from the pool. Bringing the cup to her lips, she took a long sip.

Ethan was watching her when she took the sip, so he managed to actually see cuts and wounds on her back heal before his eyes. It was like he was watching the healing process in super fast motion, only there weren't even any scars when they were done.

Nia gasped and fell back, clutching her abdomen tightly. She let the grail slip from her fingers as she brought both hands to her abdomen.

Ethan rushed forward and knelt down next to her. Her eyes were closed and her face was contorted in pain, her breath coming quickly.

"Are you okay, Nia?" he demanded. "Are you okay?"

The pained expression lasted for a few more seconds and then her face relaxed and her eyes popped open. She looked around and smiled at Ethan. Then she stood up quickly and pulled the bloody cloth from her abdomen.

Nia and Ethan both looked. Her abdomen was bloody and dirty, but there was no sign of a wound. None at all.

The foxgirl looked up with a big grin. "You were right. I am completely healed!"

"Check your abilities on your HUD. See if you have one called immortality," he told her.

Her eyes went dull for a moment while she accessed her

HUD and then they went wide. "Yes. I have an ability called immortality. This means... I will not grow old?"

Ethan nodded. "Physically, you will stay the same age. Forever."

Nia opened and closed her mouth several times, apparently as overwhelmed as Ethan had been on learning about his immortality. Finally, the foxgirl bit her lip. "This is much to think about."

He nodded in understanding. Ethan still couldn't quite wrap his head around it, let alone get a handle on all of the repercussions of immortality. But there would be time for that later.

"Par'karr drink?" the little kobold asked, stopping in front of the Grail.

"Sure," Ethan told him and then turned to Ainslee and Yuliana. "You two should drink as well."

Par'karr drank with similar results. All of his wounds were completely healed. Then Yuliana had her turn and she even gave some of the water to Luna. Both were healed completely, all of their wounds vanishing.

Then it was Ainslee's turn. The dwarf huffed and took the Grail from Yuliana. "This would be the perfect cup to drink mead from, you know."

The dwarf dipped the cup into the sparkling waters and then took a sip. Immediately the dwarf began to gag and cough, her eyes going wide. She fell back, screaming and twitching.

Ethan started towards the dwarf but stopped in his tracks. As he watched, the dwarf's wounds from the spiders healed. But not only those wounds, also the acid burns to the right half of her body she'd received from the Tatzelwurm.

The dwarf continued to twitch as the burned flesh seemed to dissolve into healthy, normal skin. The scarred tissue just disappeared. Then, Ethan watched as the white orb that had been her damaged eye seemed to bubble and reform, ending in a perfectly formed eye. In less than a minute, the dwarf lay gasping on the ground, completely restored.

"Ainslee," Ethan said. He kneeled down and shook the dwarf. "Are you okay?"

Her eyes popped open and she looked around. She blinked, probably realizing she could see out of both eyes again. She moved her hand in front of her eyes, then closed one eye, then the other. She grinned. Then she brought her hand to her face and ran it across the new, ebony skin and Ethan saw both eyes go moist.

"I'm... I'm healed?" the dwarf asked in wonder, eyes wide. "The scars are gone..."

Ethan looked at the flawless skin and grinned back at her. "Good as new."

39

———

"Go look at your reflection in the pool," Ethan suggested to the dwarf, who was still looking over her restored arm in wonder and fascination.

Nodding numbly, the dwarf let the Grail fall to the ground and hurried over to the pool of sparkling water. Bending down, she peered into the pool. Ethan wasn't sure, but he thought he heard Ainslee sobbing quietly.

Now that he was healed and out of immediate danger, Ethan noticed a nagging in the back of his head. It had been there since they started out, but with everything going on, he hadn't been able to focus on it. Now that he was healed and feeling refreshed, the little nagging had become a pulling sensation. And that pulling sensation kept pointing him at the Grail.

Testing it out, he faced different directions but each time, the pulling pointed towards the Grail. It was a very odd feeling. He looked around at his companions. "Anyone else feel a...uh... pulling sensation towards the Grail?"

His friends exchanged glances and shook their heads. Ethan frowned and walked over to the Grail. The closer he got, the stronger it felt. He reached down and picked up the Grail. The moment he did, he felt a new tugging sensation towards the sarcophagus. It was almost as if the Grail was telling him to go there.

Unsure if he should follow these odd sensations, Ethan nevertheless walked across the small bridge over the pool of water to the small island in the center where the sarcophagus lay.

"What are you doing, Ethan?" Nia asked him, her voice concerned and curious.

"I think... I think the Grail wants me to take it to the sarcophagus," he answered. He approached.

"Cup talking?" Par'karr asked, cocking his head and squinting at the golden chalice.

"I'm not sure," Ethan replied. He was right in front of the sarcophagus and now he could make out the detailed carving of a knight on the lid. No, not a knight. A king, judging by the crown on his head. This had to be it. The tomb of the king, Arthur Pendragon.

The king had been carved lying down with his eyes closed and his hands folded over his chest. The carving was clad in armor, save for the face, which was bare. The king sported a well-kept beard and a crown. He looked at peace.

Looking at the lid, what really drew Ethan's attention was the flat, circular spot between Arthur's hands. It was slightly indented and seemed the perfect place to rest the Grail. Ethan looked at the Grail's base. Mentally, he compared it to the circular spot. They seemed a perfect match.

Ethan placed the Grail on the spot. Just like he

suspected, it fit perfectly. He let go of the chalice and instantly, the pulling sensation was gone. He waited. It didn't come back. Reaching out, he removed the Grail and instantly the sensation came back. When he put it back, the sensation stopped.

```
Quest Complete.
   Starving Villagers I
   Your town is running out of food.
You have told Fearghas the Innkeeper
that you will look into lack of game
in the area surrounding the village.
   Discover why there is no game around
Hawkshead (1/1).
   You gain 500 experience.
   You   gain   +250   reputation   with
Residents of Hawkshead.
   You   gain   +250   reputation   with
Farmers of Arrowpoint Valley.
   You   have   received   a   new   quest
"Starving Villagers II"
   Report your findings to the Fearghas
the Innkeeper and tell him the game
will return.
   Report to Fearghas (0/1).
   Reward:   500   experience,   +250
reputation   with   Residents   of
Hawkshead,   +250   reputation   with
Farmers of Arrowpoint Valley
   Accept quest (yes or no)?
```

Ethan read over the messages in his HUD. According to

the messages, he'd completed the quest. Had the Grail really been the source of the sound? He couldn't hear the sound, but was he somehow sensing its magic? Maybe there was some sort of resonance to the magic. After all, what magic had caused the sound was obviously powerful enough to affect an entire valley.

"Did you all get a quest update?" he asked. He went ahead and accepted the second quest. Reporting back should be easy. He frowned. Once they found a way out of here.

The others, some of whom were glassy eyed as they looked at their own HUDs, nodded. Smiling, he turned to Yuliana. "Can you take off your magic necklace?"

"So we solved it?" Ainslee asked, face screwed up in confusion.

"That's what I want to test," Ethan responded, still looking at Yuliana.

The elf looked at him and bit her lip. Obviously, she wasn't keen on feeling the pain of the sound again even if the quest message said they solved it.

"I think we found the source of the sound." He gave her a reassuring smile. "At least, that's what the quest says. We have to test it."

Brows still furrowed, she took a deep breath and nodded. She reached down to the necklace he'd made to protect her against the high-pitched sound and slowly lifted it. Once it was completely over her head, she blinked and looked around. Then she smiled. "It is gone! I cannot hear the sound!"

Ethan nodded. "Okay. I need to do a little experiment to make sure. I'm going to lift the Grail off its spot. If I'm right, the sound will return. Just be ready, okay?"

The green-haired elf gave him a dubious look but nodded. Reaching out, he pulled the Grail off the sarcophagus. Instantly, the elf's face became pained and she quickly brought the necklace back down over her head, gasping and then rubbing her temples.

"It's much more... intense here." The elf grimaced.

"Sorry." Ethan quickly replaced the Grail and offered the elf an apologetic shrug. "I just needed to make sure it was actually the Holy Grail causing the sound."

"So that was it this whole time?" Ainslee asked, standing up in front of the pool. "A gold cup?"

Ethan considered her words and then regarded the cup and the sarcophagus. He actually wasn't sure which of the two were causing the sound. It could be an enchantment on either. He certainly sensed strong enchantments on both. Strong and complicated. He couldn't make heads or tails of them.

"I'm not sure," he admitted. "But either the Grail is making the sound when it's removed or the sarcophagus makes the sound when the Grail isn't resting on it."

Ethan looked around the room. "Where was the Grail when you found it? Was it on the sarcophagus?"

Ainslee shook her head and pointed into the pool. "It was in the water, near the pool. Nia was yelling for me to get you some water and I was going to cup some in my hands, then I saw it sitting there at the bottom of the pool and pulled it out."

Nodding, Ethan remembered they'd mentioned that before. It hadn't been on the sarcophagus when they'd arrived. He glanced around the room, his eyes resting on the collapsed wall and the tunnel beyond. He was starting to formulate an idea of what had happened.

"I think that whatever caused that hole," he told the group, pointing to the gaping hole in the wall, "caused the Grail to fall off the sarcophagus. That's when the sound started."

"Could be, wizard-boy," the dwarf replied and walked over to the hole. She had to scramble around the spider webs and cocoons but eventually made her way over to it.

Ainslee stopped just outside the hole and held up her lightstone, looking around the hole. She nodded her head and muttered some words for several minutes before turning around. "Doesn't look like it was dug out. Probably collapsed. Either the natural stress of the stone, or some sort of quake or tremor."

"An earthquake?" Ethan asked. "Wouldn't the villagers have felt it?"

The dwarf shrugged. "Maybe. Maybe not. It could have been very localized. It might only have affected the mountains nearby. They might not have felt anything that far south."

Ethan nodded. "So something happened, probably a minor quake, and it caused this wall and that passage near the spike room to collapse inward. It must have opened into some larger cavern or tunnel system where the spiders lived. They must have moved in and made this home."

He saw Ainslee shudder. She glanced towards the door where the spider queen had died. "Could be."

"This seems like a lot of spider webs for a short period of time," Nia commented.

Looking around, Ethan shrugged. "Maybe, but spiders can make webs pretty quickly. And there were a ton of them."

Nia nodded and the rest of the group nodded their

agreement. They had all fought the spiders; they were all too familiar with how many there had been.

"You....uh... think..." Ainslee muttered, backing away from the entrance. "That more spiders live... down there."

"Possibly." Ethan shrugged. He remembered all the spiders they'd found, plus the soldier spiders and then the queen spider. "But what did they eat? I mean, there were a ton of spiders. I don't know how often spiders have to eat, but you would think that with that many spiders, they'd need a pretty constant diet of... something."

All of his companions exchanged concerned looks. And with good reason. If the passages to the mine were sealed off, where were the spiders getting their food?

Ethan and the others stared into the dark passage that led out of the chamber. If they weren't getting their food from outside the mine, what else might live in the inky darkness of the passage. Was there some sort of underground realm?

Nia spoke, startling Ethan out of his imaginings. She pointed to one of the cocoons. "Perhaps opening one of these will tell us what they have been eating."

40

The group gathered around one of the cocoons and stared at it for a long moment. Ethan wondered if, like him, they were thinking about just how close they'd all come to ending up in one of them.

Walking around the cocoon, he could see that its dimensions varied from point to point and its shape was slightly irregular. He guessed it was about six feet tall and about four feet wide at its tallest and widest points. It also reeked of decay and he resisted the urge to cover his nose.

"What do you think is in there?" Ainslee asked, squinting at the webbed bundle.

"Maybe human?" Par'karr suggested, gesturing to the height. "Too tall for kobold."

"Too big for a dwarf too," Ainslee said. The dwarf looked the cocoon up and down. "Only one way to find out."

Everyone muttered their agreement and Nia stepped forward with her scimitars. The foxgirl began slicing at the wrappings of the cocoon, being careful to avoid whatever might be inside.

Ethan tried helping with his knife, but the small blade quickly got stuck in the sticky strands and he had to give up.

After a few minutes of hacking into the tough cocoon, the thing suddenly collapsed and the occupant crashed to the floor, startling them. Almost as one, the group hopped back from the desiccated corpse staring up at them with empty eye sockets.

Ainslee screwed up her face in disgust. "It stinks!"

This time, Ethan did cover his mouth and nose, as the stench of the rotting corpse filled the area. The others quickly did the same and Yuliana backed away almost a dozen paces.

"What is that thing?" Yuliana gasped, clearly trying not to retch.

Ethan stared down at the withered husk. The body was similar to a human, but very slim. Even though the limbs were shriveled, they were still thinner than most normal human's. Plus, there was something oddly long about the limbs. The fingers were longer than a humans and had an extra joint.

But that wasn't the most noticeable thing. The creature's head resembled a squid's head with six tentacles hanging down. Like the rest of the body, the tentacles were desiccated, but Ethan guessed four of them were about two feet long while two of them were at least four feet long.

The creature reminded Ethan of something out of a horror movie or some sort of H.P. Lovecraft book. Not something he'd want to meet in some dark cavern.

Despite this, he bent over and examined the body. The cause of death was obvious, but it did get him a skill up in his *Forensics* skill.

Skill increase: Forensics +1%.

"I don't know," he said. "Par'karr, have you seen or heard of a creature like this?"

"Par'karr not see this before." The wide-eyed kobold shook his head. "Par'karr glad he not see this before!"

"Do any of your worlds have creatures like these?" he asked, looking around at the women.

They all shook their heads. Ethan nodded. Another alien species maybe? Maybe even a native to this world or a channeler who'd gone through an extreme transformation. The fact that Par'karr hadn't seen it could mean it was subterranean. A thought occurred to him. "Let's open up one of the other cocoons."

"Why?" Ainslee screwed up her face in disgust. "This one smells bad enough."

"I want to know if this thing is a loner or if there are more of these creatures roaming the tunnels," he told them.

"Why does it matter?" Yuliana asked, looking down at the corpse. "It is dead now."

"True," Ethan agreed. "But if the spiders were feeding on them, there might be more. For all we know, there could be an entire underground city of them not far from here. Or, this could be some channeler who transformed fully into whatever demon he served."

"A city?" Nia asked, her face screwed up in disgust. "Underground?"

"We got underground cities like that." Ainslee nodded with a grin. "Big cities."

"Underground?" Yuliana frowned. "With no sunlight?"

Ainslee grinned. "On my world, there are crystals that

generate light underground. Some of them are hundreds of feet tall. The cities are in gigantic caverns full of them."

The elf shivered. "I could not live without being able to see the sun."

"You get used to it." The dwarf shrugged.

"Come," Nia hissed. "Let us open another of these cocoons and then leave this place. We have been in this place too long and I would like to be out in the open air. And we have yet to find a way out."

Ethan frowned, knowing she was right. He'd been hoping there would be an exit in this room but he hadn't given up hope yet. Most of the walls and floors were covered in webbing. Could there still be something behind all of the webs. Maybe a secret door?

At least, that's what he hoped. The alternative was to try and retrace their steps. Theoretically, it would be much easier now that they knew the traps and the spiders were, seemingly, gone. But he'd almost killed himself pulling Mana from some of the doors. He had no desire to go through that pain again.

Nia finished cutting open the second cocoon and another of the squid-headed humanoids spilled out onto the floor. Two of them meant they were probably a race of beings and not just some transformed channeler.

The new corpse wasn't quite as desiccated as the first. It was still... gooey. Even from a few feet away, Ethan caught the stench of it. If it were possible, it smelled even worse than the first one. Ainslee made a face and backed away. Luna whined and padded away. And this time, Yuliana did lose her lunch and went to retch in the corner.

"Eww! Loki's Balls! This one stinks worse than the first one," Ainslee muttered.

"Ethan!" Nia called out excitedly. "Look!"

Trying to breathe through his mouth, Ethan walked over to the corpse. He followed the foxgirl's gaze to a shiny medallion on a thick silver necklace around the thing's neck just visible between two of the tentacles. The most interesting part of the medallion was the circle of glowing blue Chymera crystals.

"Good eyes," he told the foxgirl. He bent down and examined the body, finding the tell-tale sign of a spider bite and earning him another skill up in *Forensics*.

Skill increase: Forensics +1%.

Having gotten his skill up, he focused on the necklace. Wary of the tentacles, he reached in and pulled at the medallion. It budged but the necklace was around the thing's neck and buried under tentacles.

Ethan began to try and get it untangled from the creature, struggling to get it underneath the two larger tentacles. After a minute, he heard a frustrated huff from Nia and there was a flash of steel as her scimitar sliced through the tentacles.

Putting her scimitars away, she raised an eyebrow. "Better?"

Looking from the severed tentacles to the foxgirl, he nodded. "Better."

With the tentacles out of the way, he was able to retrieve the medallion much easier. In the process, he learned that in the middle of the tentacles was a beak, much like the squids and octopi of Earth.

"It has a beak? Like a bird?" Yuliana asked as she caught sight of it.

"Gross!" Ainslee muttered.

Ethan barely heard the exchange. He was examining the amulet, trying to sense the spells in the crystals. Previously, he had been able to sense at least something about the enchantment. Sometimes, it was too complicated for him to understand - like most of the enchantments in the tomb.

This time, as he reached out into the crystals, he almost felt like something was reaching back into his mind. It was a strange feeling at first but then seemed to launch itself into his brain like a red-hot knife.

"Ugh!" He grimaced as he dropped the medallion and put his hands to his head.

"Ethan!" Nia exclaimed. "What is wrong?"

"My head," he said through gritted teeth. It had felt like he'd gotten an instant migraine headache but it was quickly receding.

Nia came over and put a hand on his shoulder. He looked up at her and gave her a reassuring smile. "I'm better. I think it was the necklace."

He looked down at the medallion. What had happened? Was that some sort of defense mechanism enchantment? Something to prevent another wizard from figuring out the enchantment. It seemed like that could be a thing - like a sort of encryption.

And yet. He'd felt something strange when it had happened. Almost like... a presence. He frowned down at the medallion. He was loath to pick it up again, considering the pain he'd experienced.

"We should leave it," the foxgirl said.

"No way," Ainslee shook her head. "That's probably worth an entire keg of mead!"

Still, he didn't want to just leave. Nor did he want any of

his companions touching it. He still felt like shivering when he remembered that presence in his head.

"Don't touch it," he told them, still rubbing his head. "There's some sort of enchantment on it. Maybe some sort of protection magic."

They all backed away. All except Nia, who stayed next to him. She gave him a hard look. "You should leave it."

"I want to study it," he told her. "There might be something I can learn from it."

She frowned but nodded. "You should not touch it again."

"On that," Ethan smiled at her again, "we agree."

He pulled out his dagger and, reaching down, picked up the medallion by the chain using the blade of the knife and carefully stuck it into one of his pouches. He replaced his dagger and looked at Nia. "See, not touching it."

The foxgirl rolled her eyes at him. "I still think you should leave it."

Ethan looked to the passageway that had collapsed into the chamber. Somewhere, down that passage was where these squid-headed creatures had come from. He had no desire to go down that passage. Nor did he want to leave it unsealed so that any more spiders or squid people could find Arthur's Tomb - especially not the Holy Grail.

"We need to seal this up," he told his companions.

"I would not relish entering the cave," Yuliana said, looking into the darkness. "But what if it is the only way out?"

Ethan shook his head. "If there was a way out down there, I think the spiders would have gone outside instead of coming into this chamber."

"I'm with you, wizard-boy," Ainslee said. "Let's seal those things away for good!"

41

———

Ethan and the group went to the collapsed wall and the tunnel that led into the darkness. Summoning several balls of light, he sent them into the tunnel. Unsurprisingly, they revealed a long tunnel covered in spider webs.

"Those spiders sure were busy," Ainslee muttered, eyes darting around the tunnel. "You suppose there are any more of them?"

"If there were more, they would have come by now," Nia answered, though Ethan noticed the foxgirl kept her hands on the hilts of her scimitars. "We have been very noisy."

Ethan looked around the tunnel. He couldn't even see the stone through all the webs. Still, he didn't need to see the stone to manipulate it. He stretched out his arms to help him focus.

"Whoa! Whoa, wizard-boy!" yelled Ainslee, pulling his arm down. "What are you doing?"

Ethan scrunched up his face in confusion as he looked at the dwarf. "Sealing it up. Isn't that what we just decided on?"

The dwarf snorted and rolled her eyes. "What did I tell you last time! You can't just go wizarding rock like that! You'll bring this whole place down on us!"

Ethan looked around the tunnel and then lowered his other hand. His head was still hurting from the medallion and he hadn't been thinking clearly. He remembered the dwarf's earlier admonishment about causing a cave-in with the other collapsed tunnel.

He gave the dwarf a sheepish look. "Sorry, I didn't think about that. How should I seal it up?"

"Humans!" she snorted, but there was no venom in her tone. The dwarf looked at the sides of the tunnel and then furrowed her brow. She looked back at Ethan. "I can't tell without seeing the stone and right now the webbing is in the way."

"I could burn it away," Ethan suggested.

The dwarf nodded and then gestured into the room. "You should burn the webbing in the room too. I need to see if any of the walls are cracked. We don't want the entire chamber collapsing on us."

"How will you burn the webbing, without burning us?" Yuliana asked in alarm.

"Or choking!" Par'karr said, bringing his hands up to his throat. "Smoke not good to breathe!"

Ethan bit his lip as he considered his options. He looked around the chamber and then down the tunnel. Then he smiled.

"If we all stand in the pool, the water should keep us from getting burned," Ethan told the others and they all looked back at the pool.

"And the smoke?" Yuliana asked. "Par'karr is right, the smoke will suffocate us."

Nodding, Ethan pointed down the tunnel. "I think I can burn the webs with fire and use air to blow the smoke down the tunnel. We'll get some smoke, but most of it should go out of this room."

The others accepted his idea and they all went and hopped into the pool of sparkling water. Ethan couldn't go into the water with them. There was a lot of webbing to burn and he wanted to conserve his *Mana* as much as possible. That meant being close.

Ethan should be able to control the fire, but just in case, he wet his clothes in the pool. He'd just been healed from what he had thought would be his death. He had a second chance and he wasn't about to tempt fate so soon.

Starting at the far wall, Ethan began to burn the webbing on the floor and walls. He shot out a spray of fire from one hand while funneling the smoke out the tunnel with the other hand. It mostly worked, though some smoke drifted upwards. Luckily, the high, domed ceiling should prevent it from filling up the chamber below. At least, he hoped that was the case. Smoke rose right? Wasn't that why they told you to crawl out of a burning building?

Other than the smoke, the main problem was the smell. The webs smelled foul as they burned and when he burned a cocoon, it smelled like burning sewage as they went up in flames. Soon, he was fighting the urge to vomit.

He stopped and tied a wet piece of cloth over his mouth, like a cowboy in the old films, hoping it would help. And while a kerchief might protect cowboys from dust on the trail, he quickly found it did little to block the stench.

He wasn't the only one either. Ethan heard the others complaining too, especially Ainslee. Par'karr even got sick, as did Yuliana, and retched on the edge of the pool.

Surprisingly, the only one who didn't seem affected was Nia. He found that odd, considering how good her sense of smell was. Perhaps because she was used to smelling so many different things at once, it was easier for her to block out. He made a note to ask her later.

Ethan continued for a half hour, burning away webbing and cocoons until the entire chamber was clear. Once he was done with the chamber, he cleared about twenty feet of tunnel, burning everything to ash, before he finally quit.

Throughout the process, he had gotten dozens of skill increases in *Air* and *Fire* but neither skill had actually leveled up. Ethan checked his *Mana*.

Mana: 9

Not bad. He'd cleared the entire chamber and a bit of the tunnel, using two different skills and Ethan still had a bit of *Mana* left.

He turned around. Glancing about the chamber, he was able to see it for the first time without webs. What he saw were stone murals of various battles. It seemed like depictions of the deeds of King Arthur and the Knights.

Looking around, Ethan found what he thought was the beginning. It was a depiction of a man in robes standing by a younger man pulling a sword from a stone. It had to be Arthur pulling Excalibur from the stone, just like in the legends. Did that mean the sword really existed?

Ethan glanced back to the sarcophagus. Was the sword inside with Arthur? He'd really love to see the real Excalibur, but there was no way he was opening the tomb - even if he could. He imagined an undead king rising to destroy those who had dared disturb his slumber. No thank you.

"What is that?" Yuliana asked, coming up behind him.

Ethan shook himself out of his thoughts of the undead as his companions came to stand with him, looking at the stone murals. Ethan pointed to the carving. "On my world, we have a story of King Arthur pulling a magical sword, called Excalibur, from a stone and becoming king."

"How does pulling a sword from a stone make this man a king?" Nia asked, her brows furrowed. "Did he have to face others to win the right to pull the sword?"

"No," Ethan replied, trying to remember the exact details of the story. Had he actually fought for the right to pull the sword? He'd never actually read the original myths, mostly he'd just watched the movies. But he remembered there was a prophecy. "The blade could only be pulled out of the stone by the rightful ruler of the land."

"That is a strange way to pick an alpha," Nia told him.

"Really strange," Ainslee agreed. "Didn't anyone think to just crack the stone?"

Ethan opened his mouth to reply but then closed his mouth and shrugged. "I don't remember anyone ever trying that."

Ainslee grinned smugly. "Cause he didn't have a dwarf with him."

"Luckily," Ethan returned her grin, "we do!"

"These are like kobold cave drawings!" Par'karr exclaimed. "They tell story!"

Ethan nodded to the little kobold. "I think you're right."

They walked around the room, looking at the stone images in order and Ethan told the story the best he could. It was a familiar tale to him. Arthur fighting and gathering knights. Arthur conquering what Ethan guessed was Camelot.

In addition to the pictures, each of the stone murals had a rune on it as well. Ethan used a burnt piece of wood to scribble the symbols onto an empty page of Merlin's journal. He didn't have time now, but he wanted to compare some of these runes with the runes in the book.

Moving on to the next stone carving, there was a scene showing the round table and twelve knights. It reminded him of the depictions in the room with the dragon eyes. Twelve knights around a dragon, Arthur Pendragon.

After that, there were some battle scenes. Then a scene with Arthur and a woman. Was that Guinevere? The woman featured in a few other scenes but then there more battle scenes.

In one scene, Arthur and the knights fought some sort of beast-men. In another, they fought what Ethan knew from experience were ogres. Then they fought a dragon. Ethan noticed that the man in robes, who he guessed was Merlin, stood in the background of nearly every battle.

Having seen a dragon, Ethan had no idea how even an army could bring down such a huge beast. Then again, Merlin was once again in the background. Had he somehow used magic against the dragon? That might explain it.

The murals continued the story of other battles but one in particular stood out. The entire group stopped and stared at it. The monsters depicted in the stone carving were all too familiar to Ethan. They were demons. Or at least, they looked like the horned shape that Mertin, in the Order of the Scroll, had transformed into. The only difference was, these demons had wings.

"Are those what I think they are?" Yuliana asked, pointing to one of the winged creatures being cut down by a knight.

"Demons," Ethan confirmed.

"Doesn't that sort look like..." Ainslee started and looked up at Ethan. It was clear she had seen the resemblance too.

"Mertin," Ethan finished with a grave look at the dwarf.

He looked at the scene again. It showed each of the knights killing a demon but there were more in the background. Looking more closely, he saw what he thought was a door...or a portal. Had someone managed to open a gateway to a demon realm? And Arthur and the knights had fought them off?

While Ethan hadn't actually read the original legends of King Arthur, he was certain there wasn't a host of demons in any legends, TV shows or movies about the man. That was one of those things he would remember. Moving on, there were several more panels devoted to the other battles against monsters they didn't recognize.

Finally, towards the end, there was a battle against what looked to be praying mantis-type creatures. Arthur and the knights fought them in what might be snow. There were even icebergs in the background.

Looking closely at the stone mural, he could see the bodies of dead humans on the ground. Some looked like knights but quite a few were dressed in robes. Were those wizards? On one side, Arthur appeared to behead a larger praying mantis with Excalibur. Unfortunately, it looked like Arthur had been wounded in return.

"Bugs get king man?" Par'karr asked.

Ainslee frowned. "At least they weren't spiders."

The second-to-last panel was of Arthur's death and his placement inside a tomb. The final panel was of Merlin, the robed man, taking the sword and placing it into a stone. A stone inside of a city that looked like the depiction of Camelot. Only Camelot was on fire.

"So what?" Ainslee asked as they all looked at the final scene. "The guy with the dress put the sword back?"

"That seems like a waste of a good weapon," Nia agreed.

"In the legend," Ethan explained, "when Arthur died, the sword was returned to the Lady of the Lake, not put back in a stone."

"A lady?" Yuliana asked. "In a lake?"

Ethan nodded, trying to remember the stories. "A fairy, I think."

"Fairy?" Par'karr asked wide-eyed. "What is fairy?"

"It's a..." Ethan trailed off. He had turned around to face the kobold when his eye caught something. He blinked and then pointed. "Is it me, or is the sarcophagus glowing?"

The sarcophagus was illuminated and not by anything they had. There almost seemed to be a beam of light coming down from the ceiling, like a spotlight. Ethan followed the beam up to the apex of the dome ceiling and grinned.

"I think I just found our way out." Ethan smiled and pointed up to a hole in the ceiling. A hole that had light coming through.

"How did we miss that?" Nia asked, seeing the hole in the ceiling.

"It must have been nighttime," Yuliana suggested. "This must be the first light of morning."

"It is high," Nia pointed out. "Too high to throw a rope."

"Good thing we got some magic," Ethan said with a smile. He remembered how low he was on <u>Mana</u>. He gave the foxgirl a wink. "But I will need a recharge."

Nia smiled but Ainslee just rolled her eyes and made a face. "More sex? Really?"

42

———

The chamber was large enough that it wasn't too awkward to recharge his *Mana* with Nia. They hid under the blanket again while the others went to the opposite side of the chamber. This time, with his *Stamina* nearly full, it was more energetic than the previous few times and they both enjoyed it much more than before, and he restored all of his *Mana*.

"I will be happy when we are back in your bed," Nia said afterwards as she put her armor back on. "This is not the most enjoyable place."

Ethan nodded and looked around. "I agree. This isn't exactly where I'd take a date."

"Date?" the foxgirl asked, pulling up her breeches and buckling them.

He thought for a moment, remembering her culture where the strong took the weak and women were the spoils of war or bargaining chips in negotiations. "Do you have courting?"

"Courting?" Nia cocked her head and repeated the word.

"The daughters of an Alpha are sometimes used to broker a truce, or a temporary alliance."

"Not quite what I meant," Ethan admitted with a wry smile.

"You two done over there?" Ainslee called out to them. While they had been recharging, the others had been examining the cleared passage. Glancing over, Ethan saw them waiting at the entrance.

"Coming," Ethan said. He finished buckling on his own breeches and then he and Nia walked over to the group.

"About time," the dwarf huffed, though a twinkle in her eye told Ethan Ainslee was really only kidding. At least, he thought that's what it meant.

"Can we seal it up? Or did you find any cracks in the walls?" he asked, looking at the newly revealed walls. To him, they were just rock walls. One spot looked pretty much like any other spot. Luckily, Ainslee knew much more about it than he did.

"No cracks that I could see. The rest of it looks intact." The dwarf pointed to the various walls and then walked over to the collapsed area. "We can seal this up, but you'll need to be careful. See these areas, they're still unstable. They haven't settled."

Ethan looked where she was pointing but saw no difference. He knew she was probably right, so he just nodded and tried to remember the areas she was pointing out. This went on for several minutes as she walked further down the tunnel.

Finally, she stopped and turned to him. Ainslee put her hands on her hips and narrowed her eyes. Then the dwarf looked him up and down. "You have no idea what I'm talking about, do you?"

"Not really," Ethan admitted. He shrugged and gave her a sheepish grin. "It just looks like rock to me."

Ainslee let out a sigh of frustration and rolled her eyes. She looked like she might start lecturing him on rock and stone but then she cast a furtive glance down the dark tunnel. "We can talk the finer points of stonemanship later. Just do what I tell you and try not to bring the whole tunnel down on us."

Nodding, Ethan began to follow her instructions. He used his Earth magic to harden some areas of the tunnel, then pull rock from others to form the beginnings of a wall.

It was slower and more intense than he expected and he had to wipe the sweat from his brow more than once. Something about knowing one wrong slip could bring tons of rock down on top of you was more than a bit nerve-wracking.

The slow methodical process took nearly two hours. It was just a guess and, not for the first time, he wished he had a watch. When he was finished, the passage was completely sealed with a foot of solid granite. At least, that's what Ainslee told him.

He hadn't been able to replace the original mural. It had been shattered when the wall had collapsed and his magic couldn't touch it - much like the rest of the stone that was actually part of the tomb. He was looking down at the pieces of the mural when Ainslee punched him in the arm. Hard.

"Ow!" he said, jerking away and rubbing his arm.

"We're done, wizard-boy!" the dwarf told him, pointing to the wall. "Can we get out of here already?"

Ethan frowned and rubbed his arm. He sometimes forgot how strong the dwarf was. "Fine. Fine."

Ethan brought up his HUD. During the process of sealing the wall, he had gotten a skill up in *Earth* magic, boosting his *Intellect* to 30 and his maximum *Mana* to 72. Unfortunately, sealing up the wall had also used a ton of his *Mana* and the strain had further lowered his *Stamina* to just about half.

Ainslee seemed to read his mind and she rolled her eyes again. "You're going to have to ride that little foxgirl again, aren't you?"

Blushing slightly, Ethan smiled and nodded.

The dwarf screwed up her face in mock disgust. "Well, no need to be so smug about it. Well... get to it already! I want to get out of here! HEY FOXGIRL!"

TWENTY MINUTES LATER, Ethan was lower on *Stamina* but his *Mana* was full. He and Nia were dressed again and standing with the others around the sarcophagus. All of them had their eyes cast upwards at the circular opening in the domed ceiling.

"I cannot tell how wide it is from down here," Nia said, shielding her eyes from the light.

It was now evident that it was an opening to the outside. One of the suns had moved over the opening and was streaming light down on Arthur's final resting place. Ethan thought it looked very majestic.

Ethan nodded. "I'll have to levitate one of us up there and hope it's wide enough to get through."

"You can send me," Nia volunteered.

"Actually..." Ethan bit his lip. "I need you to go last. In case I need to recharge."

"Do you think you could run out of mana while... levitating... us?" Yuliana asked in alarm.

"Not in the middle of it," Ethan assured the elf. "But possibly before I get everyone up there."

"You send Par'karr!" the kobold said enthusiastically. "Par'karr want fly! Fly like bird!"

He was about to explain that it wasn't actually flying but seeing the little kobold's expression, he simply nodded. It made sense. Par'karr was the lightest and smallest member of the group. He'd be the easiest to lift and hopefully the one most likely to fit through. "You ready?"

Par'karr's ear-to-ear grin said it all. "Par'karr ready!"

"Wait a minute!" the dwarf interrupted and pointed at the Grail. "What about the golden cup? It's got healing properties, right? Can't we take it with us? Seems like an awful nice thing to have."

The dwarf unconsciously ran her hand across the side of her face that had been scarred until the Grail had healed her.

Ethan nodded. "It does. But removing it from its place here caused the noise."

Ainslee huffed but she knew he was right. The Grail off its perch was what had caused the animals to flee and brought them here in the first place. "I guess you're right. Too bad we can't borrow it occasionally, but this seems like a lot of work just to come and borrow the cup."

Ethan started to nod but stopped, an idea forming in his head. Perhaps they could borrow it. "Ainslee! You're a genius!"

"I know." The dwarf grinned and then her brow furrowed. "Wait. What?!"

Ethan ran back over to the new section of wall and grabbed some loose stones. Using a touch of Earth magic, he fused them together and formed three unique symbols.

Running back to his confused companions, he laid the rock with the symbols on the tomb next to the Grail.

"You want to create a portal here?" Nia asked, probably remembering he'd done the same in the library.

"Not a portal," he grinned. "A portal bag. I can create a portal bag to this point, and we should be able to reach through and pull the Grail out if we need it, then replace it. I doubt a few seconds, or a minute will cause too much disruption."

"Not bad, wizard-boy." Ainslee clapped him hard on the back. She grinned. "Just remember it was my idea!"

Now that he had a plan to retrieve the Grail in emergencies, Ethan concentrated on getting them out of the tomb. Lifting something living was more difficult than lifting inanimate objects. A rock he could grab tightly with cords of air and not worry. With a person, he had to find the right balance between holding them tightly, so he didn't lose his grip on them and holding them tight enough to hurt them.

Carefully, he raised Par'karr up to the ceiling. He kept his HUD up the entire time and watched his *Mana* to make sure he didn't somehow run out. After a couple of minutes, the little kobold reached the top and easily fit through the opening.

"Looks like there's enough room for us to fit!" Ainslee stated happily. "Me next!"

At her request, Ethan levitated the dwarf next, then Yuliana. Luna whined as the elf disappeared over the top of the opening. Luna came next and despite the elf calling down soothing words, the big cat did not like being lifted.

She struggled against the bonds of *Air* and Ethan had to expend additional *Mana* to keep a hold of her. Watching his *Mana* level plummet, Ethan pushed her up as quickly as possible before he ran out. He barely had time to get her up to the top before he dipped below 5 *Mana*.

Nia looked at him with a sly smile. "Time to recharge?"

Grinning, he nodded. "Time to recharge."

A HALF HOUR LATER, they were all standing on the outside ledge of one of the mountains. The top area of the dome had been barren rock. There was no vegetation or even any outcropping of stone. When they followed it to the closest ledge, they saw that they were nearly a hundred feet above the old mining trail.

Luckily, it was easier to lower people than lift people and Ethan had them all to the bottom with only a single recharge of his *Mana*.

Once they were down, Nia pointed up the trail to a familiar sight off in the distance. It was the mine entrance. Ethan shook his head. "It feels like we went a lot further than that!"

"We did make some turns down there," Ainslee pointed out. "And if you're not careful, it's easy to lose track of how far you've traveled underground."

"I guess so," Ethan agreed.

"Enough talk," Ainslee huffed. "Let's get back to town and get some mead!"

Chuckling, the group fell into their familiar formation and began the trek back to Hawkshead.

43

———

I t took a full week before any animals were sighted near the village, but the animals were returning. Despite the assurances Ethan had given them, it wasn't until the first animals showed up that the villagers accepted his word that he had found the issue and fixed it.

Once the animals began to return and the villagers seem to agree the problem was over, they all received the reward for the second quest.

Quest Complete.

Starving Villagers II

Report your findings to the Fearghas the Innkeeper and make sure the game returns.

Report to Fearghas (1/1).

You gain 500 experience.

You gain +250 reputation with Residents of Hawkshead.

> *You   gain   +250   reputation   with*
> *Farmers of Arrowpoint Valley.*
> *You gain 3 Fame.*

Ethan had suggested, and the group agreed, that telling people the entire story might just cause issues. Instead, he simply told the villagers that Cuthbert, the former mayor, had disturbed something in the tomb and Ethan and the group had set it straight.

None of them mentioned the giant spiders or the squid-headed creatures. That would only cause a panic in the village and none of them wanted that. The threat had been dealt with and that was all they needed to know.

Michalus still had not awakened and Elspeth told them it wasn't a good sign. People who didn't wake up after this much time usually never did. After discussing it with the group, Ethan spent two days making a large portal pouch that went directly to the runes next to the Grail.

They couldn't use the water from the Fountain of Youth, it was too far from the runes. Instead they filled the Grail with river water and poured it down the old wizard's throat. The result was instantaneous. The elf's eyes went wide, and he began coughing.

"What... where... who?" Michalus sputtered as he blinked and looked around. "You!"

Ethan took a step back from the man to give him some room. As he did, he slipped the Grail into the portal pouch, placing it carefully in its place on the tomb. Removing his hand, he sized up the wizard. "Are you okay? Do you remember your name?"

The old elf stopped glancing around and fixed a glare on Ethan. "I'm not an invalid, boy. I know my own name."

"What is it?" Ethan asked, eyebrows raised. He wanted to make sure the wizard hadn't suffered any permanent damage. Despite the Grail claiming it healed all wounds, he was still skeptical.

"It's Michalus, you darn fool," the old wizard retorted. He looked around. "Where am I?"

"You're in my room," Yuliana said.

The old elf's eyes went wide, and he looked around, then looked at himself under the covers. His clothes had been ruined by blood and gashes, so he wore only a long shirt Elspeth had given them for him.

"I uh... I mean... did we... how did..." the wizard sputtered, and Ethan realized what the wizard must be thinking.

"She volunteered her room for you while you were... asleep," Ethan told the elf. Yuliana also figured out what the wizard was thinking and blushed furiously.

"Asleep?" Michalus asked, his face a mask of confusion.

Relaxing a bit, Ethan signaled the others to approach. "Do you remember us?"

The old wizard looked taken back. "Are you okay? Did you hit your head or something since the last time I saw you?"

"So, you remember us then?" Ethan prodded.

"Of course, I do," the old wizard huffed. He looked around. "How did I get here? And where is here?"

"You're in Hawkshead," Ethan told the elf. "You were gravely injured when you arrived, and you've been in a coma ever since."

"A coma?" the old wizard scoffed, looking around. "That's nonsense."

"It's true," Yuliana said, stepping forward. "I was able to heal you, but you wouldn't wake up."

Michalus looked from face to face, obviously gauging their sincerity. Finally, he let out a breath. "It's really true? How long have I been out?"

"About two weeks," Ethan replied.

"Two weeks!" the wizard exclaimed, bolting upright. "I've been asleep for two weeks? That's impossible."

"No, it's not," Ethan assured the elf. "To be honest, some people didn't think you were going to make it."

The old elf wrinkled his forehead, his face sober. "That bad?"

"You were pretty messed up," Ethan said gravely. "It looked like you had been attacked."

Michalus frowned and scratched his head. "I don't remember an attack. What attacked me?"

Ethan chuckled. "We were hoping you could tell us?"

The old wizard shrugged. "Sorry, I don't remember an attack, just the journey here. In fact, the last thing I remember was being a few days from Hawkshead."

"Maybe it will come back to you," Ethan suggested. "For now, you should rest."

"I don't need rest," the old elf scoffed, throwing back the sheets. "I feel fine."

Ainslee and Nia snickered, and Ethan had to suppress a chuckle. "Then perhaps you should wait until we find you some pants."

AT THE END of the week, a group of mercenaries from Castlehaven arrived. They asked for Ethan and explained that they had scouted the countryside and that they would report back that it was safe to resume trade.

Ethan asked the small group if they wanted to stay over but the leader scoffed. "Doesn't look like there's enough for the villagers, let alone for my group. We'll fend for ourselves thanks. There seems to be an abundance of wildlife to the southeast."

Rather than argue, Ethan let the men leave. They were right. The village barely had enough to survive, let alone feed strangers.

Fearghas and some of the other villagers had come over when the mercenaries had arrived. They nodded and muttered to each other as the men rode away on their horses.

The innkeeper turned to Ethan. "It looks like you did right by us. Once they report back, the caravans will resume. That means fresh supplies."

Quest Complete.
*   Re-open Trade with Castlehaven*
*   Your town needs trade to survive. You have told your villagers that you intend to go to Castlehaven personally and re-open the trade route.*
*   Re-establish Trade with Castlehaven (1/1).*
*   You gain 500 experience.*
*   You gain +250 reputation with Residents of Hawkshead.*
*   You gain +250 reputation with Farmers of Arrowpoint Valley.*
*   You gain 1 Fame.*

Ethan glanced briefly at the quest update. He looked at

the villagers. "Good, then we can start getting more supplies and finish rebuilding."

"About that," Hamish said and was immediately elbowed by Fearghas. The cooper growled at the innkeeper. "It's got to be asked!"

"What's got to be asked?" Ethan inquired, eyes narrowing.

"Well, you see..." Fearghas started but Hamish interrupted.

"Was there any treasure in the tomb?" the cooper blurted out. "If so, we own a legal share of it."

Ethan smirked. He should have known they'd ask about treasure eventually. "Sorry, there was no treasure. Just lots of traps. Whoever was buried there, they didn't have their treasure buried with them."

Hamish eyed him. "You're sure there was nothing?"

Shrugging, Ethan pointed at the mountains to the north. "You're welcome to go in there and look for yourself."

"Yes, well." Hamish cleared his throat. "Are the... uh... traps still active?"

"Oh yes," Ethan replied. "We made it through with magic, but you might make it. Sort of like Cuthbert."

The old mayor, Cuthbert, had been impaled in the spike room and had never made it any further. Ethan and his companions had brought the body back and the villagers had seen the marks. Apparently, Hamish remembered.

"Uh, no," Hamish said, shaking his head. "I think we can take your word for it."

"Good," Ethan said sternly. "Because I barely made it out of there alive. In fact, I would have died if it weren't for... healing. Anyone who goes into that tomb is throwing his life away."

Hamish and Fearghas both nodded and then turned and

walked off, muttering to each other as they headed to the inn.

"Do you think they will try to go into the tomb?" Nia asked.

"I hope not," Ethan said. "For their sake."

"What we do now?" Par'karr asked.

"Now," Ethan said, looking out over the village. "We help them rebuild. Help Ainslee with the forge and see what adventure awaits us next."

"Until then," Ainslee grinned, "let's go drink some mead!"

"Here! Here!" Ethan agreed and they all turned and headed back to the inn for some much-deserved rest and relaxation.

JOIN THE ADVENTURE

Thank you for reading this book! If you enjoyed it, please consider leaving a review on Amazon or tagging me on social media.
Tag me @authorjohncresı on Twitter and @authorjohncressman on Facebook and Instagram!
Reviews help readers like you find this book. More readers means more sales, and more sales help independent authors like me to be able to write more books!
To learn more about the author and his other books and projects, visit the author's website at:
https://www.johnecressman.com
Or visit him on Facebook
https://www.facebook.com/authorjohncressman/

LITRPG

To learn more about LitRPG, talk to authors including myself, and just have an awesome time, please join the LitRPG Group.

MORE LITRPG

For more information on this book and other exciting LitRPG/GameLit books, please visit the following Facebook groups:
LitRPG Books
https://www.facebook.com/groups/LitRPG.books/

and

GameLit Society
https://www.facebook.com/groups/LitRPGsociety/

EPILOGUE

The Queen was irritated. She had sent the assassin drone weeks ago to retrieve the brain of the wizard who had attracted her attention. And it had died. She knew that instinctively through the bond she shared with all of her drones.

She was doubly irritated because this was not its first failure. The first time, the drone had come back with the brain of a kobold. The thing's brain had been a wizard's brain, but it was a primitive thing and gave her no knowledge she didn't already possess.

More importantly, it was not the brain that she had wanted. The brain she wanted was a more sophisticated creature. A human. That much she knew. She had sensed it bumbling around with magic when it first arrived. The Queen clicked her mandibles in disgust. A human. Her enemy.

She still remembered her defeat at the hands of humans. The knights, as they had called themselves. And their leader, the Arthur, and his wizard, the Merlin. The ones who had killed her.

The Queen clicked her mandibles together again, this time in what the humans might call a chuckle. Yes, they had killed her, but she had been reborn. That was the way of her species. The drone who witnessed her death had escaped and laid the egg with her new body the very same day.

And like all Queens of her species, she had genetic memory. All of her memories up to the moment she had laid the egg containing the drone who had helped her rebirth. In addition, she had the memories of the drone itself.

It did mean there was a few weeks' gap in her memory, but she had seen the Arthur and the Merlin kill her through the eyes of the drone. It was an image she hadn't forgotten in the thousand years since her death. She would never forget. Not until she was avenged.

Now, someone else from Earth had come. Another wizard. She couldn't tell anything about the human, other than that it was a wizard and it had opened a portal. A powerful portal.

The Queen glanced down at the large, translucent egg sac in front of her. The new assassin drones were still growing but they would be ready soon. And this time, she would send two.

Once hatched, she would feed them her own nectar to accelerate their growth. They would still take a week, maybe longer to reach full size. Once they did, she would send it after the human. The wizard. She would drink its brain and find out where the Merlin had gone and if it was coming back.

The Queen was not afraid. She didn't feel fear. Her kind simply didn't experience it, or if they had experienced it, it was so long ago, it wasn't even in the genetic memory. No, she wasn't afraid. She was concerned.

Last time, the Merlin and the Arthur had killed her and destroyed nearly all of her brood. It had taken her almost a thousand years to recover. Even now, she kept the nest hidden from the Merlin.

Though the time was coming soon where she would no longer be concerned about the Merlin. Or his magic. Now, she had magic of her own.

She looked down at the assassin drone eggs. Its predecessor and the predecessors before it had brought her every wizard she could find. Or rather, had brought the brains of the wizards. After all, that was all she needed.

By consuming the brains, she was able to learn things from the wizards, like how to do magic. It was an imperfect process. The brains were primitive and not fresh. The amount of knowledge she could retain was tiny compared to feasting on the brain herself.

But feasting on brains herself had been her downfall before. She had been too confident. She hadn't understood magic back then. She had thought herself invulnerable, so she had led her children to the human cities, one by one, and consumed all the brains she had wanted, taking their knowledge as her own.

She clicked her mandibles irritably. She had taken over a large part of the continent before the Arthur and the Merlin and the other knights had come.

She'd eaten some of the knights' brains. That had been how she learned of Earth, the home of the Merlin. She realized that the place they came from was ripe with brains for the feasting. That was when she had decided to find a way to their world.

But then the Arthur and the Merlin had come. And she had died. As impossible as that should have been, she had died. That would not happen again. This time, she would be ready. Her and her entire brood.

A clawed foreleg sliced through the egg sac, spilling greenish liquid onto the floor of the hive. It didn't matter. One of the drones would clean it up. The second egg stirred as the other assassin drone clawed its way out of its own egg.

The Queen looked down as the assassin drones pushed their way through the wall of the egg sac, their multifaceted eyes looking around. The tiny things looked up at the Queen, straining their necks to meet her gaze.

My Queen, they clicked in unison. *How may I serve?*

Come, she replied, turning towards her chambers, where her special stores of nectar awaited. *For now, you will eat. When your brother are ready, I will send you on an errand.*

Yes, my Queen, the assassin drones clicked happily and they followed the Queen to her chambers, happy to serve her in any way she wanted.

The Queen walked ahead. The assassin drones would eat. Then, they would hunt. All too soon, she'd have the brain of the Earth human. Then, she would find the Merlin and dine on the brains of the Earth people.

<<<<>>>>

ACKNOWLEDGMENTS

I'd like to acknowledge all the members of the LitRPG Authors' Guild who helped me in so many ways! Without your help, I could never have gotten this far!

Also, a big thank you for everyone who had bought one of my books. Your support really means a lot to me.

ABOUT THE AUTHOR

John E. Cressman is an author, magician, mentalist, hypnotist, programmer, and longtime lover of roleplaying games and fantasy/sci-fi books.

As a teen, he wasted long hours creating D&D fantasy campaigns for his friends to play. He has tried several pen and paper roleplaying games from the original Dungeons and Dragons, Traveler and Star Frontiers to the new Pathfinder games.

He still enjoys computer RPGs and MMORPGs, with his current favorite being Elder Scrolls Online. He used to play Skyrim, but then he took an arrow to the knee.

John has published two books on hypnosis and is now trying his hand at the fantasy LitRPG genre with his new LitRPG trilogy, VEIL Online.